Restoring Grace

Book One of the Grace Series

Anna Christine Boulier

Anna Christine Boulier
Publishing

The Grace Series

Restoring Grace
Book One in the Grace Series

Accepting Grace
Book Two in the Grace Series
Coming September 2018

Trusting Grace
Book Three in the Grace Series
Coming October 2018

Hardships often prepare ordinary people for an extraordinary destiny.

-CS Lewis

And after you have suffered a little while, the God of all GRACE, who has called you to his eternal glory in Christ, will himself restore, confirm, strengthen, and establish you.

—1 Peter 5:10 ESV

ACKNOWLEDGEMENT

Thank you to my wonderful Beta Readers- who read my books in the midst of their busy lives. Kasey Hicks, Kristie Gentry, Diane Gaseway, Martha Slider, Erin Helm, Lauren Thomas, and Helene Horgan.

Prologue

"It's about time you got here. I called over an hour ago." Delia Anne said as she placed a large serving dish on the elegantly set table. "I've not only finished making lunch, but also potted and repotted several plants waiting for you."

"It's not my fault I'm late, Delia Anne! I couldn't find my stupid car keys anywhere." Out of breath Jill Adams came barreling through the kitchen door, walking straight to the sink to wash her hands. "I swear that dog's hiding them from me. She sits on them, and it's only when I go to walk her before I leave I find them." Wiping her hands on a pretty hand towel, she continued, "I should've gotten a cat, they never care when you come or go as long as the food dish is full."

Pushing her steel gray hair back from her face, Delia Anne surveyed the table to make sure everything had been laid out. Seeing her long-time friend standing in her kitchen, reminded her of the many meals their families shared over the fifty years she had lived in this house. "Grab a seat, Jill. I've got an idea I want to run past you while we're eating."

"Oh no, Delia Anne, no more ideas." Jill exclaimed, waving her hands. "I told you after your last harebrained scheme to raise money for the church emergency fund I wasn't getting on board with any more of your ideas. I swear, I thought the church council was going to kick us out. I mean, who in their right mind would want to purchase the widow calendar of Great Hills Christian Church is beyond me." Paling a little she said, "I thought Lauren Blake was going to die right there when you suggested a tasteful pin up for sale."

Huffing in her seat, Jill ran her hands through her dark hair, unknowingly pulling a few strands from her bun, streaked liberally with gray. She was unable to hide her nervousness when she imagined herself in a bathing suit with her body that had seen the birth of four kids, and everything else life had thrown at her. That last plan of Delia Anne's terrified her more than anything else she had come up with in a long time.

"Jill Adams, you know I was just kidding when I said that! I was tired of listening to Lauren talk about how Hillary had the best idea for raising money, yet again. The whole meeting was Lauren talking about this or that and it was giving me a headache." Delia Anne continued with force, "I know everyone else was thinking it, too!"

She had to hide a grin as she thought, *I wouldn't have been ashamed if they had jumped at my idea for the swimsuit calendar. I would like to think I look pretty good for my age. I'm active, walk constantly, and look trendy with my hair in a long, stylish bob. I'd be perfect for the month of May in a tasteful one piece of course.*

Jill began to fill her plate, but paused long enough to say, "You may've been kidding, but I was scandalized. I didn't want to show my face at the next function with you." Looking at Delia Anne pointedly she said, "You know I don't like to be the center of attention, especially if it involves a bathing suit."

"Dear, I would've let you wear a cover up in the calendar." Delia Anne told her between bites of potato salad. She paused and put her fork down beside the hand painted plate and said, "But seriously, this new plan of mine isn't for the public. It's actually a hush-hush plan to get my granddaughter married and start having my great grandchildren." Moving to refill Jill's sweet tea, she continued, "It's time she fixed things with young Cole West. He'd make a great husband for her and they just need to work out their differences, and that won't happen with her living in Atlanta.

"Delia Anne, you're acting like they're kids and argued only a few days ago. Viviane's thirty-two, and they broke up over ten years ago." Exasperation filled her voice as she tried to speak some sense into her friend. "I don't think they've even set eyes on each other in all this time. Viviane hasn't been home longer than two days since she graduated college. She's worked long and hard to avoid him, and you should respect her wishes."

Jill paused a moment, and then asked, "Why pray tell is this coming up all of the sudden... are you okay? Are you sick... is that why you want to see grandkids?" Panic at the thought of losing her best friend, especially so soon after the death of her husband a few months before had her reaching for Delia Anne's hand.

"Jill, I'm fine." Patting her hand, she continued, "Tip top shape actually, but I'd like to see my grandchildren before I do get old and can't enjoy them. It all started with Pastor's sermon last Sunday. I'm following his advice, because it got me thinking, and I feel this is what God wants me to do. I've got to help fix Viviane and Cole's relationship to get them married."

Delia Anne rose from her chair and asked, "Do you want some pickles? I do."

Jill laid down the bread she had been buttering and snapped, "No! No, I don't want pickles. You know I hate pickles... forget the stupid pickles." Jill waved her hands in animated frustration. "What do you mean Pastor Winston's sermon inspired you to help Viviane? Last Sunday's sermon was about being good Christian neighbors."

Delia Anne put the pickles on the table and sat back down. "You remember when Pastor talked about how Christians are supposed to do their part and let God take care of the rest..." Excitement caused her eyes to light up, "Well, I'm going to do my part by bringing Viviane back to town for an extended visit to see Cole and straighten out the fight the two of them had years ago."

Jill eyed her apprehensively, "How exactly? I don't see Viviane coming back for just any reason, because you've been trying that for years."

"I'm going to let her think I'm sick. I'll drop some hints, let a few clues slip and BOOM," she clapped her hands together, "She's here before I know it." Her face glowed over the simple brilliance of her plan.

"Are you out of your ever-loving mind?" Jill yelled, not pausing to let Delia Anne speak. "Let her think you're sick. You're nuts. I thought you were getting the wrong idea from the sermon, but now I know you're just crazy."

Please Lord let her see how wrong this plan is, she prayed. Her eyes filled with concern she said, "Delia Anne Mays you can't lie to the girl. That's definitely NOT God's plan."

Delia Anne remained calm as she answered, "I know lying is a sin, but Viviane must come back here to fix things with Cole and this is the best way to do it. I'd never intentionally hurt her, not with everything she's been through, but it's for the best. Once she's fixed things with Cole... well problem solved. I'll tell her how I brought them together, she'll understand and it will make a lovely story for the wedding toasts."

So secure in her plan and sure of God's divine inspiration, she radiated confidence as she spoke of Viviane's quick and eventual understanding of her little white lies. "Pastor Winston said we weren't to sit like bumps-on-a-log waiting for God to move, but to be active in helping others."

She placed a few pickles on her plate then continued, "Besides, I have to act now because I saw Cole and Hillary sitting together last Sunday."

Jill thought for a moment and finally sighed when she looked into Delia Anne's excited face, "You're my best friend and I know you mean well, but I don't think this is what Pastor Winston meant. I'll help, but under protest, in the hope of keeping this mess from getting out of hand." Pausing, she sighed, "What do you want me to do?"

Delia Anne smiled at her friend. She knew Jill would come around, she always did. They spent the next few hours deciding exactly how Delia Anne needed to act to let hints filter to Viviane. Hints that would bring her granddaughter home for good.

Chapter One

Traffic on I-75 South was horrendous at all times, but on this particular Thursday night it seemed worse than usual. "Erica, you need to be in the far-right lane, not the far left. We have to turn at this exit and you're going to miss it. Move over." Daphne said using her whole body to direct Erica.

"Daphne you're such a backseat driver. I knew you should've sat in the back, but nooo you said you'd control yourself. Well, you lied!" Erica complained as she whipped in and out of traffic, her little red Honda moving closer to the exit only half a mile away.

"Are you crazy? You're going to get us killed. Don't move over there..." Daphne screeched as she covered her eyes. "And I said I'd control myself if you'd drive like a sane person, which you aren't!"

"Guys, please calm down. We're almost off the interstate," Viviane said, secretly laughing in the back seat. *I'm going to miss the girl's antics and need to store up their laughter for the coming weeks.*

"Daph, do we go left or right up here? I can't remember." Erica asked, pulling up to the red light. "I think we turn left."

Erica leaned closer to Daphne, letting Viviane clearly see her two best friends from the back seat. Erica Caine was tall at 5'9", short blonde hair that barely curled around her ears, while Daphne Reynolds had dark, cocoa colored skin, curly brown hair to her shoulders, and was around Viviane's own 5'7" height. Erica and Viviane became friends during the first week of college, living in the same dorm, they met when they sat next to each other in a dorm meeting. The two girls immediately hit it off. They met Daphne two years after college, when she moved to Atlanta graduation.

"Right Erica, then left." Daphne said, turning her chocolate brown eyes toward Viviane, "You should've driven since you've been to this Chinese place before and said it was good." Pausing she noticed her friend's blue eyes were red rimmed and asked, "You're quiet tonight. Is everything okay?"

"I'm fine Daph. Don't worry." Viviane said pointing to a strip mall off Peachtree. "Hey, Erica it's right over there. See that big sign?"

"I see it. I see it," Erica said as she turned into the parking lot, whipping her car into an open spot near the front.

"Let's go eat, I'm starving," Daphne said while climbing out of the car, making sure her knee-length skirt was in place. She had come straight from the pharmacy where she worked.

Erica who felt dressed up wearing tinted Chapstick and jeans with a fitted shirt growled, "You're always hungry and the fact you stay so thin is disgusting."

It didn't take long for the ladies to be seated and for a young waiter to take their drink orders, "Good evening ladies. What can I get you to drink?"

A chorus of waters sounded around the table, and the women looked at each other and laughed. After the waiter went to get their drinks, Viviane said, "Grand always says a Southern lady should drink water, since it's good for you. I just never see her drink anything but sweet tea, which she calls the wine of the south."

Erica nodded her head, "My family's the same way, but I really love my coffee."

The waiter came back with their drinks and took their orders. Afterward Daphne turned to Viviane and asked, "I know you call your Grandmother, Grand but I don't know why. Is it a Southern thing?"

Daphne grew up in Michigan and was constantly told it's a southern thing. "No, it actually happened about a year after I moved in with my grandmother. You know my parents died when I was nine." She waited for Daphne to nod then continued, "It was hard for both of us, she lost a daughter and son-in-law in the car accident and I lost my parents. I spent a lot of the next year struggling to make friends in a new town and trying to make sense of my new reality. Generally, I wanted to be left alone to read." Her voice lowered thinking of the hard time she and Grand had at the beginning.

"One day, I was in Grand's parlor and was bored. I told her I had nothing to read and everything was for babies and I wasn't a baby, anymore. She had a collection of books that were special. I was never allowed to touch them when I visited and was shocked when she went over and handed one to me. She said they were very special books she read when she was newly married and my mom had started reading them when she was about my age. 'They're written by Grace Livingston Hill, a prominent

Christian author and I think you're finally old enough to enjoy them. This was your mother's favorite.'"

Viviane paused to take a deep breath, "I read it and spent the next year reading every book in her collection." She still remembered the special thrill she felt knowing her mother read those very same books. "One of the first books I read had a guy who meets his grandfather for the first time and gets to know him. He called him Grand." Tears in her eyes thinking of her sick Grandmother, she continued, "I liked it and thought of how my grandmother wasn't just a grandmother anymore, but I couldn't call her mom either. This new name fit perfectly into our situation and let her know she was more than just a grandmother to me."

She took a sip of water to give her time to compose herself, and after she sat her glass down, her two friends reached out their hands to take hers. "It's okay, Viv. Whatever's bothering you will work out," Erica said, squeezing her hand. "We've seen the sad look in your eyes and we're worried. It's been a long time since I've seen you this sad."

"Yes, you're strong and can get through anything. Look at what you've been through all ready. God can help you and give you strength to face whatever's wrong," Daphne said firmly.

The waiter came bringing their food, breaking the moment. The women divided up the dishes, and placing fried rice on her plate Erica said, "I'll pray you guys."

Bowing their heads, Erica prayed, "Dear Father, you know what's going on in Viv's heart and you're the best friend she could ever have, though Daph and I are pretty close. Please touch her heart, give her peace, comfort her, and give her wisdom for whatever situation she's facing. Amen."

Viviane lifted her head and looked at her friends. "I'm so blessed to have the two of you in my life. I'm glad we were able to get together tonight. I've been worried about Grand, but it can wait. Let's eat."

For a few minutes, the women stopped talking to eat their dinner. Viviane thought of the last conversation with her grandmother and how it went absolutely nowhere. She hadn't seen her in weeks. Grand usually came to Atlanta for long visits and Viviane had even offered to pick her up, but Grand said she was tired and maybe next week. The only problem was she had said that for the last three weeks and with other things she had slipped in a few phone conversations over the last month, Viviane was worried about her.

About halfway through her moo goo gai pan, she began to tell her friends about Grand possibly being sick, the cancellations, all the hints she accidently slipped. She made sure to mention how uncertain she felt, because Grand wouldn't be honest with her.

Feeling lost and sacred, Viviane sighed, "I just don't know, so I'm going home tomorrow to see for myself. I'll be staying a few weeks to prevent her from hiding her symptoms from me. I asked my boss Kathie for the month off from location photo shoots, since August is a slow month for weddings, I can do edits from home." Wiping a tear from her eye she added, "Kathie's wonderful, and said take all the time I need, since she will be traveling for a few weeks, and it means I can do editing work from Grand's house."

"Oh Viv, that's awful. Of course, you need to go home and see how Grand's really doing. Only..." Erica paused, looking at Daphne with a question in her hazel eyes.

"What we really want to know is how are you going to handle seeing Cole? It's been over ten years since you saw him," Daphne asked without missing a beat.

Viviane smiled through her tears, because she knew her friends understood how hard it was for her to go back. It was the place where her heart had been broken and even now she was still waiting for God to heal a crack or two.

Cole had been her best friend and first love, since high school. He had broken up with her their junior year of college and she had limped back to Atlanta to eventually mend and heal. She had never been able to go back or call Cartersville home again without it breaking her heart.

It had taken years to get to a place where she felt happy and whole again. God had been working on her for a long time, but she had never been able to face Cole. He didn't know how broken she had been, and she didn't know how to erase the hurt she still felt. All she could do was go back to Cartersville for quick visits with Grand and get back to Atlanta as fast as possible. Grand understood and spent much of Viviane's free time in Atlanta at her apartment. This was the main reason she was worried, because she hadn't seen Grand in over a month.

Chapter Two

It was a beautiful August morning, bright and sunny with lots of green trees along the drive to Cartersville. Since Viviane left her apartment in Midtown, she had been trying to focus on the traffic, instead of her growing fears the closer she got the Bartow County line. She was blasting the AC, grateful her shoulder length hair was in a ponytail. Usually she only put her hair up when she was working or running, but it had been so hot lately she kept it up all the time.

Viviane wondered if Erica's comment about the weather affecting Grand's health could be the real culprit. She hadn't told Grand she was coming home, because she wanted to see Grand before she had a chance to hide her illness. Switching off the traffic report, she put in her favorite Ella Fitzgerald CD hoping it would soothe her soul better than the top 40 songs.

Too soon for her liking, she pulled off the interstate and made the few turns toward Grand's. Passing Dellinger Park, Viviane was amazed to see the new shopping areas, and new subdivisions, evidence of Cartersville growing even with the infrequent visits she made. She smiled wistfully, it didn't matter how long she was away because Grand's house would always be special to her. She just wished her home and Cole's weren't in the same city.

Seeing Grand's drive, she turned and began the slow climb up the slight rise to the pale blue house she had grown up in since she was nine. Even before her parents died, her family visited often since they were Grand's only living relatives, because Grand's husband Walt died of cancer when Viviane was a baby.

She parked her car and got her camera bag out of the front seat, and her suitcases from the trunk. Carrying her bags up the front porch stairs, she turned the knob on the door and found it locked. She stood there shocked, unable to grasp she would need to get her key. *What's going on?*

Grand had the same morning routine for years, up at seven to make coffee, she came out to the front porch to read her devotion, and on Fridays she prepped for her Sunday school lesson. Then she made breakfast and cleaned the house that was always spotless, because the ladies committee would stop by later in the day to visit and plan future functions. Grand was a busy woman in the community, especially at church.

Viviane glanced at the little barn and saw Grand's little green Honda parked where it should be. Pulling out her key, she opened the door and stepped inside to put her luggage in the entry. She called out, "Grand? Are you in the kitchen?"

Not hearing anything, she began to panic. She walked through the empty downstairs and quickened her pace once she passed the darkened kitchen to the back stairs. Wondering if Grand had even gotten up this morning, she was surprised that her quick tour showed dishes in the sink, and a towel on the floor. *This isn't like Grand, she doesn't leave dishes in the sink?!?! It's a good thing I'm home for a month, something's obviously very wrong and now I've got proof!*

Imagining horrible scenes of Grand passed out and bleeding, she almost ran to Grand's bedroom, but made sure to slowly open her door not to scare her. She saw her lying in bed with her eyes closed still in her silk nightgown. Viviane received the second biggest shock of her adult life– Grand still in bed at eleven in the morning.

"Grand, are you okay? It's Viviane," she moved closer to the bed, "I've come for a visit." Up close she could see her grandmother's flushed cheeks and sweat shining on her brow.

Slowly Grand opened her eyes, and croaked softly, "Viviane, what are you doing here? Is everything okay?"

"Yes, Grand, I'm fine. Are you okay?" Putting her hand on Grand's forehead she didn't believe she had a fever. "I came for a visit only to find you're in bed. Do I need to call Doc?"

"Sweetie, I'm fine just a little slow today, just give me a few minutes. I'll come down and we can visit, okay?"

Grand started to move, but Viviane stopped her by placing a gentle hand on her shoulder. "Maybe you should stay in bed a bit longer. I could bring you something to eat. Are you hungry?"

"No, I'm fine. I'll be down in a minute and I can make us some lunch." Grand smiled.

Viviane hesitated but didn't see any fever in her eyes and didn't want to upset her. "Okay, I'll go downstairs, but don't worry about lunch. I'll fix us something, just come down when you're able."

"See you in a few minutes." Grand said, already pulling the covers off as she started to get up.

Viviane made sure Grand was steady as she walked to her master bathroom, and noted Grand moved slowly but did not see her wobble. Feeling safe to leave her alone, she left the bedroom door open, and went downstairs to straighten up. Dishes needed to be put in the dishwasher, and clothes put in the washing machine.

A few minutes later she walked into the laundry room and was astounded to see all the clothes piled on the floor waiting to be washed. Shaking her head, she sent silent thanks to God she was home now to help Grand get better, because she was obviously very ill. She spent the next twenty minutes starting laundry and general cleanup in the kitchen while she waited.

Delia Anne was tired, not because she wasn't feeling well, but because she had raced up the stairs five minutes before Viviane walked through the door. Wiping her brow from running a marathon sprint, she said to her reflection, "I'm going to have to find ways to exercise when Viviane isn't around. To think running up those few steps made me sweat at my age. Good grief, I'm only seventy years old."

She saw the flush on her face and scowled at how close she came to messing up the whole plan when Viviane caught her off guard, showing up out of the blue like that. She had only finished putting up breakfast when she had heard a noise in the driveway and had wiped her hands walking to the front door thinking she wasn't expecting anyone. Her committee meeting was yesterday because one of the ladies had a conflict today. When she spied Viviane getting out of her car, she had leapt into action.

Running through the kitchen to the back stairs, she ignored the dish cloth that had fallen to the floor. She didn't have time to pick it up, but instead started yanking her linen suit off, before she was completely down the hall to her bedroom. Her only thought was to get her nightgown on and in bed before Viviane made it upstairs. She barely made it, only getting the covers up to her chin when the door opened. She didn't even have time to wipe the sweat from her brow or steady her breathing.

Now, she looked at her huge walk in closet debating what to wear, her normal linen pant suit or would it serve her purpose better to wear the long caftan dress Jill had gotten her for her birthday. It had been a joke between them at the time, because even though it was a beautiful green to match her eyes, they both knew she wasn't ready to slow down and spend her days relaxing just yet. She knew Viviane would be more shocked by seeing her wear one, than anything else. "But is it too much," she mumbled. Jill would be angry to know she was wearing it to fool Viviane, but she was determined to see her great grandkids.

Deciding you might as well hang for a sheep as a lamb as her grandmother said, she slipped it on. "Hmm, it is comfortable and cool. Maybe Jill's right." Satisfied with her reflection in the mirror, she made her way downstairs, making sure she slowed her steps once she reached the kitchen.

Downstairs Viviane had finished in the kitchen and moved on to dust the living room, which looked like it hadn't been dusted in weeks. Delia Anne walked over to her and said, "Hon, you don't have to do that, I'll get to it." She didn't mention the reason she hadn't dusted in a few days was she had been cleaning out the attic, donating a lot of old clothes and things to Goodwill. In a cleaning mood, she didn't want to clean the house in case Viviane came home. *I'm glad I resisted the urge.*

Viviane turned to answer her but was shocked speechless when she saw what Grand was wearing. "It's... it's okay, I don't mind. I actually miss those Saturday mornings after cartoons dusting the knickknacks and furniture." She turned to dust the last shelf in the room to hide her tears. "You should sit and let me finish. Tell me what you're up to? I've not seen you in weeks and want to know what I've missed. Did the lady's husband in your Sunday School class get the job with the lawn care company?"

Delia Anne sat on the large gray sofa frowning, she didn't like watching her granddaughter clean her house, while she had to sit and watch. "Well, I haven't been teaching my Sunday school class for over a month now. I've been going to Grace Cartwright's women's class on the Sundays I'm able to go."

"What?" Viviane was so shocked by this, she slid into the big wing back chair across from the sofa, unable to see the checked fabric because of the tears clouding her eyes. "You aren't teaching your class? You've been the teacher for over fifteen years."

"Sweetie, don't yell. I just needed a break from the class," Delia Anne said while stretching out on the sofa as she pulled down afghan her mother had made and draped it over her. "One of the other ladies wanted a chance to teach and I felt it was time to take a less active role on Sunday mornings. I've enjoyed Grace's class." The truth of the statement was evident in her voice and she was pleasantly surprised how much she had grown to love it. The ladies had become very dear to her, and Grace always brought a thoughtful and applicable lesson each week.

Viviane was simply astounded, as her whole world crashed around her. The realization Grand had given up a Sunday school class she had fought for many years ago was shocking, but knowing she hadn't been able to attend every Sunday was awful. Grand never missed church. *A caftan, oh Lord, if Grand's wearing a caftan and missing church, I should've come home weeks ago. Please don't let me be too late.*

"Grand, I'm really worried about you." Rising from the chair, Viviane moved to get the address book by the phone to call the family doctor.

The last thing I need is a clean bill of health. Delia Anne motioned Viviane over, "I'm fine. Don't worry about me. I'll rest today and we'll go to church on Sunday. It's just a little bug, it'll pass." Grand saw the worry in her eyes, and exact mirror of her mother. "You'll go with me to church on Sunday, won't you?"

Still unsure about whether to call the doctor or not, Viviane was more than ever determined to stick around and see how sick Grand really was. Deciding not to upset her, she said standing up, "If you're feeling up to it we'll go, but you must rest today and tomorrow. In the meantime, I'll make lunch. Do you want some soup?"

Delia Anne really didn't want soup, especially in this hot weather, but she didn't want to make waves when she had just maneuvered Viviane to attend church. It had been four years since she had stepped inside the building, not since Cole came back from Virginia to be the youth pastor. Her girl only visited during the week now, claiming her job was working weekends. She went to church in Atlanta, and was very active, but it was time she moved back home permanently. Sunday, whether Viviane liked it or not, she was going to Great Hills Christian Church, and if Delia Anne had anything to say she was going to enjoy it. After all, she had been planning for this moment since June.

Chapter Three

Up since seven am, Viviane tried on her third outfit of the morning, worried about what to wear, how to fix her hair, and even how much makeup to put on. She was a wreck and her morning devotion hadn't helped. She was in the middle of reading Song of Solomon right now, and the last thing she needed to hear about was love. She pulled off the red top and black pants she had on and walked over to the closet surveying the clothes she brought from Atlanta. She was determined the next outfit she pulled out would be it. She wasn't some silly high school teenager trying to impress a boy.

Not seeing anything, Viviane put her face in her hands, as her soul cried out to God in despair, *Lord, I'm so messed up. It shouldn't be so hard. It's been ten years since I've looked at Cole, but I feel Sunday is Your day and I shouldn't be focused on anyone, but You. Please help me!*

Immediately she began to feel peace wash over her. As she was still, she felt God speaking to her heart, "Daughter, I love you with an everlasting love and if I clothe the lilies of the valley in beautiful garments, what makes you think I would not do the same for you?"

Resting a moment in the quiet strength, Viviane began to think of all God had brought her through, the wonderful people he had brought into her life, and she knew she would make it through this morning, as well.

Suddenly she remembered about a month ago, she had been shopping with Daphne and Erica when in the back of a trendy store downtown, she had spied a black jersey dress with cap sleeves. She had fallen in love with it, because it had a blue wrap belt the exact color of her eyes. Both girls told her it was a knock out dress, simple enough for any occasion, plus it was on sale.

When she had gotten to the cashier, she discovered it was being put on clearance and the owner would go ahead and give her the extra markdown a few days early. Daphne had said, "If that isn't a sign from God to buy it, nothing is!" She had bought it, calling it her God-given dress.

Standing up, she walked to her closet thanking God for the dress and the reminder to pack it. She only wished she had remembered it earlier, before she had gotten upset over nothing. With a new smile on her face and in her heart, she proceeded to put on a touch of makeup, sticking with her usual routine of just enough to feel feminine and look natural, her favorite look.

Seeing it was almost 8:30, she grabbed a light shawl from her closet before going to check on Grand. Standing outside her bedroom door, she knocked but didn't hear anything. She was sure she heard her moving around this morning, and cracking open the door, she saw Grand wasn't in the room. *She must be downstairs, which is a good sign.*

Grand rested all weekend but seemed restless. Viviane sympathized, knowing it must be hard to want to do things, but couldn't because of your health. When she reached the bottom steps, she smelled cinnamon in the air, and walked in the kitchen to see Grand sitting at the large kitchen table with a small plate of a half-eaten cinnamon roll and cup of steaming coffee.

Grand smiled at her and said, "I've got a plate for you."

Filling her plate with two cinnamon rolls, Viviane said, "I'm so glad you're feeling well this morning, and I'm especially glad you were up to making my favorite breakfast."

Biting into one she sighed with pleasure, "I'll have to run an extra few miles this week to make up for this, but it's so worth it. It's a good thing I live in Atlanta, or I'd get fat from all of your cooking."

Grand's heart tightened at the thought of all of her efforts wasted if Viviane went back to Atlanta, but didn't react as she simply said, "You could do with a little more meat on your bones my girl. Which is why I put a pot roast in the crock pot for lunch. You eat out too much."

Panicked Viviane said, "You shouldn't have worried about lunch. I could easily fix us something. I don't want you overdoing it when you're feeling better than you have in days. Did you get up early this morning? You always were up at the crack of dawn on Sundays to prepare for Sunday school."

"I actually enjoy sleeping in and spend my time praying more. I thought it would be really difficult to walk away from my class, but I've truly enjoyed Grace's." Taking a sip of her coffee, she sighed, "It's been a real blessing."

"How did you end up in Grace's class? Doesn't she teach a class for new Christians?"

"Not since June, she felt led to start a women's class which delves deeper into a woman's heart through God's eyes. I've been amazed at what I'm learning at my age. I wish I had known some of these things when I was younger, especially newly married."

Grand enjoyed watching Viviane eat the rolls she made after getting up early to do something special for her girl. She knew today would be difficult for her seeing Cole for the first time in years but knew sometimes medicine tasted bad even when it's good for you. She had been praying all morning that Viviane and Cole would see each other, fall in love again, and quickly move past their argument. She was sure they didn't even remember what the fight was about anymore.

She reached out to take Viviane's empty plate, put Viviane stopped her, "No, sit back down, I'll put them away."

Putting the dishes in the dishwasher, Viviane asked, "You still haven't explained how you ended up in Grace's class?"

Not wanting to make too quick of a recovery, she let Viviane baby her and clean up. "Grace came to me in May and mentioned she wanted to start a women's only class with a very specific goal to include women of all ages and walks of life so they would grow, lean on, and learn from each other. She asked if I knew some ladies who'd be interested in finding out what God finds captivating about women. I was intrigued and said I'd let her know, then June came and well..."

Grand quickly cut herself off, she didn't want to tell Viviane about Pastor Winston's "help your granddaughter" sermon as she called it, which was what lead her to step down from her Sunday school class. She knew when Viviane came she would attend her class and wouldn't interact with other women her age. She needed Viviane to embrace living in Cartersville again to make getting back with Cole easier, and Grand decided to find a Sunday school class to fit them both.

Viviane heard Grand stop mid-sentence and thought to herself, *June- that's when Grand got really sick and I'm just now learning about it.*

"Well, I'm glad you're enjoying the class. I'm looking forward to it. It's been ages since I've seen Grace."

Hearing keys jingling, Viviane put her hand on Grand's and said, "Let's take my car, it's right out front." She helped her up and steered her to the front door, not allowing her to protest, "It'll be easier for you to get in and out of."

Unlocking her car door, she realized with her worry over Grand she had forgotten about seeing Cole in a short time. Her nerves came rushing back, and Viviane started praying scriptures, *I can do all things through Christ who gives me strength. I can do this.*

Grand had been a member of Great Hills since before Viviane was born. It was a nondenominational church that when Viviane still attended had around 400 members. She knew the church had grown, because Grand was on most every committee and kept her up to date. She said it kept her busy, especially after her husband Walt died.

Viviane had always loved the old church, her church in Atlanta couldn't compete with its quiet charm and beauty. She knew every nook and cranny, all the best places for hide and seek after visiting Grand every summer to attend their Vacation Bible School. One summer she had even followed Andy McCain around everywhere, because she had the biggest crush on him at the tender age of seven. Before her parents died, she had been very active and outgoing.

After her parents died, it became hard for her to make friends, because she was constantly worried they would leave her. That changed when she met Cole the summer before ninth grade when Grand had been working on a project with Cole's mother, Lynn. She and Cole, along with his brother Nathan had been dragged to church every day for six weeks to help clean and organize for the big fifty-year celebration planned for September.

Cole's mother was the new church secretary in charge of the anniversary committee and since the family had just moved from up north, Grand had volunteered to help guide Lynn, which meant the kids had been volunteered, too. Mostly they cleaned, scrubbed and polished everything in sight. It was a boring summer, made bearable with Cole's funny antics and the discovery of their mutual love of books.

In between furious cleaning sessions, Viviane had been trying to read Clive Cussler's latest thrillers before school started. The first day, Cole teased her for going off to read romances, but when he saw what she was reading, he made a stupid comment about girls not reading action books, and she wasn't a girl. She punched him, yelling how girls weren't supposed to be able to hit either, but she could.

He rubbed his arm most of the afternoon, not speaking to her, only sending angry looks her way. The next day he had brought her the next book in the series for her to borrow. They spent several weeks reading and talking of all the places they wanted to explore.

It was the beginning of their friendship, something Viviane had desperately needed because she had no real friends. It was hard for her to explain to people why she lived with her grandmother, called her Grand, and why she cried sometimes. Eventually she stopped trying and spent all of her time reading. She had a high reading comprehension for her age, but very few social skills.

The great thing about Cole was he never asked questions about her family. She always thought it was because his mom and Grand became close and he knew the situation from his mother. She wasn't sure, but he never asked or seemed to care one way or another.

Grand didn't realize Viviane had grown quiet, she was too busy trying not to get mad at the way Viviane was babying her. She had to remind herself this is what she wanted and to calm down. *It's all part of the plan, but when I do actually start to get old and slow down around ninety-two or three, I'm not going to be babied. No, ma'am,* she promised herself.

Chapter Four

When Viviane reached the church parking lot, she noticed a lot of cars were here for Sunday school. She turned to Grand, "You said the church had grown, but... wow."

Grand looked around at the people, and nodded, "Yes, our children and youth programs have really expanded to bring in a lot of families as Cartersville's grown. It's wonderful to see the church sanctuary so full."

Viviane hesitated in the vestibule, hurt by the thought of all the things she missed by hiding from Cole. She attended the church when he was away at college and working on a church staff up north. It wasn't until he moved back she had quit coming. Squeezing her hand, Grand said, "It's going to be okay, honey." Pulling her to the right, she continued, "Our class is upstairs, room 204."

Viviane's heart was pounding as she struggled to hold onto the peace she felt this morning. It was very hard when she was unsure of when she would run into Cole. She kept praying she wouldn't have to speak to him at all today, but ease into it gradually. Unconsciously, she ran her hands along her dress smoothing out the imaginary wrinkles.

Grand waltzed into the room and immediately greeted the five women seated in a semi-circle in front. In the midst of greetings, Viviane heard Grand say, "You remember my granddaughter, Viviane."

She nervously smiled and stammered, "Hello... everyone."

Walking to the first open chair, Viviane sat down and tried not to show how nervous she felt. She reminded herself she knew many of these ladies because they had watched her grow up.

Grand turned to a young woman with long, dark red hair standing in front of the classroom, "Good morning, Grace. How are you today?"

Grace had a huge smile light up her petite face as she rushed to hug Delia Anne, "I'm wonderful. It's so good to you. I've missed you the last two Sundays, but assumed you were with Viviane."

Grace still held onto Delia Anne, as she turned to Viviane to ask, "How are you Viviane? I haven't seen you in ages. You look beautiful with the belt that brings out your eyes." Barely pausing for breath, Grace continued quickly, "Oh, I love your shoes. I'm a pushover for shoes, just peek in my closet and you'd know."

Viviane looked at Grace's simple black, strappy sandals and wondered about this much more outgoing woman versus the shy girl she remembered in high school who always had a book in her hands. *We probably would've gotten along well with our mutual love for reading, but somehow, we never hung out with the same people. Grace was surrounded by a group of girls, quiet and smart like her, and I was more of a loner.*

Sensing the compliment was genuine, Viviane responded, "Thank you. I like your dress and hat, too! I know you love hats, I remember that from high school."

Grace really did look elegant in a beautiful ruby red dress with matching floppy hat, like women wore for the horse derby. She had never dressed like a typical teenager.

Grace smiled back and said, "Thank you. Why don't you both get something to eat?" Pointing to a small table with food she continued, "We'll get started soon."

Viviane put a few pieces of fruit on her plate, while Grand went for the coffee pot at the end of the table. "I'm not hungry but would like some coffee."

Grand got a cup and moved to sit where Viviane placed her purse. When Viviane sat down, she asked, "How many women are in the class?"

"The class started with just five, but now we usually have ten to twelve. I know Grace has been praying for God to use her to speak to the women through the lessons she teaches to help us grow closer to God and hear Him for ourselves."

"That's wonderful, I know I'd love to understand more about what God would say to me."

Grace moved to sit down in the circle, and formally welcomed everyone. When she reached for her Bible, Viviane opened hers and waited to hear what Grace would talk about this morning.

"I wanted to continue our discussion about falling in love with our Shepherd and sensing His presence more and more. Last week we covered how the first chapter in Song of Solomon points to Christ's love of his bride, the church. We learned how to apply it to us personally as women." Grace shuffled her papers and continued, "But more importantly, how to sense His presence daily in a relationship with God, our Shepherd, and Savior."

Viviane was amazed to hear the confidence and authority in Grace's voice. The girl she knew in high school was not this self-assured woman speaking before her.

"If you turn to chapter 2 verse 6 the Amplified version says, 'I can feel his left hand under my head, and his right hand embraces me'." Pausing just a moment, she continued with a smile, "I don't know about you ladies, but I find a lot of comfort in this verse. Each one of us has different circumstances in our lives, some are married, some divorced, some are still single, and some are widows and this verse reminds me that God says He will hold you in an intimate embrace and it doesn't matter who else is in your life, He will hold you up."

I can't believe the verse Grace is talking about is the very same verse I read this morning that felt so pointless. In the margins of her Bible she began to write, Lord thank you for embracing me whether I'm married, single, alone or in a crowd of people.

She looked up as Grace said, "If you turn to Deuteronomy chapter 13 verse 8, it says, 'The eternal God is your refuge, and underneath are the everlasting arms."

"This is one of my favorite verses," a small woman quietly said to the group. Viviane remember she had only nodded hello and quickly sat down when she arrived. "I love thinking of God as big enough for me to run into His arms. He doesn't even flinch when He sees me running to Him at a fast gallop full of fear and worry. He just scoops me up and says, 'It will be okay, I won't let those mean people keep you from being everything I want you to be.'"

Grace nodded in agreement, "That's perfect, Sharon. God's big enough to not only hold us, but to take care of us, and dry our tears. As women, we need to learn to embrace a comforting Savior, caring God, and most importantly learn to run to Him in every circumstance." Grace thought, *I love it when Sharon gathers her courage to speak. She's very insightful. Though new to the group and recently divorced, she struggles to feel God loves her when her own husband said he didn't.*

Another woman spoke up, "I've had a hard time running to God, and seeing Him as someone who'll care if my feelings have been hurt over something trivial like my daughter saying how she hates the dinner I made, or a coworker's mad because I didn't turn in a report fast enough."

"That's one of the reasons why I love God so much, because I know how much He cares about the little things," Grand said. "God cares when someone cuts us off when we're driving, when I have broken a vase I love, or when a neighbor's mad because they think my grass is too high. I know He cares about every moment of my day, because He says He counts the number of hairs on my head, and that changes daily." She waited for the chuckles to die down, and then continued, "If I go to Him before I get a chance to become upset or worried, He'll guide me through it, so I don't grow angry or overwhelmed."

"Don't you think He gets tired of all our whining and complaining?"A different woman asked, and Viviane thought she was the youngest in the group. "I mean, I know when my friends come to me about the same boy problem over and over, I get fed up. Doesn't God?"

The ladies laughed and Grace still chuckling answered, "Yes, Zoe, humans easily get fed up, but God isn't human. He loves us completely, and we don't bother Him, because He truly loves to hear from us, even about the same old problem."

Grand spoke up, "But that doesn't mean we get a free pass to complain. We have to remember to give thanks in all things, pray constantly for His will to be done, and listen for what He wants us to do."

Sharon nodded, "Yes, God wants to be in a relationship, which means communicating back and forth, not just a one-sided lecture from us."

Several more ladies told of ways God cared about the small incidents in their lives and before Viviane knew it the class was almost over. *I'm going to see Cole soon.*

Grace spoke up again, "Okay ladies, we have to end a few minutes early today. Sharon would you close us with prayer?"

With the simple request, Sharon bowed her head and said with a voice full of humility and dignity, "Dear Daddy, I'm so happy to be here today surrounded by these special ladies. I've felt your presence in our midst. Please continue to teach us how to be closer to you. Calm our hearts, and steady our fears in your precious Son's name, amen."

Viviane looked at Sharon's smiling face and felt her fears melting away as peace filled her heart again. *I've always marveled how God orchestrates teachings to bring better understanding of His word when you need it most. I'd forgotten the entire Bible can be applied to my life, even the Song of Solomon if I will just look closer and ask God for help. In James it says to ask for wisdom, because God gives liberally and ungrudgingly,* she reminded herself, *I just need to ask for help.*

Most everyone had left by the time Viviane put her Bible and notebook away. Grace came over and said, "Ms. Delia Anne, I have to put up the breakfast things if you would like to go downstairs and get our seats."

Grand smiled and said, "We can help you, and it'll be done in half the time."

"Thank you both," Grace said, putting the dishes in a canvas bag. "Viviane did you enjoy the class?"

Viviane didn't stop cleaning up the coffee things, but said, "I read the very same verse this morning and thought it didn't apply to me, but you reminded me it all matters. I just need to look at it in the right perspective and ask God for help." She looked at Grace, and smiled, "Thank you!"

Grace with a look of understanding in her eyes said, "You're welcome."

Soon the ladies finished cleaning, and Viviane prayed on their way down, *Lord, I want today to be about You- worshiping and learning from You. Please help me to not even notice Cole but keep my focus on the service. Put blinders on my eyes and a lock on my heart. Amen.*

Grace interrupted her prayer, "This is where Ms. Delia Anne and I usually sit."

Viviane turned her attention to Grace and noticed her pointing to a pew close to the front left of the sanctuary. Grand nodded saying, "We sit here so we aren't distracted and can focus on the stage."

Viviane smiled at God answering her prayer, "This is perfect, ladies, just perfect."

As they were seated, Viviane heard Grand say to the couple behind them, "Welcome. I'm so glad you could join us. This is my granddaughter, Viviane." She could hear the pride in her voice.

Viviane shook their hands and thought they were in their mid-thirties. The woman mentioned it was their first time and she was glad when Grand told them about all the different classes. *It means Grand's still pretty involved and couldn't have been sick for very long. Lord, please just let her need some rest, extra care, and be good as new very soon. I'm not ready to move back to Cartersville yet, not with my heart still hurting.*

Grand finished speaking as Pastor Winston made his way to the podium and soon Viviane was caught up with the service. The praise and worship was wonderful and she looked forward to Pastor Winston's preaching. She always enjoyed his sermons, because they were full of wit and wisdom. She was surprised what felt like a short time later that his sermon was over.

After the closing prayer, she put up her Bible and stood to say goodbye to Grace when she saw Cole standing across the sanctuary laughing with one of the teens. Her heart stopped, as she froze, blatantly staring.

He looked the same in a lot of ways with his dark brown hair streaked with blond from the sun. It was longer in the front, but he looked more mature, and sure of himself. He didn't seem to have noticed her and she was grateful, because she felt waves of both anger and shame washing over her.

Grand must have seen her freeze, because she heard her say repeatedly, "Viviane are you okay?"

She nodded her head slightly feeling like she was in a fog, "Yes, I'm fine. Just thinking about something Pastor Winston said." *Lord forgive me for lying in church.*

She grabbed her purse and moved to exit the aisle when Grand stopped her to ask, "Did you want to stop and speak to someone dear?"

Ignoring the wistful hope in Grand's voice, she replied, "No, let's go home and eat the pot roast you fixed. I've been looking forward to it all morning."

"You sure? I don't mind waiting; we could always go out to lunch. The pot roast can wait."

"No, it's fine." Trying for a light note, she took Grand's arm to steer her toward the exit. "I'm hungry and nothing but your pot roast will satisfy me now."

Grand saw she wasn't going to budge and let the matter drop for now, "If you're sure. I'm a bit hungry myself."

Back straight, Viviane looked neither left nor right, and didn't see Cole's eyes following her, but people in church watched him tracking his high school sweetheart right out the door.

Chapter Five

Cole West stood alone in the sanctuary after saying goodbye to several teens in his youth group. The lights had been turned off, but he could still see his way to his office. He unlocked his office door and moved to sit in the big, leather chair he prayed in when he wanted to be comfortable. He felt the old, brown leather give way as his body fell into the familiar grooves of the soft, cool fabric. The cleaning lady often threaten to trash it, but he had spent too many hours praying in this chair to give it up.

His thoughts drifted to when he had woken up this morning and prayed for God to move in people's lives today. He prayed for his students, especially the ones having a hard time with family or school problems, for the service to touch lives in the congregation, and for God's will to be done. While at breakfast, he had prayed specifically for God's will in his own life. He had been struggling lately with knowing God's direction, battling for a few months a restless feeling, which he couldn't seem to pray away. *What I definitely did NOT pray for was Viviane Stanton-Mays to come back into my life.*

Running his hands through his hair, he told himself he needed a haircut this week, which reminded him Viviane's hair was longer than he had ever seen it. She kept it in a short bob in school. He knew she had cut it when her parents died, because it was hard for her to brush it without missing her mom braiding it before bed every night.

Viviane, he kept thinking. He spent the first year after their break up, praying specifically about a godly wife. A woman who would be an asset to his ministry and career and began to look around college at his female classmates, wondering if one of them was the woman God destined him to marry. When he graduated still single, he thought God meant for him to meet someone while he was interning at a church near the college, but even a year later after he become an official part of the staff, he still had no wife. It wasn't his age that bothered him, he knew several guys his age still single, including his best friend, but he never knew of a minister not to be married by the time he was in full time ministry.

Gathering a few things for the evening, he packed his bag and locked up. As he passed a few cars in the parking lot, he remembered driving up to the church four years ago to apply for the youth pastor position that had opened up. Cole pulled open the car door to his blue Nissan, *I was so sure of myself, even resigning my position in Virginia to move and apply, because I was so confident in God's timing.*

The heat blasted him, and he got in to crank up the AC. He turned his car to drive home, thankful he wouldn't be eating lunch with his parents today because they were in Rome visiting his brother. He needed time to think. It had been Cole's mother who had told him about the job, always keeping him up to date on church news, including the fact Pastor Winston didn't feel any of the current applicants were who God wanted. Lynn had been wanting him to move home for years, and both felt this was a God given opportunity. Cole had moved back as quickly as he could.

He made an appointment with Pastor Winston and the two men talked a great length about his single status, youth ministry, and future plans. He was honest about the disappointment he felt with God about not being married, and the Pastor promised to partner with him in prayer about the situation and if God wanted him as the youth minister for the church.

For the next two months, the two men met weekly to talk, and a friendship developed, allowing Pastor Winston to see Cole's heart and gain a better understanding of his love for God and youth. Eventually the Pastor went to the council to recommend him for the job, and even though they were hesitant, everything worked out.

Cole pulled into his driveway, glad he lived on the outskirts of Cartersville in the downtown Cassville area. His home was on the edge of his parent's property, but far he enough away he had privacy. Growing up, his parents had always rented out the ranch house, but a few years ago after the last tenants left it had sat empty. He was positive his mother hadn't let his dad rent it out, because she thought renting it to him would be an incentive to move home. He wouldn't tell his mother, but it did make the decision easier.

As he pulled into the garage, he wondered what the congregation thought of his single status. Lately he noticed more and more mothers hovering around him with their daughters. He didn't want the church to become a dating service. *But none of this explains why Viviane was here. I hadn't seen her since we broke up junior year and now here out the blue she's worshipping God with an openness and honesty I've never seen before.*

The garage shut, he was able to hear his dog barking, and walked toward the kitchen, he called out, "Hush, Moses. I'm coming."

The house was built in the forties and renovated by his mother six months before he decided to move back. She had put in granite countertops, stainless steel appliances, and new furniture to tempt new renters, she said. A two bedroom, one and half baths with lots of architectural details, including large windows and long back porch, with a large plot for a family to add more space to grow, as his mother often reminded him. *I know better than to tangle with Mom, and everyone knows the real reason she renovated, but since I've always loved this house, it wasn't even a hard choice.*

Before he could walk into the open living room, a big chocolate lab jumped on him getting hair all over his suit. "DOWN, Moses. Get down girl," Cole said in a loud, commanding voice as he shoved the dog. "I really don't want you to ruin another pair of pants, Mo."

"Your dog isn't going to settle down, a storm is headed this way."

Cole whirled around to face the deep, masculine voice coming from the darkened living room to see rising from the couch a tall, thin black man about Cole's age. He continued speaking, "Mo always freaks out when it rains, and would be a great weatherman except she goes crazy."

Cole recognized his best friend, as Mike continued talking, "The problem, man is this is Georgia and it always rains. Want a coke?"

The two men met at the local two-year college while he decided whether to go into full time ministry or not. They played a flag football game and had been best friends since, which is why he wasn't too surprised to find him at his house. Mike came over a lot to watch sports.

Chuckling at Mike's funny expression, Cole sat in a large recliner, and said, "Sure, I'd love one of my cokes, and by the way, I gave you a key to my place to take care of the dog when I'm away, not to break in and steal my food."

Ignoring him, Mike asked, "Why'd you name that dog Moses anyway, she's a girl and afraid of water." He brought the coke and made himself comfortable on the couch.

"She was from a litter one of my youth kids gave me and I didn't want to disappoint him. It wasn't until I brought her home I found out he was a she and then our first thunderstorm together I found out she was terrified of storms." Cole petted Moses and murmured in her ear. "After I'd had her a few weeks the kid's mom told me she had caught her six-year-old daughter trying to baptize poor Mo, who's been afraid of water ever since."

Turning to Mike he said, "I gave her the name Moses to encourage her to stand up to her fears, like Moses embraced his speech problem and went on to part the Red Sea. I thought it would be inspirational."

"Well, I didn't come to talk about your dog."

Cole raised his eyebrow but didn't respond. He watched Mike squirm on the couch.

"Yeah, I... um... felt I should be here for support... you know."

"Shouldn't you be eating with your girlfriend? You and Devin always go out to eat with the singles group at church."

Mike looked away, "I saw Viviane at church this morning and being the sensitive Christian guy that I am, well I'm here for moral support, plus we could watch some baseball, there's a game on soon."

Cole laughed, "That's gracious of you since I know you don't get the channel the game is on."

Mike didn't hide his grin, "Maybe, but I know it was probably hard to see Viviane. I mean," turning serious he continued, "You've never talked about the break up. I still don't know what happened, and that's fine, but it's been more than ten years, man."

"I'm fine, Mike. Just surprised to see her is all. Let me go change and we'll watch the game. You know where the remote is."

"Well, if you need to talk I'm here for you man. Seriously!" Reaching for the remote, he patted the couch for Moses to hop up next to him. Cole left the two of them sitting together and went to his bedroom to change.

He struggled to pay attention to the game, too busy trying not to think of Viviane, he kept seeing her midnight blue eyes that still haunted him. Her eyes were the first thing he noticed when he had met her twenty years ago.

He had been sent down a long hall to find a girl wearing a large purple Cartersville Hurricane t-shirt, and jean shorts. He found her in a storage room, her back to him reading a book completely surrounded by boxes covered in dust.

"Hey, I'm Cole. Are you Viviane? I'm supposed to help you."

"Oh, my God!" She turned quickly around, hiding her book as she looked for her grandmother to see if she would get in trouble. Not seeing her, she started to laugh.

He loved that laugh, loud and unafraid, and decided he would enjoy spending the summer with her. It wasn't until later he learned that laugh would be rare until they got to be better friends. *It had been worth it to win her friendship,* he thought. *She was funny, smart, and good company, not like most girls always talking about boys and makeup.* She liked reading action books, watching football, and would play outside with him and his brother when they had breaks from cleaning up the church that summer.

Cole kept up a running commentary about the game to keep Mike from becoming suspicious. He was worried if he didn't yell at the Giants playing against the Braves every once in a while, Mike would want to talk about Viviane. He knew if he talked to anyone it would be Pastor Winston, because he was the only person besides Viviane who knew what really happened over winter break their junior year of college. *I know Mike thinks I'm paying attention. I'm totally multitasking this- Viviane who?*

Mike knew Cole wasn't paying attention when Chipper Jones hit the possible last ball of his career, and Cole only nodded his head, not saying a word. He would let him stay silent on the subject and hope Viviane left soon. He had never spoken to her, but he knew trouble when he saw it, his momma raised no fool.

Chapter Six

"Don't you dare move!" Viviane had been out shooting with her camera all morning, which explained why she was telling a large black cow to stand still. She started early, out the door before the sun was up to get some sunrise shots. She wasn't a morning person and was getting a bit cranky from the hot sun and hunger. After five hours she was finishing up at one of the pastures near Grand's home when her stomach rumbled, and a glance at her watch said it was almost noon. *If I hurry, I could eat with Grand.*

Carefully she put her extra lens up, the spare batteries back in the side pocket, and zipped the bag to make the short trek to her car. She put her bag in the front seat and started for home.

Viviane's phone rang and she struggled to grab it while still managing to stay on the road. Worried it was Grand, she answered in a panicked voice, "Hello?"

"Viv, it's Kathie. How's your Grand?"

Viviane slowed down the car. "It's good to hear from you. Grand's doing better. I know being here has helped, but I'm still trying to determine if she is going to need someone with her full time or not. How are you? How's work?"

"Work's good, steady appointments starting in September. I'm actually calling to see if you could do the engagement photo shoot for the Landon woman a week from this Saturday, because she has to go out of town. Can you do it?"

"Sure Kat, not a problem. Tell Tara Landon I'll meet her in Decatur near the tracks for pictures. If you'll send me her contact info, I'll email her about wardrobe changes."

"I will Viv, you're a gem. Keep me up to date on Grand. I care for you like family and will keep you both in my prayers."

"Thank you. I'll be praying for your travels. Talk soon." Pulling into the driveway, she hung up.

Inside she discovered Grand sitting in the living room with TV on mute. She noticed her wearing a purple caftan with white flowers, and walked up to check on her, worried because she looked to be staring off into space. Laying a gentle hand on her shoulder, Viviane asked, "Grand, are you okay?"

She turned to Viviane, a slight smile on her weathered face, "I'm fine honey. I just got off the phone with Lauren Blake. Do you remember her from church? She has a daughter near your age."

"Of course, I remember her and her daughter Hillary. The woman is on just about as many committees as you."

Grand began to fidget with her hands, "She called to remind me I'm supposed to help during the silent auction this Saturday. I signed up months ago, it's one of the biggest events at the church to raise money for the youth group's winter mission trip."

"Oh, it's for the youth group?" Viviane sat down on the sofa, not wanting to hear what she knew Grand was going to say next.

"Yes, Lauren called because some volunteers have dropped out and they need help," she continued, unable to look her in the eye, "You know she can make me a little insane and was talking about how we all need to help the youth and our Christian duty, and well, before I knew it I had signed up for the whole shindig."

"This is the thing you were helping Grace find items for the silent auction early this summer, right?"

"That's right, I was only going to help with the phone calls, and finding donors for the auction, because we wanted the items early this year to use in the advertising. Now I'm signed up to help on Friday for set up and help run the auction on Saturday," she paused, "I've just been so tired this week, and I've been trying to keep you from noticing."

Viviane replayed the past few days in her mind, and realized Grand hadn't done much, mostly resting on the sofa and watching the cooking channels. Not the usually busy schedule she kept all of Viviane's life. She could hear the anguish in Grand's voice, and said quietly, "Grand, it's okay. I can help Friday and Saturday. Then you can just show up for the event that evening if you feel up to it. That will take care of Lauren." *Lord, I'm going to have to do some serious praying to work side by side with Cole, because I know I won't be able to avoid him like I originally planned.*

"Oh, sweetie, thank you so much," Grand said, hugging her tight. "I know it will be hard for you, because Cole will be there. The event is his idea, they've done it several years in a row, because it raises so much money for the kids." She sat back looking Viviane in the eye, tears shining, "I hate not being able to help."

"It's all settled." Viviane clapped her hands together, "I came home for lunch. I've been taking pictures all morning and now I'm starving. What can I get you to eat?"

"I'm not hungry right now, but I'll sit with you while you eat."

While Viviane made herself some lunch, Grand sat in the living room waiting to join her. Lauren Blake's call this morning was better than she hoped. *Wouldn't that woman be angry to know she was helping Viviane and Cole get back together?* It was perfect, she couldn't have planned it better if she tried, because now Viviane and Cole would be forced to speak to each other civilly, which would get the ball rolling. She knew they would quickly resolve their differences after they started talking. They were perfect for each other after all.

She bit her lip, feeling a twinge of guilt lying to Viviane about her health. She had put on another caftan this morning and ate breakfast so when Viviane came home later, she would be too full to eat. Sick people don't eat much. She was tired of only watching TV every day, she was use to cleaning, and going out. Plus, not being able to try all the new recipes she was learning was driving her crazy, but what was really hard was this was the first year she wasn't co-organizing the fundraiser with Cole.

It was a huge event with food, entertainment and the silent auction. *I love this fundraiser, but I love Viviane more,* she reminded herself, *and this is about her happiness. Which means if I live on this sofa for six months, I'll do it.* Hearing Viviane singing in the kitchen, she continued, *It's worth it.*

After lunch, Viviane refused to leave Grand and they spent the rest of the day with more cooking shows. At seven, the phone rang, and Grand picked it up, "Hello?"

Viviane couldn't hear who was on the phone, but they seemed to be talking rapidly and was upset.

"It's okay, Grace. We'll find something to replace those two items. No, you're right we need to have them and a picture isn't enough." Grand kept nodding her head, "Yes...yes... I'll call you as soon as I think of something. Don't worry, I won't breathe a word to Lauren, wouldn't dream of it."

She ended the call and then turned to explain, "Grace called in a panic to say one of our huge donors dropped out. They offered to get the two items to us eventually. Now we've got to find two expensive items and I'm not sure who's left to ask at this late date."

She started to rise, but Viviane said, "Wait, would one of my big framed photos work? I have several that are from around Cartersville."

"That would be perfect sweetie, thank you. Now, I only need one more item, hopefully several hundred dollars."

Excited to help, Viviane thought a moment and said, "I think I can help with that, too! I can offer to do a photo shoot for either a graduation or engagement. I can let them change outfits, produce some shots, and give them a cd. That should be in the $200-300 dollar range."

"Oh, that's wonderful, and helps a lot."

Grand came over to hug her, and Viviane said, "It's not a problem, it won't cost me much, but time. I'd like to help raise money for the kids. It's a good fundraising idea," she paused, "but don't tell Cole I said that."

"Deal. Let me call Grace back, so she can stop hyperventilating. She didn't want Lauren to hear we hadn't met our donation quota."

"You do that. I'm going to run to the printer here and see if they can print one of the new photos I took this morning. I got some really good shots of the sunrise around Cartersville." Packing up her things she said, "I need to see if I can get everything done here or if I need to go back to Atlanta and pick something up from my apartment. I can definitely have the display pictures for the photo shoot printed here."

Grand watched her walk out the door a few minutes later thinking, *Lord, is it wrong I hope she goes to Atlanta for a bit, so I can get out of the house for a few hours? I'm going stir crazy stuck here.*

Chapter Seven

Viviane put a box of tablecloths on an empty table. She wiped her forehead, feeling hot and sweaty, but the work the volunteers had been doing all day was really coming together. She had gotten to the church at nine and hadn't sat down since she had received her orders from Grace.

The fellowship hall was a large room with a long row of windows connected to the gym where the food and entertainment were designated to be Saturday evening. She couldn't believe all the items donated by the church and surrounding community that had to be sorted and labeled for display.

Thankfully, Cole had been busy directing everyone, and working directly with the entertainers setting up. She had barely seen him all day which is good, because she wasn't sure if all of her extra praying last night about their first face to face meeting would make things easier. She had been jumpy all day, worried when he would show up and how she would react. Grace had left her to cover the tables, while she went to get food. Neither woman stopped for lunch when the others did, because Grace needed to be finished by five to meet a friend from out of town.

"Here, let me get that for you," Cole said as he bent over to pick up a tablecloth that had fallen out of the box.

"Thanks." Viviane took the fabric from him and busied herself covering the tables. *Lord, what do I do? Ignore him, be indifferent or cool and mysterious?*

"I could help you and Grace. We finally got all the musicians hooked up to the sound system."

She forced herself to look at him and could see the hope in his eyes, almost childlike. *I can't understand his desire to speak to me after so long.* Remembering her prayer this morning not to hold onto any hurt or bitterness, she said, "I'm sure it would help Grace out, she has to leave by five to drive to the airport." Diving into the whole Christian forgiveness stuff, she continued, "I remember Grand talking about this event over the past few years, but I had no idea it was this elegant."

He smiled, "Thanks. I wanted to do something different that would have a big impact on helping the kids earn money for the mission trip. I can't see a kid not being able to serve the Lord, because a family couldn't afford to send them."

She could hear the pride in his voice, and remembered he always had a heart for missions. *It's wonderful he's passing that love to future generations, but Lord, I'm not quite ready to tell him that!*

The two of them spent the next twenty minutes covering the tables with black and white tablecloths, and they talked about the mission trip planned for next February. Viviane had no idea how much time, money, and energy the youth put into a five-day mission trip over their winter break. Cole talked quite a bit about past trips and the impact it had on the community, and the kids who donated their vacation time to serve. *It isn't too hard talking to him as long as it's about the youth.*

As they finished covering the last table, she said, "I'm really impressed with the kids."

Cole shrugged, "It really rose out of SPLASH, and the kids wanting to help more than once a year. So, after some planning, we started this trip to go outside of Cartersville and help others."

"I've heard a lot about SPLASH from Grand but have never been here in July to help."

He walked over to a cart full of items and began moving them around, "It started in 2008, the year before I moved back, and it's grown into a huge event, over a thousand people from multiple churches come together to serve Bartow County in mission type projects. It's really about the teens and teaching them the mission field is right where you're at. We usually have over 400 teens paying their own money to work during the day and worship and learn in nightly services. It's great to see all the different ages working together. I've seen men and women in their eighties working side by side with teens, it's a lot of fun to help. I know they have a photo team that documents the work every year. If you're around to help, I know the woman in charge and could send her your way."

Viviane hesitated, she could hear the passion in his voice, and it's something she knew she would love, "I just don't know if I'll be here next summer."

"Well, it's really a cool event, and I know you would enjoy it. The service projects range from running Backyard Bible Clubs to building handicap ramps and washing windows to painting."

"Sorry that took so long. I thought grabbing a pizza at 2:00 would be fast, but I was wrong," Grace said carrying a large pizza box. She stopped when she saw Cole and Viviane talking. "Sorry to interrupt."

Reaching for the box to hide the awkwardness, Viviane said, "It's okay, I'm just glad you're back. I'm hungry."

"I didn't realize you two hadn't eaten. You should've said something." Cole also looked a bit embarrassed.

"Cole, where did you... oh sorry to interrupt. I guess you two ladies were too busy to eat when the rest of us stopped for lunch?"

Viviane looked up from her slice of pizza, cheese dangling down her chin to see a tall woman dressed in a pant suit of dark blue, which set off her platinum blonde hair. She looked to be in her late forties with blue eyes that sparkled with dislike toward her. Viviane grabbed a napkin to wipe her chin to respond, when she heard Grace speak.

"Mrs. Blake," Grace said with only a trace of frustration in her voice, "Viviane was gracious enough to work through lunch to make sure we would finish sorting and cataloging the items, because I have to leave to drive to the airport at five."

"How can I help you Mrs. Blake?" Cole asked trying to ease the tension in the room.

"Well, yes, I needed to ask you about a few things regarding the food setup and if you're not too busy..." she said pointedly glaring at Viviane. "I need to go over a few other things as well." She didn't wait for an answer but pulled him toward the gym.

When they walked off, the two women looked at each other and burst out laughing. Watching Lauren Blake dragging Cole off by his shirt was extremely funny. She thought he hid the panic pretty well, but she could read his face and knew he wished he could disappear. As their laughter slowed down, Viviane said, "Thanks for lunch. We can eat quickly and be done well before five so you can get on your way to the airport. Traffic's going to be crazy on a Friday night."

"I know, but my best friend is coming into town and I haven't seen her in ages. I hope she enjoys silent auctions, because I'll be here tomorrow night."

"Don't worry about staying for the whole evening, especially any clean up. Grand and I will be here to help."

"Oh, we do most of the cleanup on Sunday afternoon, because the event goes so late and we don't want to give anyone an excuse not to go to church the next morning."

"That makes sense," Viviane said as she grabbed a second slice of pizza. "Now explain how we organize the items on the tables for display."

Grace spent the next few minutes while they finished eating, explaining the set up for the auction. The items were grouped by category with a suggested retail price listed at the top of the bid sheet. Numbers were used instead of names because some people bought items for gifts to be given later. At the end of the night, the winners were announced and people came to pick up their item and pay.

"What about the people who don't win, but want to donate money?" Viviane asked.

"Cole came up with a solution to that very problem," Grace said as she threw away the pizza boxes. "He has the youth kids walk around with baskets at the end of the night for people to donate any last money they brought with them. He mentions this money goes directly to the help the kids who wouldn't be able to afford to go without scholarship money."

"That's a good idea." *Lord, I don't want to be impressed with all of Cole's forethought and prep for this big event.*

Grace gathered up pens and papers and began to move around the tables, "It's the big event for fundraising, but he's done smaller things to help the kids raise money as well, car washes and bake sales. His cakes are actually a big hit, a pound cake from a favorite aunt that everyone raves about."

Wondering if Cole really bakes the cake, she said, "Well, let's get this done quickly so you can get on the road."

Grace began to sort, and quickly both ladies began to lay out the tables, creating eye catching displays to lure potential bidders. Since they spent all morning organizing and labeling, the table set up went quickly.

A few minutes after four, Grace wiped her brow, but smiled, "It looks great! Your artistic eye really helped create a great display. Your framed photo is going to be a big hit. The sunrise of downtown with the fog is stunning."

"Thank you! It's one of those perfectly timed photos with everything just right, and I only snapped the picture." Viviane smiled as she remembered the funny, excited feeling she got when she shot it, and knew it would be one of the special ones.

Grace caught her eye, "I'm sure it was more than that." Moving to get her purse, she continued, "I don't know if I thanked you for also donating the photo shoot package? I called your grandmother in an absolute panic, and not even twenty minutes later she called to say you solved the whole problem. We have several families with graduating seniors this year and I'm sure that will be a hot item as well."

"I think the auction will do well this year, and I'm excited to be able to help the kids."

"Well, you've helped me tremendously." Walking over to hug her, Grace smiled.

"Your welcome, drive carefully and we'll see you tomorrow night."

Waving goodbye, Grace ran out the door and Viviane laid the last bid sheet down and stepped back to see fifteen tables covered in prizes. Working with Grace made her wish they had been better friends long ago. *But that's okay, we're definitely friends after today!*

She moved around the tables one last time to make sure everything was perfect, thinking about the long, cold shower she was going to take once she got home. She was so focused on her task, she missed Cole watching her, his gaze intent on her every move. It was only when someone called his name that he shook his head and turned away, hoping no one noticed he had been staring. He answered one last question and began to finish the last task Lauren had given him.

Cole thought he hadn't been noticed, but Lauren had been keeping an eye on the two of them. She noticed both of them watching each other throughout the day. *This will not do,* she thought to herself, *my Hillary would be a better match for Cole, and the good mother that I am, have been working toward that goal for months. Viviane Stanton-Mays isn't going to ruin all of my hard work. Hillary would've been here today, but she had school. Tomorrow night I'll make sure they work the event together. That would show Viviane that Cole has moved on, and she won't get a chance to break his heart a second time. Hillary would be a perfect pastor's wife.*

Chapter Eight

Viviane ran down the steps taking two at a time, *I'm late Lord, and I can't find my purse.* Landing on the bottom she called out, "Grand, have you seen my purse?"

"I have it," Grand called from the kitchen.

Viviane found her holding a small purple clutch, sitting at the dining table in a stunning gray pantsuit. "You look lovely, but you don't have to be there for another hour. I'm going early to help Grace." Viviane reached for the purse, "She called to say her friend had jet lag and won't be there tonight."

Grand put her hands on her hips, ready to do battle, "Viviane, I'm going with you tonight. I know Grace's friend is in town and with both of us there, she can leave right after the bidding closes."

"Now, Grand..." but Viviane never got to finish.

"I'm leaving now. We can either go together, or I can drive myself, but we're both walking out this door in a minute."

"It'll be a long night, and you want to go to church in the morning."

"I'll be fine, sweetie. I've rested for two days and this is a big event for the youth. I'm going. Let's go, we're running late."

Realizing she was determined to go, but wanting to have the last word, Viviane said, "Fine, I'll drive, but you're going to do a lot of sitting tonight."

Marching to the door, she paused as she turned around to ask, "Do I look dressed up enough for this event? I didn't realize... and you look stunning..." She tried to hide her nervousness but was failing miserably.

Grand looked at Viviane standing uneasily before her in a long fuchsia ball gown skirt with a dark gray sleeveless sweater top, accented with a long-beaded necklace that matched the skirt. Her hair up in an elegant bun, the ensemble seemed to say Viviane was artistic and was very eye catching. "Dear, you look beautiful. It suits you and has just enough sparkle for the perfect hostess for tonight's event." *Cole won't be able to keep his eyes off of her.*

Feeling a bit better, Viviane hugged her and said, "Thanks, Grand."

Fifteen minutes later, the two women walked through the crowded gym to the equally crowded fellowship hall. Some of the youth were scrambling to bring in more chairs. Grand moved past all the excitement and went to the main auction table. She and Viviane made sure the tables were all set, when Viviane heard a shrill voice say, "Well, I'm glad to see you're finally here ladies. Hillary and I have been here since 3:30."

Turning around, she saw Lauren Blake barreling down the aisle toward them with a young woman trailing behind her. Lauren was moving fast and everyone instinctively moved out of the way. Both women were dressed in black, Lauren in a long evening gown, and her daughter in a short cocktail dress. *It must be Hillary behind her, because they even having matching pearl necklaces to set off their platinum blonde hair.*

Hoping to prevent Grand from saying a biting comment, Viviane said, "You both look stunning. Hillary, I love that dress on you. We're all set up here, and came a little later, since we knew we'd be here so late handing out the auction items."

Hillary smiled, "I love your skirt, Viviane. The color looks nice on you."

"Thank you! How's teaching been this year? Your mom said you're teaching third grade?"

Eyes sparkling, Hillary gushed, "I love it! Third graders are the best age to teach."

As she listened to Hillary tell a funny story about two of her little boys, Viviane could see how much she truly loved her job. After she finished, her mother said, "Hillary, aren't you needed in the gym to help Cole tonight with the entertainment?"

Blushing, Hillary nodded, but said to Viviane, "It's good to see you. Have fun tonight."

Viviane waved at her as she left, noticing Lauren leave without even glancing her way. *I'm not sure why that woman seems to dislike me so much.* She and Hillary had never been in the youth group at the same time, since she was five years older than the girl. *I've always been nice to her, because her mother demanded such perfection and I felt bad for her.*

Shrugging her shoulders, she turned to see if Grand wanted help, but couldn't find her. She walked around and saw her standing near the restrooms. "Grand is everything okay?"

"Yes, just a quick and timely break," she said, eyes twinkling.

"I understand. Ready to help the kids earn some money?"

Grand grabbed her arm smiling and said, "Of course. Let's go help people empty their wallets. My Walter always said I was very good at that!"

The fellowship hall, gym and most of the parking lot were packed all night with adults and kids, once the bidding started. Viviane, Grace and Grand had been constantly moving all night promoting the auction and reminding bidders to keep an eye on their items to not lose out to someone else. It was a fun evening, and Viviane understood why Grand insisted on being here for the entire event. Seeing the church community supporting such a worthy cause reminded her why she loved Cartersville.

"Viviane?" When she turned to see who was calling her name, she saw a petite looking woman with long brown hair and big green eyes looking at her.

"I'm Viviane."

"Cole sent me. I'm Christy Boulier and I'm in charge of the SPLASH photography team. When I saw your photo, I knew I had to meet you."

"Thank you. Yes, Cole told me about you yesterday. I've heard of SPLASH but haven't been here in the summer before."

"We'd love to have you next year if you're around. We don't take photos quite so artistically for SPLASH, but it's a fun way to serve, because you get to see a little bit of everything. I understand you live in Atlanta, but if you can fit a day or two into your schedule, please let me know."

"I don't know what my schedule will look like, but I'd love to help."

"You'll love it, Viv. I'm a team leader and it's so much fun." Grace said walking over to where the women were standing.

"Let me give you my contact information, Christy." Viviane moved to get her purse, she had a business card she could give her.

After exchanging contact information, Christy said, "It was really nice to meet you, Viviane. I'll talk to you soon."

"Thank you, I really hope I can help next year."

After goodbyes, Viviane turned to Grace and said, "I'm going to mingle a bit. I need to mention to one of my bidders his bid on the golf clubs isn't the top one anymore."

Walking away, she found the gentlemen and laughed when he hustled to the table to up his bid.

"Have you eaten anything? I've seen you running around all night and haven't seen you slow down once. I can't let you starve like yesterday."

Viviane turned around to see Cole smiling at her. She noticed his causal look of dark khaki pants and linen shirt rolled half way up to reveal muscled, tan arms. Looking at the crowd, she gave herself a moment and then said, "I'm fine Cole, thank you. I ate twenty minutes ago, we've been taking shifts since it's so busy." *Just friends, just friends*, she told herself, angry she noticed how handsome he looked. Turning to smile at him, she said, "I'm having a great time. The event is amazing. You must be proud."

He could hear the excitement in her voice and was glad she was having fun. Her smile was genuine and he loved seeing it all night. She had been working the event, talking to everyone like she had never been away. "Thank you. I'm glad you're having fun. Everyone's talking about your photo. I've seen it and wow, I knew you're talented, but it's amazing." *I think she's been avoiding me.*

She blushed, hearing his praise over her work still had the power to make her sing inside. "Thanks, it means a lot to hear you say that. Cole..."

"There you are. I've been looking for you. Mother sent me, because one of the bands can't find an extension cord. Can you help me?" Hillary asked. She turned to Viviane, "Sorry to interrupt, it's a little hectic and the musician's a little temperamental."

"It's okay, Hillary." Turning to Cole, she said with only a little hesitation, "Maybe we can talk later?"

Cole placed his hand on hers, "I'd like that."

She watched him walk away. *It's easier to talk at the event surround by people, since I'm still battling a desire to be near him. Stupid heart.* Sighing, she told herself, *Now isn't the time to discover if it's a good idea or not. I don't know if we could be friends, again. That's the civil thing to do right? But what if my heart can't take it, knowing we weren't friends anymore?*

Lauren Blake watched her lost in thought. She had seen Cole walk over to her and didn't like the way they were looking at each other. Thankfully, Hillary came to ask her a question and she sent her to Cole. She turned to Tessa Green, a mom of one of the youth, "Have you noticed anything between Cole and Viviane since she came back?"

Surprised by the turn in conversation, Tessa said, "No, I haven't seen her much. Isn't that Delia Anne's granddaughter? I thought they broke up years ago."

"Yes, they did. Poor Cole," Lauren said as she put more cupcakes on the table, "I don't know if he ever got over her coming home one day out of the blue and breaking up with him. It was such a surprise to all of us, we thought they'd get married."

"Oh, that's awful. I didn't know she'd broken his heart." Tessa held her hand over her heart feeling sympathy for the young youth pastor. "I knew he wasn't married. Sad, because would he be such a great husband."

She grabbed another woman's arm who was walking by, "Carol, did you know about Cole and Viviane's break up? I didn't know she'd broken his heart. It must be so hard having her around."

"No, I didn't know. We're pretty new, only been here two years. So, Delia Anne's granddaughter broke Cole's heart. That's awful."

Lauren didn't stay to hear the rest, she had to keep things running smoothly and couldn't stay in one place for long. However, anytime she saw a teen's parent, or caught Cole and Viviane looking at each other, she spoke to whomever she was standing near to ask what they thought of the breakup.

Chapter Nine

The night passed quickly for Viviane, and too soon they were collecting bid sheets to determine the winners. Viviane couldn't believe how much she enjoyed an event started by Cole, but she had loved every moment. She hadn't seen him much after they talked, but once in a while she would catch his eye and they both would smile.

"Viviane your photograph was one of the top money makers tonight," Grand said waving a sheet of paper at her. "It raised almost a thousand dollars. People had to use two sheets for bidding."

"Wow, that's wonderful." She handed the sheets she tallied to Grand. "I can't believe it."

"The only thing is it's an anonymous bid and I don't know who got it. It's probably a Christmas gift." She took the papers, and continued, "Your photo package did well too, $400! A family with a graduating senior scooped that one up." *I knew my girl was talented, but a thousand dollars talented, well that's something you tell people, especially a nosey blonde with exceedingly rude manners.*

When Grace walked up, Grand said to her, "I'll take your sheets. You scoot on out and see your friend. I'll let Cole know the winners to announce for the big-ticket items."

"Thank you, Delia Anne. I'd like to get home and check on Bailey. Traffic out of the parking lot will be horrendous soon." She turned to Viviane, "Thank you so much for everything, the two items you had in the auction did so well and helping me Friday and tonight. I had so much fun working with you."

The two women hugged, and Viviane said, "Me too! See you at church tomorrow.

Cole walked up, and after waving to Grace, he said, "Do we have the winners, ladies? The natives are getting restless."

Grand handed him a short list, "These are the names for the big-ticket items. Viviane is going to type up the items for people to find out if they've won." She turned to Viviane, "Make several copies, we'll need one to mark off who picks up their item."

"Okay, Grand." She ran to the church office and typed quickly, noticing the master sheet listed several anonymous bidders. *I'd love to know who bought my photograph, but I guess I should remember pride goes before a fall.*

After she printed several copies, she rushed back to the gym to hear the end of Cole's speech, "...thank you again for a great night. All of the money goes to help the youth and further their efforts to reach people for Christ. The last donations you make tonight will go in a special fund to make sure every youth at our church can go on the winter break mission trip. I've always felt kids should have a chance to serve God, and your donations will make sure our youth can achieve that goal. Let's pray."

Viviane bowed her head but didn't listen to his prayer as she prayed for one of her own. *Lord, I don't know every reason for my being here, but I do hear the love Cole has for these kids and I know we're both in the right place, because of Your guiding hand. Help me to put away any hurt or anger I might still have and extend true friendship to him.* She wiped a tear, but continued, *God, I believe it's Your will for me to mend our broken friendship. Help me to walk in Your will for my life and not be bitter. Amen.*

She felt better after she prayed, and when she looked up to see Cole smiling at her she was confident God heard her prayer. She and Grand were busy for the next hour making sure everyone went home with the correct item and collecting money. As the line began to thin out, she asked Grand, "What happens with the items that aren't picked up?"

Grand finished handing a spa package to a young woman, and then turned to her and said, "We load them on a cart to take to Cole's office. He'll make sure over the next week each person gets their items." Taking the check from the lady, Grand thanked her and then said, "We can start loading the carts now. I think that's it for the evening. I'm ready to head home. I'm tired tonight, my love."

Viviane rushed over to her, "Are you okay? Do you need to sit down?"

She pulled out a chair, but Grand only nodded no, "I'm fine, just tired. We've worked hard, but it's such a worthy cause."

Viviane stepped back but kept a close watch on Grand to make sure she didn't pick up anything too heavy. She felt exhausted herself. "Do we have a key to Cole's office?"

Grand frowned, "No, and I'm sure it's locked. I don't want to walk all the way down there and find we can't get in. Why don't you go find him and get the key?"

She watched Grand sit for probably the first time all evening, and quickly agreed. She wanted to get her home as quickly as she could. Rushing out of the hall toward the gym, she searched all over but couldn't find him. Confident he hadn't left yet, she went out to the parking lot to find him helping someone load a brand-new mountain bike into their car. She waited until he finished, and then they both thanked the gentleman for his support.

Suddenly nervous to be completely alone with him, she blurted out, "Great evening, wasn't it? I've been looking for you. Do you have the keys to your office? Of course, you should, they're your keys.... Um..." *SLOW DOWN*, she told herself sternly, *it's just a normal, everyday conversation.* "Grand and I wanted to put the leftover items in your office and need a key."

"I can take the cart. You two don't need to that. Take Grand on home. She's probably exhausted, she was busy tonight."

"Thanks. She's been running around all evening, but I know she loved every minute."

He fell in step with her as they made their way back to the fellowship hall, "Did you get a chance to have fun? I know you were a big help to Grace and Grand."

"Oh yes, I listened to a few bands, ate some of the most wonderful cupcakes, and even sat for a few minutes. I'm glad there will be another one next year."

He loved hearing her talk about next year's event. He liked seeing her interact with the church members, looking right at home. He wondered if she was as surprised as he was how well she fit in. "I'm glad."

She heard a lot of extra meaning in those simple words but didn't want to say anymore until she had a chance to think and pray. *I'm NOT losing my heart again to this man.* Coming around the corner, she saw Grand pushing the cart down the hall, and called out, "Grand, we're coming. Wait a moment."

She and Cole rushed after her, and heard her say, "I'm going slowly, don't worry. I didn't want anything left out in the open." She stopped and said to Cole, "It was a great night, young man. You did this church proud."

"Thank you, Ms. Delia Anne. You've certainly helped me make this a must attend event these past few years."

She smiled at him, "Did you see how much Viviane's photograph went for? It was probably one of the highest bids tonight."

She was hoping Cole would tell her who won it but was disappointed with his reply.

"No, I don't know. I've not looked at the list, but you know I couldn't tell you. It's part of the pastor's code of honor, you know."

Viviane laughed at Cole's polite attempt to out maneuver Grand and said, "We're leaving now. See you for the cleanup after church." She grabbed Grand's arm to steer her out the door, but leaned forward to quietly say, "I'm going to make her rest tomorrow afternoon."

"Why don't you let me drive you home afterwards? That way you could drive to church in the morning, and Grand could leave after the service without waiting for you."

Grand started to protest, but the thought of the two of them alone in a car made her quit balking at being treated like a child. "Fine, treat me like an invalid. I don't care." She knew if she didn't make a fuss, Viviane would get suspicious. *Walk slow, I can't ruin this positive turn of events by skipping.*

"Grand, I'm only thinking of you." *A car ride?!? I'm not sure how I feel about that!* Looking at Grand moving slowly to the car, she thought, *but it IS for Grand, I have to think about what's best for her.*

Chapter Ten

The next morning everyone was talking about the auction with a focus on Viviane's photograph that went for a lot of money. However, whenever her name was mentioned, it was quickly linked with Cole's and gossip began to spread throughout the church. Most of it was harmless, people were curious about whether they were getting back together, but some made harsh comments about her breaking his heart.

When Viviane walked into church that morning, she was feeling calmer and wasn't dreading the afternoon with Cole. Her prayers during her devotions this morning focused on guiding her in mending their friendship. She was positive God was working, and she would finally have complete closure.

Walking through the Sunday school classroom door, she spied Grace standing next to her friend, waving her over. "Viviane, this is my best friend, Bailey Evans. She's visiting from Colorado."

Viviane noticed the two women could be sisters, both had long, red hair, green eyes, and neither topped 5' 4". Grace was slightly taller, but it was the only difference. Extending her hand, she said, "It's nice to meet you. I hope you're enjoying your visit. Is this your first time in Cartersville?"

"No, I've visited Grace's family a lot when we were in college, since my family's so far away." Bailey pushed a lock of hair behind her ear, "I've always loved Georgia, it's one of the only places I feel is as beautiful as my Colorado."

Liking her immediately, Viviane said, "I haven't been to Colorado, but want to go and take pictures. The mountains are gorgeous." *Lord, I'm happy to be making new friends here and I know this goofy grin on my face is because I'm finally able to make girlfriends in Cartersville.*

The three ladies continued to talk, telling funny college stories, and Grand watched feeling proud to see how well she fit in. She knew she had done the right thing in bringing Viviane back to Cartersville. *The happy glow on her face this morning is proof, because I'm sure it's Cole who put it there. The ride this afternoon is just the thing to jumpstart their relationship and get me the grandbabies I want.*

When class started, Grace led them in a discussion about Hosea with a beautiful description of God chasing after a woman's heart. The women talked about how God specifically wooed them at different points in their lives. It made Viviane remember the times in her own life, and she felt the breakup with Cole was one of the biggest, because it was when God really began to speak to her heart, both as a woman and daughter of God.

After the class was over, she helped clean up. There was a lot of laughter, which made the chore easier. The four women walked to the sanctuary with Grace leading the way to their usual spot. Viviane was on the lookout for Cole, because she discovered he taught a middle school boys class held in the gym.

Grand watched her craning her neck, and asked sweetly, "Is your neck bothering you love? You seem to be twisting it funny. Are you looking for someone in particular?"

Viviane ignored the implication and said, "No, I'm fine. I was reacquainted with half the church last night and I'm looking at all the familiar faces."

Grand smiled knowing the truth but kept walking to their pew. She laid down her Bible and said, "There's Mrs. Beverly. I need to let her know what she missed last night."

"Tell her I said hello." Viviane said, but Grand was already gone.

She turned to talk to Bailey and Grace until service started, when Grand came rushing back to slide into the pew. Out of the corner of her eye, she saw Cole seated in the front next to some youth kids. She started to wave until she noticed Hillary slip in next to him and put her hand back down. *Help me focus, Lord.*

After the service was over, Pastor Winston asked for volunteers to stay after and Viviane was glad many people raised their hands. *Hopefully, Grand won't make a fuss about leaving.* Turning to her, she said, "I'll see you later this afternoon. Please rest some." *I'll watch her closely once I get home.*

"I'll be fine, hon. Don't worry about rushing home." Grand winked at her as she packed up her things. She hoped she wouldn't see her for a few hours, because she really wanted to go home and clean something. *If things keep working out like I hope, in a few weeks I can put away the sick lady act and get back to my normal pace of life!*

Grand waved a goodbye and was gone before Grace and Bailey could speak. Viviane said, "If I didn't know better, I'd say she was making a break for it."

The three women laughed as they made their way to the fellowship hall. "Do you two want to go to lunch? I think there'll be plenty of people to help if you want to sneak away. I know Bailey leaves in a few days."

"Yes, the two of you should sneak out," Cole said as he came up to stand beside Viviane. "We have lots of volunteers, plus the youth group to help."

Grace looked at Bailey, who was nodding yes, and then turned back to Cole and Viviane, "Well, if you're sure it's okay... Let's go Bailey. I'd love to eat at Jefferson's. If we leave now, we can get a good seat."

Bailey smiled, and said thanks to Cole and Viviane, before she followed Grace outside. Waving goodbye, Viviane suddenly realized they were completely alone in the hallway. *Too soon, Lord. I wanted to ease into this.*

"Are you still letting me take you home?"

Unsure if she could speak, she nodded. Having him so close was making it hard to focus on what she was supposed to be doing.

"We'd better go, it'd look bad if I didn't help clean up after my own party." He bowed to her and said, "After you."

She began to walk, feeling a little stupid with her inability to speak and spent the next thirty minutes telling herself she was being silly. *You're not a lovesick teenager. You want to be friends, nothing more. This is ridiculous, he broke up with you. Remember that!* She was so preoccupied, she didn't notice how empty the fellowship hall became as the cleaning was finished.

She saw a lone box of decorations sitting on a table but didn't see a teenager to take it to the storage room. Deciding to take it herself, she grabbed it and walked down the darkened hallway to the offices, glad the light from the windows allowed her to see where she was going. Having grown up in this church, she knew where everything should go.

She turned the doorknob and without pausing, walked to the back shelves to slide the heavy box next to other decorations used throughout the year. Wiping her brow, she heard someone speaking, and turned slightly to see where the noise was coming from. She thought it might be one of the pastor's walking to the front offices. She would say hello and then find Cole. *Maybe we can leave soon and get lunch. I know he'll be as hungry as I am. We used to hang out all the time and it'd be nice to be able to do that again in a crowded restaurant.*

"...I didn't believe you, but then I saw her with my own eyes. She made a fool of herself following him around all night."

Viviane froze, *what should I do?*

"I know, it was embarrassing to watch. Someone really should tell her to quit acting like a love-sick puppy. She broke up with him and she's crazy to have walked away from a wonderful man like that. It's sinful what she did to him, breaking his heart. Cole deserves better than Viviane Stanton-Mays, I tell you. He should marry that Blake girl, she'd make a wonderful pastor's wife and a beautiful bride."

Viviane felt the tears welling up in her eyes. She couldn't see who was talking, but now knew who they were talking about and felt hurt. She couldn't believe what these ladies were saying about her and she thought, *they're probably not the only ones.* She felt herself sliding down to the floor, tears rolling down her cheeks. Not caring she was still in her dress, she leaned her head against the wall and sobbed. *So that's what the church thinks. That I broke his heart and he's the one who never got over it.* It made her headache, as she thought, *It's Cole who didn't care. He broke up with me by saying he didn't care that way anymore.* "Lord," she whispered, "I can't hurt like this, not again."

Over and over the hurtful words played in her head. She kept seeing tall, thin and beautiful Hillary sitting next to Cole. The ladies were right about Hillary making a perfect pastor's wife. She didn't examine how this thought hurt her more than the others.

She stood up quickly wiping the tears from her face and took a deep, wavering breath. *I'm stronger than this. I've been through this before and I can move past this again. It's time I go home to Atlanta for a few days. I need to remember Cole isn't supposed to be anything, but a passing acquaintance. I need time to close my heart to him. I thought I was stronger, but I was wrong.*

She walked back to the fellowship hall, glad no one was in sight. *I want to find Cole and have him take me home.* She prayed he wouldn't say anything to upset her, because she didn't know how she would react shifting between feeling angry and hurt.

"Hey, I've been looking all over for you. Everyone's gone, so do you want to go to lunch Vee?"

"Angry it is..." She had worked herself up thinking of him letting the church believe she was the one to break his heart. His insensitive, arrogant use of the special nickname he had for her when they were dating made her see red.

"What Vee? I missed that." He walked right up to her and in that short amount of time her anger flared to the surface.

"I said I... AM... ANGRY. How could you let this church believe I broke up with you? That's the most insulting and arrogant thing I've ever heard." She stepped forward to point at him, "YOU broke up with me."

He started to reach out, but she pulled back, her voice rising even louder, "You gave me this long speech about how you'd been called to be a pastor and I ... I ... I wouldn't make a good pastor's wife." Tears pouring down her face, she could feel her mascara running.

"Vee."

"STOP CALLING ME VEE. You haven't called me that since you broke up with me. Don't you ever use that name again."

He could see the pain she was in and his own heart broke knowing he caused it. He knew he had been a jerk that day. "I'm so sorry. I thought we'd get a chance to talk today and I could apologize. Please let's go somewhere and talk."

He touched her arm, but she jerked away from him. "Take me home, Cole. Now."

"I don't know why you're upset all of the sudden, you've been fine all week."

His hurtful remarks only angered her more, she yelled, "I was fine. I thought we could be friends, but then I found out you've been using me to score points with the church by playing the broken-hearted pastor to make yourself look better. I'm through Cole, take me home." Arms crossed, her eyes flashed as she spoke through gritted teeth, "Don't say another word to me. We're done... forever, as far as I'm concerned."

"But I never told anyone you broke up with me..."

She didn't let him finish, "Lying by omission is still wrong, you...you... jerk." She grabbed her purse and stomped out to the parking lot.

After a few minutes Cole followed, and opened the car door for her to get in, but she refused his offered hand. On the drive to Grand's house, he opened his mouth to speak several times, but quickly shut it and kept staring straight ahead.

Viviane was fuming and couldn't wait for the ride to be over. As soon as he was in the driveway she didn't wait for him to stop the car but jumped out slamming the car door. Walking stiffly up the porch steps, she didn't say a word, but went quickly into the house.

Cole knew he needed to pray. *I should've told her I was sorry years ago, and explain what an idiot I was back then, but kept putting off waiting for the right moment. I've made things worse by waiting all these years.* He hoped she would forgive and forget, but that would be impossible now. He didn't remember everything he said that night, but he knew it was some terribly untrue things, which she might never forgive him for. *Right now, I don't blame her.* Starting the car, he prayed, *Lord, what have I done?*

Viviane walked into the house and leaned against the wall. She didn't want to see Grand, because she didn't want to deal with what just happened. She started up the stairs, when Grand came out of the kitchen holding a scrub brush, "Viviane, what are you doing back so early? I thought you two would go out for lunch."

"I'm not hungry, Grand. I'm just going to lie down, I must still be tired from last night."

Grand watched her walk slowly to her bedroom, and knew something was wrong, Viviane was obviously upset. She had hoped their first chance to talk would have gone better, but she had always been a stubborn child. *If they don't fix things soon, I'll have to do something.*

Shaking her head, she went back to the kitchen to finish cleaning the stove. It wasn't until later she realized Viviane hadn't chastised her for cleaning and not resting after church.

Chapter Eleven

Monday morning found Viviane lying in bed not wanting to get up and read her Bible. She knew she desperately needed God's word, but she didn't want to go to the throne to find Him not meeting her need again. She felt extremely tired hurting over Cole. *I don't need this now, I was happy in Atlanta. So I'm not big on dating, I just haven't found anyone I feel chemistry with and feeling any with Cole only proves I need to stay away from him.* She rolled over, pulling the covers over her head. *I'm staying in bed until ten when I need to start cleaning. I'm going to Atlanta for the photo shoot and I don't want Grand doing too much while I'm gone. I'm not running away, I just need time to think and recharge.*

At the same time, Grand was already dressed. She knew Viviane was sleeping in and wanted to enjoy her quiet time at her favorite spot on the wrap around porch her husband had built. Walt had called it her special place, because she loved spending her devotional time outside in God's beautiful creation. Sitting at the table and chairs he made, she opened her Bible and began to read. She took time to pray about how to get Cole and Viviane back on speaking terms. *What I need is another project they could work on, but the auction is the last thing for the year. Well, that was what God was all about wasn't it? Making a way when there is no way.* She decided to call Jill, who had been out of town visiting grandkids in North Carolina. *She needs to know how well the auction went and Viviane's items doing so well.*

While Viviane slept the morning away, Grand called Jill, but didn't mention the fight because she was sure it was a temporary setback. After her call, she found a book to read, not wanting to be caught cleaning. Finding a new one, she sat down with her feet propped up, quickly becoming interested in the story.

Viviane felt the sun on her face and rolled over to see what time it was. She had set an alarm for ten but was shocked to see it was after eleven. Throwing off the covers, she hurried to get dressed, pulling on a t-shirt and shorts before running downstairs to check on Grand. In a rush to start cleaning, she told herself she would take time tonight to pray and read her Bible.

In the kitchen, she discovered Grand sitting at the table reading. "Morning, Grand. How are you?" Viviane yawned out.

"Fine, sweetie. Did you sleep well? I noticed you were up later than you thought." She put down her book, marking the page she was on.

"I slept well. A little too well, because now I'm behind on the schedule I set for today."

Grand perked up, hopeful, "Oh, I didn't know you had plans this morning. Are you going somewhere? Meeting someone, perhaps?"

Viviane pulled bread and butter out of the fridge, "No, I'm going to do some cleaning and cooking today. I know how you like to keep the house spotless and I'm going to take care of it since I know you haven't had a chance to." Making her breakfast, she missed the angry look that crossed Grand's face.

"Cleaning? Viviane, I don't want you here cleaning my house. I thought you came for a visit? Why on earth do you want to spend the morning cleaning? You should go out, meet someone for lunch..."

Viviane placed the buttered bread in the toaster, "I have to go to Atlanta this weekend for a photoshoot and I won't be home until Monday. I DO NOT want you cleaning while I'm gone. You've been doing too much lately."

Grand bristled at her comments. *My house isn't dirty. I might not be polishing the antique silver every week and dusting every nook and cranny, but this house is spotless. Why, the child could eat her toast off my floor. How dare she tell me differently!*

Viviane took her silence for frustration and said, "I know you want to do more than you can right now, but I'll do some work today and then we can spend the rest of the week doing fun things. Scott's Walk Up BBQ on Wednesday and maybe the Booth Museum on Thursday? How does that sound?"

Grand took a long look at her and could see the dark circles under her eyes. Her anger melted away as she reminded herself this was all part of the plan. Maybe a weekend in Atlanta would be good for Viviane, give her a chance to calm down. *I just need to make sure she comes back.*

"Okay, but you're not going to do too much, my house doesn't need THAT much cleaning."

Plus, if she's in Atlanta, I'd have several days to get out of the house, maybe do some shopping, and even meet a few ladies for lunch. There's some definite possibilities here.

"That's settled then. Why don't you go to the living room and watch some television, while I start in the kitchen?" She sprinkled cinnamon on her toast, missing Grand's face at being told to watch TV.

Grand moved to the living room, thinking, *Maybe I'll watch a game show, and work on my mental abilities since I can't work my body. I really need to see about signing up for a gym while Viviane's gone. I haven't gone walking in weeks!*

Cole also had a rough morning, getting up with a heavy heart and little sleep. He knew he needed to talk to Viviane and straighten things out but didn't know what to say. He moved into the kitchen to feed Moses and decided to take her for a run. Hoping to clear his head, he dressed and went to put a leash on an excited Mo. They hadn't been able to go for a long run with all the extra work he had put into the silent auction.

He groaned thinking of the auction, Viviane's face yelling at him. He spent all night trying to get her hurt face out of his head. The two events would forever be linked in his mind, and her tears haunted him. Moses pulled on the leash, and Cole gratefully followed her on their usual route around Cassville.

The sun was rising high enough to burn off the rest of the morning fog, and he waved at a school bus as it drove by but didn't pay attention to where he was going. He followed Moses lead, having named the dog very well. He might have kept running forever, but Moses became hungry and led the way home.

Cole gave her some extra food and went to his bathroom to shower and change for work. He made sure the door was locked, because his dog often panicked when he was taking a shower. If he didn't, she would burst through and try to drag him out, thinking she was protecting him, even as he howled in pain. It was nice to know she would face her fears to protect him, but he really didn't like her teeth sinking into his naked flesh. Last time he forgot, he couldn't sit for a few days. Maybe Mike was right and his dog needed therapy.

After taking a few extra minutes to get ready because he had a staff meeting this morning, he grabbed his computer bag and other papers he had been working on last night and told Mo to behave as he walked to the garage. On the drive, he prayed for God to show him how to handle Viviane.

When he realized he wouldn't be able to sleep, he had crunched the numbers for the silent auction. He knew Pastor Winston would be pleased, especially since they reached their goal. Last year they needed to do a few smaller fundraisers to raise the rest of the money. If only the happiness over success of the auction was enough to keep Viviane's face covered in tears out of his mind.

Cole pulled into the parking lot later than usual. The staff meeting had been pushed back an hour, and he had taken advantage of the extra time at home. He knew Mrs. Misty; the church secretary would have been there at ten minutes to eight. He walked into the front office and said, "Hello, Mrs. Misty. How was your evening?"

Misty Owens, a tall woman with curly hair framed by large glasses kept typing. She never looked up, but called out, "Morning Cole, you're late. Been in trouble on a Sunday evening?"

Cole laughed, "No, Ma'am. I was up all night working on the numbers for the auction. They look good." She was a formidable woman and like his mother before her, she knew everything that went on in the church.

She looked up at him, and sternly said, "You should let me know when you're coming in late. I'm not saying you can't, but I need to know where everyone is in case of an emergency."

Cole sincerely apologized and promised it wouldn't happen again. He knew she took her job seriously and ran the office efficiently. She had helped him out too many times for him to take it personally. "I'll be in my office until the meeting starts."

Misty watched him walk away and thought, *He doesn't look preoccupied thinking about Viviane. The ladies talking about him being a love-sick puppy must be out of their minds. I know a love-sick man when I see one and he doesn't look it. Lauren must be wrong this time.* Resuming typing, she mused, *It wouldn't surprise me a bit if Lauren was trying to push Cole to her daughter. He's much too sensible to marry Hillary, if only because it would make Lauren Blake his mother-in-law.*

Cole walked to his office and finished typing the report he started. He went over the Sunday school numbers and was pleased the youth classes' numbers were up. It was good to see on paper his efforts were working. If only his personal life would fall in line so well. He turned off his computer, and reached to grab the papers he had printed, hoping to beat Misty to the door before she came to remind him about the meeting. He liked to think he was faster, at least occasionally.

As he rounded the desk, he tripped over his computer bag, and reached down to untangle the strap from his foot. He heard his door open and a voice say, "It's time for the meeting, Pastor West. You don't want to be late."

Cole sighed, *Misty 32, Cole 2.* "Thank you. I'll be right there." *Maybe next week I'll beat her to the door.*

He straightened his dark gray chambray shirt before he picked up his papers once again. He made his way down the hall to the conference room to see most of the staff already seated and being served coffee. "Thank you, Mrs. Owens." He said, taking the water she always got him, because she knew he didn't like coffee. He could have brought his water from his office but was afraid to offend her with the audacity that could take care of himself, at least during office hours. Smiling at her, he picked up the chocolate doughnut with sprinkles she saved for him, because she knew he liked sprinkles.

Taking a bite, he winked at her as Pastor Jennings arrived. He was younger than Pastor Winston, quiet and more reserved, he had been on staff for ten years now. Cole liked him and enjoyed the new insight he brought to a subject.

"Morning everyone," Pastor Winston called when he walked through a few moments later. He sat next to Cole, greeting him personally before turning to Jeffrey Collins, the church accountant.

While Pastor Winston began the meeting with prayer, Cole wondered why Pastor Carrie Quinn wasn't in her usual seat across from him. She was usually very punctual.

"Dear Lord, thank You for bringing us here today. Thank You for a wonderful Sunday, a growing church, and a growing community. Give us wisdom as we make plans and give us Your heart for helping those who walk through our doors. Please be with Pastor Carrie today as she goes to the doctor for the flu. Thank You for Your blessings. Amen."

Cole lifted his head after saying his own prayer for Carrie and then listened as everyone went around to give a report on their area of ministry. Mrs. Owens gave Pastor Carrie's report she sent in last night. Cole made a mental note to do the same, determined to send a typed summary even if all it said was dying on Monday during scheduled meeting.

He nearly missed the chuckles over Pastor Winston's comment about welcoming growing pains for the church, when everyone looked to him to give his report. He shuffled his papers as he cleared his throat and went quickly through the numbers. The entire staff shared his happiness with the money raised.

"Does this mean you have all of the money for the items auctioned off?" Misty asked as she was taking notes.

"No, I still have about fifteen items waiting for owners, but should have everything taken care of by Wednesday at the latest. Then I just need the adult chaperones to pay for their spots." He grabbed another sheet from his stack, and after glancing over it he said, "I have four confirmed chaperones, but won't know the total number until closer to the trip. I estimate I'll need around six adults total."

"Wonderful, Cole. I'm excited how well this has come together," Pastor Winston said. "Any other business ladies and gentlemen?"

People shook their heads no, and Pastor Winston smiled, "Let's close out in prayer then. Pastor Jennings will you do the honor?"

Pastor Jennings spoke with a clear, authoritative voice, and soon the meeting was over. Cole began to stack his papers together walking by Pastor Winston standing in the door speaking to each person as they left. "Do you have lunch plans, Cole?"

"No, Pastor. I have some leftovers Mom sent me before they left to visit Nathan in Rome. She made enough food for a month, but I won't complain. I missed her Southern cooking when I lived up North."

Pastor Winston said, "I thought we could eat lunch together in my office, since we didn't get to meet this month with all the prep for the auction."

"I'd like that and it just so happens that I have enough of Mom's lasagna for two." Pastor Winston loved his mom's cooking and missed it since she wasn't the church secretary, anymore. The two men often met for lunch with Cole sharing any leftovers his mom sent over.

Pastor Winston's eyes perked up, "Well, in that case, meet me in my office in ten minutes, and I'll bring an extra fork."

Chapter Twelve

Cole chuckled as he walked back to his office to get the little cooler he packed last night. *I'm glad I included the whole container, because the good pastor will eat several helpings.* He carried the cooler and his Bible back through the kitchen to grab an extra plate, before he walked down the hall to the back-office Pastor Winston used. Since he was expected, he walked through the open door holding up the container, "I've got an extra plate from the leftover auction supplies."

"Excellent!" I've got a fork and the appetite." Pastor Winston patted his large stomach, "I love my wife, but she doesn't have the same culinary magic your mom does in the kitchen."

Cole sat down at the small table, "I'd tell her you said that, but she'd tell your wife and then we'd both be in trouble."

"True." Pastor Winston said with a chuckle.

Both men bowed their heads while Cole prayed and then spent several minutes filling their plates. Cole had eaten many meals in this office, always enjoying the peaceful room with its big windows that let the light stream in. The office had changed little over the years, and he spent a lot of time in it. When he had first felt called into ministry, one of the first people he talked to besides his parents was Pastor Winston. The man had given him great advice over the years, and he admired him greatly.

"Cole, I saw Viviane in church Sunday, and I know she helped with the auction."

Pastor Winston didn't ask a question, but Cole knew he wanted to know if he was okay with this new complication in his life. *And it's a complication I've been thinking about nonstop.*

Cole laid down his fork, now isn't the time to be munching on his mom's lasagna. "At first I thought God was bringing us back together to mend our friendship. I've always felt the hardest part of our breakup was losing my best friend, but now... well?" He paused, trying to think of the best way to explain his feelings.

Pastor Winston finished eating, and then sat back to look at Cole, concern showing on his lined face, "What happened to change your mind?"

Running his hands through his hair, Cole said, "I'm confused to be truthful. Yesterday, we had an argument after the cleanup. I left to put some chairs in a classroom, and when I came back she started yelling at me."

Unable to stay seated, he stood to pace in front of the windows, "I mean, Viviane doesn't yell. I've seen her angry before, but it's a seething, quiet anger. Yesterday for the first time, I saw the pain and anguish in her eyes... in her voice. I'm shaken."

He turned to face Pastor Winston, "It hurt to know I caused it."

"Break ups hurt, son. I don't mean to make light of it, but you had to know she'd be upset."

"This was more than upset, this was pain, real and continued. She told me I said she wasn't fit to be a pastor's wife and I don't remember saying that."

Pastor Winston sighed, "Cole, you might not have said those exact words, but you did tell me how you cared for her, but felt she was too artsy, too much of a loner, and you needed someone who could embrace the ministry life God was calling you to."

Cole stopped pacing, frozen at Pastor Winston's words. Feeling the strength leave his legs, he fell into an empty chair feeling sick. Hands covering his face, he mumbled, "What have I done all in the name of ministry, my ministry?"

"This is something I've known you've needed to face, but I've been waiting for the right time." Pastor Winston leaned forward to place his hand on Cole's back, "I've been praying God would show me how to help you. It's a problem all ministers must face, how do we keep ministry from overtaking our personal lives."

Cole lifted his eyes wet with tears, "Why?"

Wrinkling his forehead Pastor Winston asked, "Why what?"

"Why did you let me take this job? You said I admitted I did this horrible thing to Viviane years ago and you still went to the board for me. Why? A minister can't treat people like that and still lead others."

Pastor Winston had been waiting for this question for a long time, and even with years to prepare an answer, he was unsure how to respond. *I was hesitant to hire an unmarried man, not because I feel he needs to be married to do the job just that it helps to have someone to share the burden.* He remembered his hesitation and thought meeting weekly to talk would help him to get to know Cole better. *We began a friendship that day, like none other I've ever had. God's taught me so many Biblical principles about mentoring, sons, and even God's love for His own Son that I couldn't have learned without befriending this young man. How do I explain that to him? I'm sixty-five and barely understand myself.*

He looked into Cole's green eyes and could clearly see the pain and anguish. *I know his heart and determination to follow God, and most importantly, I know about God's restoring grace.*

"I need you to understand something, Cole, something you've needed to hear for a while. Ministers, none of us are perfect! Only Jesus, who ministered for over three years without a wife, I might add. The rest of us just struggle along and let the Holy Spirit do the rest. Some days, the Holy Spirit has to work harder than others."

"I don't know what to do now. She won't even talk to me." Cole felt like his heart had been shattered. *I don't see how I can fix this. How can Viviane forgive me for throwing away something wonderful?*

Pastor Winston's brown eyes filled with concern said, "I don't know if you and Viviane are right for each other. To be married to a minister is hard work, but I do know the two of you need to clear the air and discuss what happened. You need to apologize, ask for forgiveness from both God and her, and then move forward." He paused to let his words sink in, and then continued, "No matter how Viviane reacts when you ask for forgiveness, you must let it go and her go, if need be."

Cole lowered his head and whispered, "I really want her to forgive me."

"I know." Pastor Winston looked out the window, seeing the sun shining he said, "If I were you, I'd get out of here, take a drive and go somewhere you can be alone and pray. Talk with God, tell him everything and pray for Him to show you how to mend your friendship with Viviane. I don't know if it can be done, it will take both of you, but pray about it and don't quit until something happens, or God says stop."

Lifting his face, Cole asked, "And if she won't ever see me again?"

Putting his hand on Cole's shoulder, Pastor Winston said firmly, "Pray Cole. Pray for God to soften her heart and arrange a way for you two to talk. God has created big and mighty things, and He can make a way for the two of you to work this out."

Nodding his head, Cole got up and began to gather the plates. *It's hard to believe God could make this right, when I keep seeing her blue eyes filled with pain.*

"I'll take care of this. Take the rest of the day off and go talk to God. Think of it as a special assignment from your boss."

He walked up to Pastor Winston and extended his hand, "Thank you, and thank you for bringing me on staff even knowing how messed up I am."

Pastor Winston ignored his hand and moved to hug him, "If I only hired perfect staff members, I'd have to start by firing myself."

Cole half smiled at those words as he thought, *I know there's a lot of truth in that statement, but it still hurts to think of using God's calling as justification for hurting someone I truly care about.*

Chapter Thirteen

By Thursday, Viviane was exhausted and didn't know if she would make it to Friday to drive back to Atlanta. She needed to escape to sleep for at least a week. Grand decided to embrace her idea of a good cleaning, and Viviane had spent the past three days cleaning every dish, spoon, and piece of furniture Grand owned. If there was a dust bunny left in Cartersville, it was only because it had escaped out of the house in the dead of night.

Viviane was still in bed, because she didn't think she could move her body. Her alarm had gone off ten minutes ago, but she couldn't get up to turn it off. They were to meet Grace at the Booth Museum and then have lunch. She knew Grand would be up to it, because she spent the whole cleaning process sitting in a chair to make sure she cleaned each item according to her high standards.

Viviane groaned, but stopped because it hurt too much. She attempted to roll over to turn off the alarm; this was the closest she had gotten to succeeding since she had woken up. Gritting her teeth, she propelled herself forward, excitement welled up when her hand touched the alarm, but disappeared quickly when she squealed as her bedroom door burst open.

"Viviane will you turn off that horrible racket?" Grand crashed into her room dressed in a beautiful pantsuit in shades of pink, which set off her gray hair elegantly.

Viviane looked up from the floor where she landed, "Grand, don't you look nice early this morning."

She didn't succeed in keeping the sarcasm out of her voice, but Grand ignored her, "Get dressed and come to breakfast, please. We've got to be at the museum by ten and it's already eight-thirty!"

Viviane had a flashback to high school of Grand always trying to get her up much earlier than needed. She could sleep until fifteen minutes before she needed to be out the door. *Maybe it's a grandparent thing.*

"There's plenty of time, it doesn't take me long to get ready."

Grand bent over to pick up clothes lying on the floor. "Don't worry about that. I'll do laundry when I get to Atlanta. It will give me something to do." She silently added, *besides sleeping.*

At her words, Grand dropped what she had in her hands. She slowly walked up to the bed to see her face up close. It was the same bed Viviane had since she was nine, the four poster bed her parents had owned. "Are you still planning on coming back after the photo shoot?"

Viviane saw fear in Grand's eyes but didn't understand. *I thought she was feeling better this week.* "Yes, I'm staying until the end of September when Kathie gets back from her travels, and business picks up."

Grand nodded and simply said, "I'm glad we'll still have some time together."

Viviane slid out of bed to hug her. "I'll get dressed and meet you downstairs. We can leave soon for the museum."

Grand brightened and told her she would see her in a few minutes and began humming on her way downstairs. Glad she sounded happy, Viviane quickly got dressed in a pair of comfortable dark wash jeans and light half-sleeve green top with matching sandals. Twenty minutes later, she grabbed her purse and went downstairs to help Grand clean up breakfast. She knew she had another long day ahead of her, but thankfully no cleaning. She planned to put every dish they used for the rest of the week in the dishwasher, whether it was dishwasher safe or not!

She told herself for the third day in a row, *TONIGHT I need to read my Bible no matter how tired I am.* She rationalized, *I've just been too busy cleaning the past few days to spend time in prayer.*

The three ladies spent almost two hours walking around the Booth Museum. Viviane hadn't been before and was excited to see the wonderful art collection, and now inspired by several photographs she was itching to grab her camera and go west. This reminded her of how she discovered in college she was better at photography than drawing and switched concentrations her first semester at UGA. Her love for art spanned all forms of media, but she had a special talent for photography.

When Grace called late Tuesday to let them know how well the auction did, Grand mentioned their plans. Grace said she had never been, and Grand quickly invited her for a tour and lunch. Viviane was excited to spend the day doing something that actually felt like a vacation. Glad she had dragged herself out of bed, because once she started moving she felt better.

After they finished touring the exhibits, they went to eat in the museum's Café. The ladies ordered and sat down to wait at one of the tables near the large window. It gave a stunning view of the front grounds of the museum, showcasing the shops downtown under the bridge. Viviane stared out the large window, not paying attention to the conversation.

"Viviane... Viviane are you listening? The food's here."

"Sorry, Grand." She jerked her head and saw a young waitress bearing a tray with their orders. "Oh, thank you." Viviane took the food the waitress had been trying to hand her for some time.

After she walked away, Grand brought up her lack of conversation, "What's wrong with you today? You're not paying any attention."

"I'm sorry." Viviane turned to include Grace in her apology, "It's a stunning view of downtown. I was trying to think of ways to take a picture."

Grace wasn't offended seeing the pain in Viviane's eyes, she knew there was more to her lack of focus. She played along, praying she would get the chance to talk to her alone. "It's a beautiful view. I love watching the train go by."

Eating her lunch, Viviane made herself focus on the conversation after she sent up a silent plea for God to forgive her for lying. The bridge was one of her favorite spots, but she actually had been thinking of the fight with Cole.

Conversation centered on exhibits they had seen and other museums they visited. Grace made it easy to pay attention with the wit and humor she wove into her stories. She went to college in Atlanta and had seen a lot of the same exhibits at the High Museum. "I took an introductory art course and loved it. My art teacher was a funny woman who made art come alive for me. She told us that when she went to the Louvre on a high school trip, she walked up a grand staircase to see the Winged Victory statue and was so completely awed by it, she fainted falling down the stairs and broke her leg."

"Oh, that's awful." Viviane exclaimed.

Grace nodded, "Yes, she spent the rest of the trip on crutches. I can't remember all the details it's been ten years, but I think she went back to the museum to finish the tour!"

Laughing, Viviane said, "That's dedication. I don't know if I'd have gone back."

"Oh, I would've," Grand said in between bites of ham and swiss, "Think of all the money that went into the trip and how awful spending it in the hotel would be."

Still smiling, Grace went on to say, "She said it was a medical condition called Stendahl syndrome. I remember, because I was worried I might have a similar problem. Growing up, I fainted a lot because my blood sugar would drop."

"That's terrible. Have you ever passed out over a piece of art?" Grand asked.

"No, but I passed out in a Michael's once with my mom. I'd forgotten breakfast, and the employees in the store panicked wanting to call an ambulance, but Mom was used to it by now, told them I was fine and she'd take me to lunch. We went for Chinese after she bought the craft supplies she came for."

Everyone was laughing by the time she finished her story, and Grand said, "I can see your mom saying that with everyone crowding around you."

Viviane remembered Mrs. Cartwright as a tiny lady who attended Grand's Sunday school class for years. Finishing their meal, Viviane and Grace took the trays to the counter while Grand went to the gift shop. Seeing it was just the two of them, Grace paused in the lobby, "I didn't want to ask in front of Ms. Delia Anne, but how did your car ride with Cole go?"

Viviane had told Grace that Cole would be giving her a ride and knew she would understand the significance of the event and asked her new friend to pray about the first time they would be alone in years.

"It didn't go well at all." Tears welling in her eyes, she sniffed and forced them back. "I've not been able to talk about it, and I'm leaving for Atlanta tomorrow."

"If you want to talk when you get back," Grace hugged her, "I'm here if you need me. You have my number."

Glad they were becoming good friends, Viviane was comforted. After making sure her eyes weren't red, they went to find Grand. *Lord, I could use some help.* It was the first prayer she said in days.

Chapter Fourteen

Late Friday morning found Viviane stuck in traffic on I-75 South heading toward her midtown Atlanta apartment. An accident clogged the interstate, and she had been staring at the same billboard sign for over thirty minutes. She turned up the music on her iPod determined not to think of anything related to Cartersville but was failing miserably.

Ready for some alone time in her apartment, she wanted to see Erica and Daphne on Sunday to talk about the fight with Cole. *Not really a fight, since I did all the talking... well the yelling, anyway. Though I don't want to admit to them I haven't prayed about the situation, because I know they'll ask. I don't want to go to God and discover I'll never be fully healed. I don't know if I can accept that!*

In another twenty minutes she was able to move close enough to get off the interstate and take the back way. With the AC and her music blasting, she didn't hear the honking horns when she pulled out of the long line, lost in thought. *Can I fall in love with someone else with these unresolved feelings? That first fight cost me more than a boyfriend- my best friend.*

The closer she got to her adorable two-bedroom apartment the more excited she got. She loved her little haven painted in soft greens that was open and airy with a large balcony. Having a spare bedroom gave Grand a place to feel at home when she visited. Cartersville would always be home, but since she couldn't stay in the same place as Cole, this apartment became a much loved second home.

Viviane pulled into the parking deck and whipped her car into her assigned spot and ran to check the mail. Stifling a yawn, she realized sitting in traffic for hours had completely worn her out. Her original plan had been to order take out and then veg on the couch, but now she thought a nap sounded wonderful. When she unlocked her front door, she stepped into her cool apartment and breathed a sigh of relief. *It's good to be home. People might think I'm crazy having two homes, but my heart was torn in two long ago, and each piece wanted to live in its own place. I've learned when I get lonely or uncomfortable in one to visit the other.*

In the entry way, she placed her keys on the little side table and pulled her luggage inside the front door. She walked into the dark living room and collapsed on the sofa. She fell asleep immediately and hours passed while her phone rang and rang. She was sleeping soundly and never heard a thing.

Hours later, Delia Anne rushed through the back door to grab the phone. "Hello?" she answered out of breath. She had just gotten back from signing up at a gym close to her house and was looking forward to exercising in air conditioning. *If Viviane would wise up about Cole,* she thought, *I wouldn't have to hide my exercising anymore.*

"Grand, it's Erica. Is Viviane still there? I can't get a hold of her."

"No, she left for Atlanta this morning."

"Oh, I guess she isn't answering her phone."

"Well..." Grand paused, unsure how much Erica knew. *I've got a feeling she's not talking to anyone about what happened.*

"Grand is something wrong?" Erica couldn't hide the worry in her voice.

Knowing how close the two girls were she decided to take a chance and tell Erica what happened. *If anyone could get Viviane to fix things with Cole, it's Erica Caine.* "I think she's really upset, because she fought with Cole on Sunday. She's not talking to me about it."

"Well it's good she spoke to him. I'm sorry it went badly though. I don't understand why she isn't talking. The two of you are close."

Grand thought, *I've always felt we had a close relationship, but it seems we talk about everything but Cole.* A little worried, she said, "I don't know, she's always been so determined to get over him and move on, but in reality, she hasn't at all. I don't know what to do anymore, she wouldn't eat with me before she left."

"Don't worry, Grand. Daph and I will talk to her. Pray for us to help."

The two ladies chatted a few minutes more, and Grand made sure not to mention how busy she would be this weekend. *I don't want to contradict any of the work I've put in the past few months.* "Keep in touch, hon."

When Grand hung up, she felt much better about the situation. *I should've gotten Erica to speak to Viviane about fixing the mess with Cole weeks ago.* Grand mused, *it's almost mid-September and I hope by Christmas there'll be talk of an engagement. A summer wedding would be lovely.*

Viviane woke with her head pounding, and noticed it was pitch black. Still groggy from sleep, she fumbled around for her phone to check the time but couldn't find it. It had to be late if the sun had already set. The pounding kept getting louder and she realized the noise was coming from someone banging on her front door. Grateful she didn't have a migraine, she yelled, "I'm coming, just a minute."

She ran her hands through her hair, before she opened up the door with a yank, "Yes?"

Outside stood Daphne and Erica looking overheated and frustrated still dressed in their work clothes. "Finally," Erica said, "I thought we'd have to break down the door. We've been standing out here for twenty minutes."

"I was about to tell the manager we smelled a dead body or something," Daphne said in a huff.

The two women walked past Viviane, Erica waving Chinese takeout in front of her face like a full access pass. Viviane struggled to speak, trying to wake up from her deep sleep, "What are you guys doing here? I thought you had plans this weekend and I'd see you Sunday."

"No big plans," Erica called from the kitchen as she grabbed forks. "I've been calling you all day and finally talked to Grand who said you had a fight with Cole. I called Daph and we decided to come over."

Daphne nodded her head while sorting food and Viviane noticed they were pulling out more than their usual takeout order. She grabbed some water for all three of them, and went to the living room to ask, "What's with all the food? You've got two different restaurants."

Daphne answered, "We've got your usual from your favorite Chinese restaurant and dessert from Café Intermezzo."

Viviane collapsed on the sofa, "I'm dying and you're trying to break it to me gently."

This much food meant serious girl talk. More than two years ago, Erica had been dumped by her fiancé and they stayed up all night talking, eating and crying. Erica felt better and told them whenever she needed to heal from a broken heart again to bring food from her favorite restaurants. It would work every time.

Erica laughed, "No silly, but we felt you needed a bit more TLC than normal takeout would provide. Plus, you normally eat PF Chang's twice a week and being in Cartersville so long, we knew you're probably going through withdrawal."

"And we decided if we're going to harass you about Cole the least we could do is feed you first."

"Daphne," Erica said through gritted teeth, "we were going to ease into that subject!"

"Guys, you don't have to bribe me to talk. I'd planned to tell you at lunch on Sunday." Viviane began to scoop out food as she talked. "I'm glad you did though, I've been craving PF Chang's for weeks."

She filled her mouth with noodles, thinking as she chewed, *I don't want to talk about this now. I know what they're going to say and I don't want to hear I need to pray about it. God's not helping me.*

"See I knew it." Daphne said sounding smug. It was her idea to get food and see if Grand was right about her not talking or eating. *If that's true, it's bad.* They each cancelled their plans to find out how upset she really was about Cole. Their friend was more important than any plans they made.

The next ten minutes were spent catching up in hope Viviane would bring up the fight, but she only skirted the subject of the church fundraiser. Finally, Daphne said, "Viv spit it out. Why did you two fight? Grand seemed to imply you two were getting along. What changed?"

Viviane put her fork down and looked at them, "I don't think I can talk about it. It's embarrassing to think about... I was humiliated and don't feel like discussing it. Maybe by Sunday, but I don't know."

"Viv, we're your friends and we love you. Pushing away your feelings isn't good, and you know that." Setting her own fork down, Erica implored, "Talk! We're here to listen and we're not leaving until you do. Why do you think we brought enough food for a few days? I know how stubborn you can be."

Erica stared at her expectantly, seeing her shutting down. She knew her feelings for Cole were scaring her, because she hadn't seen her this messed up since the original fight.

Viviane whispered, "Fine," but started yelling, "I'm angry at God about all of this!"

Finally talking about what had been bottled up for days, everything came out in a rush. "It isn't just Cole breaking up with me, but the stupid gossip the church ladies are spreading. They have the story all wrong. I'm furious with God for not healing my heart after all this time, because... because..." she paused trying to catch her breath, "it means Cole was right not wanting to marry me, because I can't be a good pastor's wife."

She pushed up from the table to walk back and forth, crying out in anguish, "God was right to tell him to dump me, because obviously I couldn't handle it. I had an eating disorder to prove it and I HATE THAT ABOUT MYSELF!"

Her whole body was heaving as she struggled to catch her breath. Erica could hear the racking sobs and ached for her friend. She spoke with as much sympathy as she could, "It isn't true about you not being a good pastor's wife because of an eating disorder. That isn't something to be ashamed of. You conquered that issue with God's help years ago. It's in the past."

Erica came over to sit next to her, "I don't know what you mean about the church ladies, but Cole breaking up with you had nothing to do with God feeling you're unfit to be a pastor's wife- eating disorder or not."

Daphne moved to sit on Viviane's other side, putting her hand on Viviane's shoulder, "You've got to forgive yourself. The eating disorder isn't a reflection of who you are, but of you trying to make sense of your life. Until you can let it go completely and give it to God, He can't fully heal you."

"I can't! No one knew about my eating disorder, because I hid it so well.... but..." she paused to wipe tears with the back of her hand. "But when Cole broke up with me, I didn't care anymore and after all these years I see Cole was right."

Daphne handed her a tissue, and Viviane smiled a watery thanks, "I hate to admit I shouldn't be angry at him. I thought we could be friends, since I'm healed from the disorder, and learned how to handle things, we could be... I could be a better wife for him, but now..." She shrugged, saying no more.

"You still love him, don't you?" Erica was afraid to ask but had suspected this for some time.

"I don't know how I feel." Viviane paused and her friends waited for her to process her thoughts. They knew she was working this out for the first time herself.

I was friends with Cole before I fell in love with him. It's more than physical attraction, but knowing what a kind, thoughtful guy he is. He cares about people, it's obvious after seeing him at the auction. It's hard to admit I still have strong feelings for him, when he might want to be friends, nothing more. Admitting it now could mean a lot of heartache with me staying until the end of September. This caused a deep ache to lodge in her heart. Oh, God, she prayed, *what do I do? Can I admit I still care deeply for Cole? Can I say it out loud?*

For the first time since the fight, Viviane felt a quiet peace settle into her heart and when she looked up, she spoke in a strong voice, "I still care, but I don't know what kind of love, a first love that lingers or a real lasting one, but it's love."

The two women could hear the change in her voice, and Daphne being the blunt one asked, "What changed?"

"I prayed," she ducked her head ashamed to admit it.

"You know you can't stop praying, because you don't like the answer." Erica said knowingly.

"I know guys, but it isn't so much not liking the answer as feeling God is ignoring the whole question. I've prayed about all of this for so long and for God to heal my heart, but He hasn't. It hurts."

Her voice cracking, she continued, "Part of the reason I ran when things got bad again with Cole was because I felt all the shame and anger welling up all over again. I really want to move past this."

Erica said, "God likes for us to get an A on the test, before He moves onto the next lesson."

Daphne agreed, "Yeah, a lot of times the next lesson is harder if you don't learn the previous one. God's timing is perfect. You can't have a relationship with anyone if you can't let go of the shame you feel."

Erica stood to get her purse and dug through her simple black shoulder bag to pull out the Bible she always carried. She moved to sit between Daphne and Viviane, "I wanted to read from the Message Bible, because I love the way it phrases the passage about no condemnation in Christ."

When she found it, she read aloud, "This is from Romans 8: 1-4, 'With the arrival of Jesus, the Messiah, that fateful dilemma is resolved. Those who enter into Christ's being-here-for-us no longer have to live under a continuous, low-lying black cloud. A new power is in operation. The Spirit of life in Christ, like a strong wind, has magnificently cleared the air, freeing you from a fated lifetime of brutal tyranny at the hands of sin and death.'"

As Erica continued to read, Daphne reached for Viviane's hand, noticing the tears start to fall freely down her cheeks. "God went for the jugular when He sent His own Son. He didn't deal with the problem as something remote and unimportant. In His Son, Jesus, He personally took on the human condition, entered the disordered mess of struggling humanity in order to set it right once and for all. The law code, weakened as it always was by fractured human nature, could never have done that."

When Erica came to the last verse, she took Viviane's hand with her free one and continued, "The law always ended up being used as a Band-Aid on sin instead of a deep healing of it. And now what the law code asked for but we couldn't deliver is accomplished as we, instead of redoubling our own efforts, simply embrace what the Spirit is doing in us."

The three women sat quietly, each one with tears rolling down their cheeks with the reminder of how Jesus died to set them free and to accept the healing act to truly be free.

I've forgotten to choose Jesus' healing every day, and got so bogged down in worry, I forgot to ask God about His feelings for me. I know He loves me, because of Christ's death on the cross. The trouble was I forgot to embrace the wonderful, healing love of God. It's an act I must choose to do every day.

Feeling free for the first time in a long time, she bowed her head and prayed out loud, "My savior, my God thank You. Thank You foremost for dying on the cross for me and thank You for bringing these wonderful women into my life to help lead me back to You."

She squeezed her friends' hand as she continued, "Lord, I want to learn the lesson You're trying to teach me about trusting You and walk away from condemnation You don't mean for me to hold onto. Help me to walk in Your truth and follow the path You've set for me."

Tears rolled down her cheeks, humbled by the outpouring of love she felt, "God give me clear guidance with what to do about Cole. Help me to see the situation through Your eyes. In Jesus' name, amen."

She felt much better and was blessed to have these friends in her life. When she said that, Erica laughed and said, "Hey at some point I'm sure you'll be reminding me of God's love and restoring grace. As humans, we tend to forget that too easily."

Daphne laughed in agreement, "Oh yes, this could be me in a few weeks. You never know what life will throw at you."

Erica pulled everyone into a hug, "That's why we stick together, because you'll always need a friend."

The women dried their tears and moved to clean up. Halfway to the table, Erica said, "Let's forget the cleanup now, and have some of the amazing tiramisu. After that emotional rollercoaster we need major sustenance."

Viviane and Daphne laughed, but liked her idea. Walking to the kitchen to get the dessert, they returned to the table to spend the rest of the night talking, laughing, and eating. It was a healing time for all of them.

Chapter Fifteen

"Finally," Viviane said under her breath, wiping the hair falling into her eyes. She pulled open the door to her hot car after she finished running all of the errands on Grand's list. She glanced at her watch to see it was almost one. *I left the house before eight, and I've been moving non-stop since then. Now, all I want is something to eat and to get out of this heat.*

Twenty minutes later, she was happily munching on fries with the windows down, music blaring. Already Thursday, she had been home since Monday after having a wonderful time in Atlanta. Able to recharge, she hadn't dreaded the drive back to Cartersville, but focused on how to best clear the air with Cole and move on. Hoping God would show her how to run into him, she prayed for direction while she waited. So far, she hadn't seen him and decided to keep trusting God by waiting.

Viviane pulled her car next to the front porch and grabbed as many bags as she could carry in the first of several trips. Huffing up the stairs in the heat, she almost missed the note taped to the front door. She ripped it off and carried everything to the kitchen.

After the third trip, she asked herself, *Is Grand planning some kind of cookout for the entire county to make this much food necessary?* She wiped her forehead, *I can't believe how hot it is still. I'm glad I took Grand's list from her last night, because her the three-page list of errands was too much, but I should've said it was too hot for anyone to be out!*

After putting away all the groceries, she went to get a cold glass of tea and sit down at the table. Savoring it, she remembered the note and turned to see it still on the counter. Leaning back in her chair, she was too tired to move and nearly fell backward.

"Almost... got it..." Viviane felt a brief moment of triumph but was puzzled to see the note had her name on it. *Who'd leave a note for me?* Opening the envelope, she recognized Cole's handwriting.

> *Viviane,*
> *I'm sorry. Could we meet- face to face? I'll be at*
> *our spot in the park until seven tonight. I don't*
> *deserve a chance to apologize, but I'd like to.*
> *Please?*
>
> *Cole*

She was glad to be sitting down, a little nervous to face him alone. She had assumed they would talk at church on Sunday. *I'd tell him sorry for yelling and he'd apologize for being an insensitive jerk, and we'd move on.* Viviane sighed, putting her head on the kitchen table. *I need to let Grand know I'm going back out again, but I'm NOT saying where I'm going!*

She pushed herself off the table, *the sooner I meet Cole the better. It's like ripping off a Band-Aid, best to get it over with. I can speak my peace and move on, because it's closure and that's what I've been praying for.*

Leaving a note for Grand by the kitchen phone, she took the backstairs to change from her sweaty yoga pants wanting to meet Cole in something that didn't look like she had slept in it. Twenty minutes later, she was out the door to Dellinger Park where she and Cole often went in high school to play tennis or run. She knew immediately the place he was talking about. It was across from the tennis courts, behind the miniature golf course. It became their special place to meet.

It didn't take long to arrive and she quickly parked her car to sit for a moment to pray for God to give her strength and the right words to say. *I'm pretty sure God wants me to tell Cole about my eating disorder and I need strength to tell him. Erica and Daphne were right and I don't need to be ashamed of my past anymore. I'm proud of who I've become and all that God has done for me. As Daphne says, you can't be both a victim and victorious.*

Determined, she walked to the spot where she knew Cole would be waiting. He was sitting on a log off the beaten path, and he smiled with he saw her walking toward him. *He looks relieved,* Viviane thought. *Apparently, he was worried I wouldn't show up.*

Cole had been praying for this meeting for days. Pastor Winston was right about him needing to ask God for forgiveness. That was easy but finding a way to see Viviane and ask her forgiveness had been much harder.

Last Sunday he expected to see her after service and convince her to talk to him but had been surprised to see Grand sitting alone. He casually walked over to ask how she was doing. Grand was no fool, but God love her, she said Viviane was in Atlanta for work this weekend. *She grinned the entire time, too!*

It's silly to expect things to go my way when I never asked God if he wanted me to apologize at church, I just assumed. The idea to write a note and meet at their spot came out of the blue while he had been praying yesterday. Cole felt at peace for the first time over the situation, sure it was divine inspiration.

Waiting over an hour he prayed, *Lord guide my words and intercede in the situation. I really want to clear the air, but also to mend our broken friendship.*

"Time to face the music," he whispered. He stood up and walked to Viviane. *It's time for me to face the woman whose heart I broke ten years ago. God help me.*

"Hi."

"Hi, Cole."

Both greetings were said at the exact same time, quiet and reserved as if they were unsure how the other person would react. Each seemed hesitant to speak, but Cole decided to start since this was his idea. "I wasn't sure you'd come," he said moving to stand close, "but I'm glad you did."

Viviane took a deep breath and said, "I want to apologize for yelling at you. I got angry about what some people said, but that's no excuse to take it out on you. I'm sorry."

She started out by staring at her feet, but when she said sorry she was looking him in the eye. *She still takes my breath away,* Cole thought. *She's stunning in a pink t-shirt and white shorts with her matching pink running shoes, but it's her honesty that blows me away. An apology I don't deserve shakes me to my core.*

"Viviane you don't need to apologize, not for telling me how you feel. I'm sorry," he ran his hands through his hair, "So sorry for the things I said years ago." The anguish on his face evident as he continued, "I ruined a wonderful friendship and I'm sorry I waited ten years to apologize. I shouldn't have said those things."

She could see how upset he was, but after talking with Daphne and Erica, she realized their breakup had ultimately been a good thing. God used it to heal her both physically and emotionally from her eating disorder. She needed to tell Cole to move past the shame she felt.

"Cole, I don't know how to say this... but," Viviane paused a moment and then in a rush said, "You were right to break up with me. You really should've done it differently and not used God as your excuse, but you were right to say I wouldn't have made a good pastor's wife, not with how I was at the time."

Cole's eyes widen, *my biggest hope was she'd forgive me, not tell me I was right to end things.* Suddenly he realized, *I know nothing about women.* "I don't understand."

"Well, it was wrong of you to say I wasn't good enough to be a pastor's wife to let yourself off the hook because it was mean spirited, but there was truth in it. You just didn't know that. Our breakup ended up being a blessing to me after some time."

Cole collapsed back on the log and threw his hands up. "I'm so lost. I don't understand anything."

Viviane knew she was talking in riddles, but he needed to know he couldn't treat people that way and expect God to work it out. "Let me start at the beginning, but I need to warn you it's a long story."

Seeing him nod, she started, "After my parents died, I had weekly counseling. It was hard coming to terms with the loss of my parents, but Grand and the school were great in helping me. I think everyone was a little surprised how quickly I adjusted, except for some crying spells and nightmares I moved forward with my life."

She moved to sit on the other side of the log, leaning against him because it would be easier to not see his face. *If I watch the changing emotions, it will make this harder.* She could feel him tense a bit, but once she was leaning completely against him, he relaxed and soon so did she.

Cole was deeply engrossed with her story, losing track of time as she talked, he realized he was hearing a part of her life he knew nothing about.

"If anyone would've asked me at twelve, I would've said I was okay, but when I was about to enter high school I became depressed about not having my mom to talk to. I knew Grand was trying, but it wasn't the same. She wasn't my Mom and I didn't say anything, because I didn't want to upset her. I began to feel insecure, especially around other girls. I felt like an outsider and it became unbearable. I began to go through times of not eating, then eating everything in sight. I panicked, because I knew if I started gaining weight I'd get fat and the girls would make fun of me."

I can't believe what she's telling me. I don't remember seeing anything that would point to her having any problems. Cole said quietly, "I remember you ate with us all the time."

With a sad smile, she said, "I worked hard not to be noticed, taking laxatives when I got home and when I wasn't around people, I didn't eat. I skipped a lot of meals with Grand, saying I'd eaten already."

"I can't believe I missed this. I thought we were close and I should've seen something big like this."

"I wanted it that way Cole. I thought if no one knew, then it was okay. I never lost a lot of weight, only maintained an already skinny body type."

I need him to understand it was something I never planned to tell anyone. If it hadn't been for the breakup, I might have continued hiding my secret. Needing to finish her story so he finally knew everything, she continued, "After we broke up, I didn't care about anything. I stopped taking care of myself and hiding my not eating. I quit going to classes, seeing Grand and lying to her about being busy with school, until one day I was so hungry, I gorged myself on everything in the fridge. Erica had been worried for weeks and came back early from class to check on me and found me sick in the bathroom. That was the day my life began to change for the better."

Trying to hide the tears in her voice, she continued, "With Erica's help, I went to the school counselor and was diagnosed with bulimia and entered an outpatient program near the school. I stayed on campus that summer making up the classes I missed and going through the eating disorder program. Erica even stayed with me and with her support, I began to get better. We started attending a local church and did a Bible study together written by a woman who overcame an eating disorder." Smiling a little, she said, "We worked through the entire book that summer, it was hard but a really rewarding time of emotional and spiritual growth."

She turned to face Cole and said, "I realized I'd been living my life based on Grand's view of God, attaching myself to her relationship with Him and never developing my own."

He started to speak, but she laid her hand on his knee to stop him, "I was saved, but not acting out a changed life. Through therapy and really getting into God's word, He began to speak to me as a daughter of God. He healed my heart where my parent's death had left a hole that couldn't be filled before. Through all of this He taught me about restoring grace, something I'd never understood before."

She became tongue-tied, unsure what to say next. *I know this wasn't what Cole was expecting to hear, but I really feel it's something he needs to know, especially if we're to ever be friends again.*

"Cole?"

"I didn't know, Vee. I'm sorry you felt you had to hide all of this from me." *I can't believe she hid something so big for so long. How could I have missed this?*

Relieved to hear him call her Vee, she thought, *As long as he keeps calling me by my special nickname, we can resolve anything.* "I hid it from everyone because of guilt and shame. I kept it from you and Grand." Sighing she said, "Grand still doesn't even know."

I can't tell Grand, because I know it would break her heart to know she wasn't enough.

Cole realized he was being stupid and understood why she hadn't told anyone but couldn't seem to get past her even having a problem. *What about my youth group? What are they going through that they're hiding from everyone, even their best friends? Lord, please protect my youth group and let any harmful secrets come out in the open to be dealt with in your timing.*

Viviane could see a range of emotions cross his face, but his continued silence worried her. She used to be able to read his thoughts as easily as her own. *Maybe it's best if I leave and give him time to come to terms with everything. It's a lot to process.*

When she rose, she felt his hand grab hers and squeeze tight as he said, "Don't go, Vee! I'm sorry, I was praying for my youth kids. Your story made me realize I need to start covering them with a whole new type of prayer."

Touched he was using her story to pray for the youth group, she knew why he was a great youth pastor. *He really cares for his kids as he calls them.* "I was a little worried by your silence."

"I'm glad we're being truthful. I'm sorry my words hurt you, but I'm glad God used my insensitive self to help. There's a lot of truth that God causes all things to work together for the good of those who love him. God took my arrogant words and used them to bring healing and a stronger relationship with Him for you."

"Yes, it still amazes me how much more real God is to me now. It wasn't until our break up that I was forced to learn how real He can be."

Cole thought for a moment, *I'm glad for her, but what does it mean for us? I've had enough silence between us for a lifetime.* "Can we be friends, again? Even knowing how I treated you all those years ago?"

Viviane thought for a moment before she answered, *I really do want to be friends again, I loved him once, first like a brother and then more. We need to face the fact we've changed and might not be suited for each other. God might have different plans for us now that we've moved past the fight.* "I'd like to be friends."

"Good, let's forget the past and move forward."

Viviane shook her head, "You can't forget the past that's a myth. We must learn from it and remember how good God's been to us and keep moving down the path He wants us on."

"So where do we go from here? How long are you in Cartersville?" He leaned back against her.

She sighed, "I'm back until the end of September, because I've noticed Grand isn't doing well. She's tired all the time, cutting back from her usual activities." She whirled around to face him, nearly toppling him over. "Did you know she gave up her Sunday School class?"

Steadying himself, he nodded. "Yeah, I was shocked when I heard, but she joined Grace's class and I thought she wanted a change. She'd been teaching the class for over fifteen years."

"There has just been too many little things I've noticed that have me worried. Just when I think she's on the mend something happens to worry me all over again." She twisted her hands, continuing, "I wonder if I need to move back permanently. I love my life in Atlanta, but if Grand needs me, I'm home no hesitation. The trouble is she won't come out and tell me if she's sick or not."

Cole smiled, "Vee, no one doubts your devotion to Grand. She's always been independent and stubborn!"

"Don't I know it!"

"I know you've prayed about it, any leads?" Cole could feel her fear, *knowing Grand is the only family she has left I can't imagine how worried she must be.*

"No. Sometimes I think I need to hog tie her and take her to the doctor," she said in a huff.

He laughed, *I can imagine the two of them struggling and could see Grand trying to get away as Vee shoved her in the car.* "If you do, promise me you'll call so I can come watch."

She lightly punched his arm, "Please, now that we're friends again you're bringing the rope to help."

Sobering at the thought he said, "I just got one female to stop being mad at me, I don't need to add another one. Besides, Grand scares me more than you."

Laughing, she said, "Funny." Leaning against him, needing comfort she said, "Seriously though, I could use a fresh perspective." *I hope he has some ideas, because I've been struggling about what to do for weeks.*

"I'd need to watch her up close to see her in action. At church she always seems on the move."

Viviane nodded, but was still lost in thought when Cole said, "How about I take the two of you out Saturday? Maybe something in the afternoon and then dinner? That would give me a chance to see how she acts."

"That's a good idea. Because if she's tired around company, I'll know something is wrong." *It's a good plan and with Grand there, we won't be alone. I can do friends... I think.*

"Good. I'll call you tomorrow to set it up. Tell Grand to keep Saturday free."

"Grand will like that."

Viviane and Cole both stood up and after only a slight hesitation hugged before saying goodbye. As each went their separate way, both were happy with how well the first real talk went.

When she told Grand later that night, Grand sent up a silent Hallelujah. She made herself wait until Viviane went up to bed, before she did a little dance of celebration. *Finally, my plans are working. Part of me wants to cancel on them last minute, but it would be good to see how they interact with each other after all these years. Things for my granddaughter are definitely looking up.*

Chapter Sixteen

Grand looked at the clock to see she still had a few minutes before she needed to get dressed. She felt content and decided to lie in bed a little longer praising God for the past few weeks. The smile on her face shone brightly as she thought about two weeks ago when the three of them spent the day in Atlanta sightseeing and eating like old times. *I enjoyed watching the two of them rediscover their friendship. They still finish each other's sentences, have similar likes and dislikes, but the most encouraging thing happened at dinner when Cole's salad came with olives. He picked them off to pass to Viviane, who ate them and passed him her hated cucumbers. They didn't even notice but kept talking as an ingrained habit from over ten years ago came back without conscious thought.*

Grand had been smiling every day since. *They aren't officially dating yet, but that will change soon. I can see it in the way they look at each other. Even the church has noticed the change, because no one could miss the looks back and forth during the service, and leaving to eat together, causing church ladies to ask if they're serious again. I do love smiling sweetly and saying they're just good friends, especially to nosey Lauren Blake.*

Grand knew Lauren was pushing her daughter at Cole, but Viviane was perfect for him. *Lauren only wants to say her son-in-law is a minister. I want Viviane to be happy, not have another notch on my Christianity belt.*

Rising from bed she decided some light work was called for since things were going so well. *I can resume some of my normal activities without sending Viviane packing. It won't be long now, before I can give up all this lying around watching TV stuff.*

Looking in the bathroom mirror, she was pleased to see positive results from the gym already and decided as soon as they were an official couple, she would be open about her fitness regime. *It's doing me a world of good.*

Tiptoeing past Viviane's closed door, she went to the kitchen for her coffee and devotion time, already deciding to make biscuits. Viviane was up late last night doing some editing rushes Kathie called about. *I'll have to forgo all my usual breakfast sides, but that's okay. Appearances must be maintained a little longer, but at least I'm able to cook some.*

Viviane woke to a growling stomach and came fully awake at the smell of Grand cooking her famous biscuits. Stretching, she smiled to see how late she had slept. *It's wonderful to wake up happy with the world. The truth is I've enjoyed the past week with Cole, talking on the phone every day, sometimes more than once. It's been nice to learn things about him I never knew before.*

Dressed in her favorite cargo pants and t-shirt, she went downstairs to hear Grand singing in the kitchen. *I hope that crazy woman hasn't done too much. She's been doing so well the last two weeks. If my budding friendship with Cole helps Grand stay strong and healthy, then I'm even more grateful we mended our friendship.*

Walking through the doorway, she saw Grand pouring a cup of coffee and said teasingly, "I hope that's decaf. You've got too much energy this morning."

"Morning love. No, it's not decaf, you know I don't like decaf." She frowned, "I thought you would sleep later? You were up late last night."

Viviane came around to hug her, "It's okay. I got a lot done, and I'll be able to finish everything by the deadline. I want to have my weekend free."

"No plans with Cole until Friday, huh?"

"Yeah," Viviane grabbed a cup to pour some coffee, "We're going to Atlanta for dinner and movie tomorrow night with a group from my church in Atlanta."

Grand hide her smile, "I made biscuits this morning and there's jam in the fridge. Help yourself while I do some light picking up. Jill will be here soon to start working on the Thanksgiving dinner for the church."

Snagging a biscuit, Viviane said between bites, "It isn't even October and you're already planning?" She started to fix a plate thinking, *I need to make sure Grand doesn't do too much before she's back to full strength.*

"You know the church does a huge dinner the Sunday before Thanksgiving. I usually handle it by myself, but I'm having Jill help me this year, because it is an important community event." Trying to hide the frustration in her voice, she thought, *I always plan it alone, because I enjoy being busy. It keeps me young. I volunteered poor Jill, because I thought with some help Viviane would let me be. Obviously, I was wrong. It's only for a little longer,* she reminded herself.

She watched Viviane sit down and decided to move to the living room where she could clean without someone hovering over her. On her way out the door she called back over her shoulder, "Clean up after yourself. I wiped down the counters this morning." Smirking, she added silently, *I also polished all of the cabinets, and put Old English on the furniture in both the kitchen and dining room. What Viviane doesn't know won't hurt her.*

Viviane only shook her head, *Grand will be Grand and as long as she doesn't seem too tired I'll let her keep up this pace for a while. I have less than a week before I'm back in Atlanta full time and need to know now, if she'll be okay when I leave as planned.*

Frowning at the thought of leaving Grand, she was also torn about not seeing Cole. *How will our friendship progress if I'm not here? Do I want to move back to Cartersville? Would I be able to stay here knowing we're only friends?*

Mumbling a prayer for guidance, she picked up a jelly biscuit and remembered her lease wasn't up until next June. *I have time to discover what God wants me to do. I won't make any hasty decisions unless Grand makes a turn for the worse.*

Satisfied with her answer, she took a big bite. *Nobody makes biscuits like Grand.* Excited for the upcoming weekend, her head was in the clouds the rest of the week.

"That was a great movie, but I'm hungry. Let's go eat guys." Daphne said while walking out the theater to throw away her empty tub of popcorn.

"Daphne you ate almost all the popcorn and part of my candy. You should be sick." Erica complained.

"Where are we eating?" Viviane asked, having arrived late because of traffic.

Cole rubbed his stomach, "I'm hungry, too! Chinese?"

A tall, skinny guy named Paul laughed at Cole, "You're definitely a friend of Viv's if you want Chinese."

The group laughed at the accurate statement before they settled on PF Chang's because it was open late. Viviane watched Cole after they were seated and saw he was smiling and talking to the guys around him. *I was worried how he'd be around my friends but should've remembered he always made friends wherever he went. Everyone must like him, since I've been getting thumbs ups and winks all evening, even though I mouth we're just friends. It doesn't help that he's being extra charming to Erica and Daphne, because he knows they're my best friends.*

Enjoying the fellowship, it was an hour later when Daphne leaned over and rather loudly whispered, "Viv, you never said how cute Cole was, I mean pictures don't do the guy justice."

"Shush Daph. You're being silly." Viviane whispered back. "I don't want him to think we're whispering about him like kids."

She saw Cole laughing out of the corner of her eyes, and frowned, *He isn't talking to anyone, and unless he just happened to think of something funny, he heard Daph's comment.*

Determined to ignore him, she was sidetracked when he leaned over to whisper, "Your friend thinks I'm handsome, huh?"

Viviane rolled her eyes, "Daphne's sheltered, and she only said you're cute, not handsome. Cute as in a puppy!"

Cole laughed loudly, and everyone turned to stare. *I don't care, I like her friends and I'm having a great time. I did the right thing coming with her tonight. It's great seeing her interact with people she feels comfortable around. She's never this relaxed at church, and I don't know why. She's comfortable around me and Grand, even Grace, but after church she's hesitant, very controlled in her movements. It is frustrating, because I've watched her during worship, and can see the openness and joy on her face. It's great to see her around her friends, but I want to know why she holds back in Cartersville.*

Chapter Seventeen

"Why does time always move quickly when you least want it to." Viviane asked herself while getting ready for church Sunday morning. She was happy to be attending service, until she remembered this was her last day in Cartersville. *I leave tonight and I've got to pull myself together. I'm messing up my makeup crying like this.*

Staring herself down in the mirror, she said out loud, "Stop this! It's not like you're going to Africa." Squaring her shoulders, she continued sternly, "You're only an hour and a half away."

Still feeling tears welling up, she prayed for strength for when she saw Grand. Last night when she started packing, Grand became very subdued. *Please Lord, don't let her have any health setbacks because I'm leaving. When I said Cole volunteered to check on her and even eat with her a few times, she didn't crack a smile knowing how much Cole enjoyed her cooking. I heard her say under her breath Cole should be with me, not her. I know she's unhappy we're not dating, but it's too soon.* Wiping one last tear, she thought, *At least that must be what Cole thinks since he's never brought it up and I'm fine with that. Even if we were dating, I'd still be going back tonight.*

Picking up her Bible, she grabbed her purse to walk downstairs. She stayed up late reading Psalms hoping for guidance about leaving Grand. *I don't want to hurt her.* Viviane bit her lip hoping to hear Grand humming in the kitchen, but there was only silence. *A pin could've fallen and I'd hear it from the upstairs landing.* Sniffing the air, she thought, *No delicious smells is a bad sign.*

She found Grand seated at the table with only coffee in her hands. She moved to stand directly in front of her, and asked quietly, "Morning, Grand. How are you today?"

Grand looked up from staring off into space, "Hi, Dear. I'm fine. Coffee?"

"No thanks. Are you hungry? I could fix some eggs."

She started to move to the fridge, but stopped when Grand said, "Don't worry about it. I'm not hungry now and will have something in class."

Viviane could see Grand was tired and hated knowing she was the cause. *Please Lord, let me know if I'm doing the right thing. I've got to get back to work. Grand will get use to me being gone again. Please let her health hold up, she's been doing so well the last few weeks. Should I have insisted she go to the doctor? If the doctor said she needed someone to stay, I wouldn't hesitate. I love her and hope Grand knows that!*

Viviane made herself a cup of coffee, seeing Grand wasn't in a talkative mood. She sat at the table staring out the window, *Thank goodness we're leaving for church soon, because I can't handle this silence much longer.* Finally gulping down the last of her coffee, she said cheerfully, "Ready to go?"

Grand looked up without a smile and said, "Yes."

The two of them moved to the car, neither speaking. Grand felt a bit contrite since she felt fine, only her heart hurt with Viviane leaving. *I'll miss her and understand she has a job in Atlanta, but she isn't where she needs to be. I want her happy and that happiness is with Cole. It's time the girl realizes she needs to move back and into a married phase of life.*

Viviane was hungry by the time they reached the classroom. Grand quietly sat down in one of the folding chairs, and Viviane sighed before moving to get breakfast, neither woman speaking.

Grace watched them and knew something was wrong. She moved to stand beside Viviane. "You're leaving, today aren't you?"

"Yes, this evening." Wiping a stray tear, she glanced at Grand.

"It seems Ms. Delia Anne isn't happy about it."

Viviane chuckled, "More than just a little."

"It'll be okay. I've been praying for both of you. I think she's feeling better, but I'll keep an eye on her for you."

Through watery eyes, Viviane said while hugging her, "Thank you. I can't tell you how happy I am we've become friends."

"Me too, and I think today's discussion will help you. I read something last night that had me completely change my lesson. It fits perfectly with something I've been going through and I think will help you as well."

"I look forward to it."

Grace moved to the front of the room and pulled out her Bible and notes. *I wasn't kidding about changing my lesson at the last minute. My evening devotion really spoke to me and know it'll be good for Viviane, too! I was up late last night, but it looks like God's prompting was perfect as usual.*

"Good morning, ladies. Please open your Bibles to 1 Kings 8:56. 'Praise be to the Lord, who has given rest to his people, Israel, just as he promised. Not one word has failed of all the good promises He gave through His servant Moses.'"

Viviane thought, *I don't see how this verse applies to me. I've been resting for a month. This whole vacation has led me to my problem. Now, I'm not only leaving Grand who's used to having me around, but I'm also leaving Cole.*

Grace continued, "This verse is important, because we all could use a little rest. Not just in relaxation, but rest from worry about the tomorrows, the what-ifs, anxiety about everything that affects our day. This verse promises God given rest, and reminds us God has never failed to keep even one of His promises."

Sharon spoke up, "And that's a big promise to make."

As the ladies laughed, Grace smiled, "Yes, and I don't know about you, but I can't say I've kept all my promises."

The ladies sobered at Grace's statement each thinking of promises they had broken. Grace continued, "It's a blessing He keeps His promises and it's these very promises which mean we can give Him our worries and troubles knowing He will take care of them. Can anyone think of a verse from the Bible we can claim as a promise that God will take care of us?"

Zoe said, "The one from Deuteronomy about how God will never leave us. If He promises to be with you and protect you that's one less thing to worry about."

"Perfect Zoe. Deuteronomy 31:8 says, 'The LORD himself goes before you and will be with you; He will never leave you nor forsake you. Do not be afraid; do not be discouraged.'"

Viviane felt encouraged to speak, "It's important to remember God loves us enough to care for us. He cares about our day, our plans, and even our worries. We just have to remember that when we don't feel it."

Grace smiled broadly, "That's perfect and leads me to my favorite verse Jeremiah 29:11. The Message version says, 'I know what I'm doing. I have it all planned out-plans to take care of you, not abandon you, plans to give you the future you hope for.'" She paused to let it sink in before she said, "I love this verse, because it's a reminder God knows what He's doing and gives us what we need."

Viviane made notes in her Bible thinking, *I've always loved Jeremiah, but the Message version really spoke to my heart. I really want to do the right thing, but need direction on what to do, and where to go. I'm tired worrying about Cole, Grand, my job, where to live, it's a never-ending cycle. It's time to walk away and let God handle it. I need to go back to Atlanta and trust God to help me with all my problems.*

While the group kept talking, she prayed about releasing her fears to God, putting Cole and Grand in His adept hands. After she finished, she lifted her head with a beautiful smile on her face and Grace could see the change in her. Happy her friend was embracing God's promises, she continued the discussion for another fifteen minutes, before closing with announcements and prayer requests.

When class was over, Grand spoke up for the first time all morning, "I need to find Jill. I promised to get her these figures for the dinner. I'll meet you downstairs." She turned to say goodbye to Grace and was gone before Viviane could say a word.

"Thank you for the lesson. It was well timed." Viviane said moving to the table to help clean up breakfast.

"You're welcome. I'm glad it spoke to you like it did to me. I really felt lead to share it this morning and I'm glad to know God used it to help others." *I always try to let God have His way with this class, because these ladies mean a lot to me.*

Putting the last dish in Grace's bag, Viviane said, "I've decided to put Grand's health and my friendship with Cole in God's hands. I'm going to let Him tell me when I need to move back to Cartersville. I want to walk in the path He has for me, not my own."

Hugging her Grace said, "I know how hard that can be. I spend much of my time reminding myself to do that very thing."

Laughing, Viviane said, "I'm glad I'm not the only one."

Grace joined her in laughing, "Not by a long shot."

The two ladies went downstairs and at the last moment Grand slid into the pew next to Viviane just as Pastor Winston moved to start the service. *Everything must look normal to outsiders,* Viviane shook her head. *Remember I'm trusting God with all of this, but it's harder than I thought.*

After the service was over, they said goodbye to Grace and started toward the car. Cole made his way over to them and asked about their plans. Viviane started to tell him she planned to spend the day with Grand, when Grand spoke up, "No plans, Cole."

Cole's face broke into a wide smile, oblivious to any tension, "Well, how about I take both of you to lunch?" When he saw Viviane hesitate, he said, "My treat!" *I know they'll want to spend all the time together they can, but I really want to spend time with Viviane, too!*

"Thank you, Cole, but I'm tired. Why don't the two of you go to lunch and you can drop Viviane off at home later."

"Grand are you okay? I don't mind driving you home and making us something to eat."

"I'm fine, dear. Go have lunch. I'll see you later. We'll still have time together before you leave this evening." Grand hugged her and walked off, leaving Viviane struggling with what to say.

Chapter Eighteen

Happy with how things worked out, Cole gently took Viviane's arm and propelled her to his car. He asked, "What are you in the mood for besides Chinese?"

Viviane laughed, "Mexican?"

Cole smiled, "Mexican it is. Our usual place?"

Smiling, she said, "Yes, I'm hungry."

Discussing Pastor Winston's sermon kept them busy even after they were seated. While the waitress took Viviane's order, Cole thought, *I've got a degree in theology and I can't believe how much Vee knows. She's carrying on a discussion most divinity students wouldn't be able to handle casually over lunch.*

Finally, Cole blurted out, "How do you know so much about all of this, Vee? I mean the gap theory of creation? That's pretty deep stuff."

Viviane laughed, *it's nice knowing so much about a subject Cole clearly loves.* "After I realized I was living on Grand's Christian coat tails, I decided I needed to learn everything I could about Christianity. I always loved to learn and started reading a lot about Biblical history and theory. I even took some classes in college, because I was desperately searching for answers."

"It's really great to talk to someone besides Pastor Winston about all of this. I was..." Cole was interrupted when Lauren Blake and her daughter came up to stand at their table.

"Good afternoon Pastor West. How are you?" Lauren asked without even apologizing for interrupting. "I'm glad we ran into you, because I wanted to ask you about Wednesday. Could we get together and talk?"

Viviane could tell Mrs. Blake wasn't happy to see them sitting alone together, her frown directed at her an obvious indication. Viviane smiled at Hillary and mouthed hi. The poor girl was completely drowned out by her mother. Viviane prayed, *Please let him send her away, because I really don't want to share our last meal with anyone.*

"I'd be glad to meet with you. Just call Mrs. Owen to set up an appointment. She knows my schedule better than I do."

Lauren moved closer to the table almost blocking Viviane, "I hoped we could meet today, possibly now? I've got a lot of things to get done this week." She turned to smile pointedly at Viviane, "I'm sure Viviane wouldn't mind, seeing how it's church business."

Viviane could swear the woman was being rude on purpose. *Lauren Blake hadn't even looked at me before. Poor Hillary, she's such a sweet woman to have such a controlling mother. I'm so glad Grand isn't controlling. Please send them away Cole.*

She couldn't believe her ears when Cole said, "I'm sorry Mrs. Blake, but I can't now. I promised Viviane a special lunch since she's leaving to go back to Atlanta tonight."

Choking on her tacos, she took a gulp of water. *That isn't true, he never promised me any such thing.* Hiding a smile behind her glass, she thought, *but I'll take it.*

Surprised at Cole's words, Lauren was pleased to know Viviane was leaving. *The sooner that girl is out of Hillary's way, the better. I'll make an appointment for tomorrow and invite him over for dinner one night. Then he'll see for himself what a wonderful hostess Hillary will make. She's a fabulous cook.*

"I'll call Misty. Between the two of us, we can find a way to meet soon."

"I look forward to it."

Cole prayed lightening wouldn't strike him dead for lying as he watched the two women walk away. He turned to Viviane, having caught her face when he was speaking to Lauren. *She knows what I'm thinking without me saying a word.* Smiling, he thought, *It's nice to have someone who knows you so well.*

Coughing, Viviane said, "I don't seem to remember you saying anything about a special lunch today?"

"What can I say? I want this to be a great lunch. I know you're weekends are busy until Christmas and I work during the week, and it will be hard to see each other. We'll work it out, won't we?"

Unsure what he meant, she only nodded in agreement. Picking up their discussion, Lauren Blake became a distant memory.

An hour later when the waitress took their dessert plates, neither made a move to leave. Cole kept thinking how hard it would be not to see her. Sipping his almost empty water, he struggled with what to say.

Viviane told herself in the growing silence, *It isn't as if he's actually said anything about a long distance relationship. Men can be so confusing.*

When the waitress started cleaning the table, the two stood up to leave. Cole grabbed the check, "My treat."

Viviane nodded, "But I get the tip."

Speaking very little on the way to Grand's house, Cole pulled into the drive, and neither moved. Viviane stared at her purse thinking, *I don't want to say goodbye, but I don't know what else to say.*

Cole spoke quietly, "Call me when you get to Atlanta. I want to know you made it okay."

Viviane gave him a half smile, *That's what he always said when we were dating. I loved that.* "I promise like always."

She watched to see if he remembered her familiar reply, but forgot everything lost in his deep, sea green eyes. He started to speak but froze when their eyes locked. The two of them staring, when Cole leaned forward.

Suddenly a banging front door caused them to jump apart as Grand yelled, "Viviane, it's Kathie. She's been trying to reach you."

Viviane opened the door, "Okay Grand. I'll be right in." Unsure if frustration could be heard in her voice she turned to Cole and said an awkward goodbye. Sad the moment was broken, she walked with a heavy heart inside. She picked up the phone wondering, *what did we miss out on? Will we ever get it back?*

After she hung up with Kathie who called to check on Grand, she walked into the living room to see Grand knitting and watching TV. Looking up, Grand asked, "Did you have a nice time with Cole?"

"We had a nice lunch. I'm glad we had a chance to say goodbye."

"I trust you didn't mind having some alone time together? I really hoped the two of you would've talked about being more than just friends."

I'm not telling her she interrupted what would've have been a definite move toward dating. I don't want to disappoint Grand, I'm disappointed enough for both of us. "I'm going to change and then we can spend some time together." She moved up the stairs, trying to hold back tears. *It wasn't until we almost kissed that I realize how much I wanted it. The next few weeks are going to be hard, because I won't be back until Thanksgiving. That's two months away!* With a silent groan, she prayed, *Lord this is really hard. Is this a test to see if I really trust You? If it is, please let me pass this one.*

The two women spent a few hours together watching TV and talking. Neither one mentioned her plans to leave at six, but the hours passed quickly as Viviane found herself praying for Grand to be healthy and take care of herself.

A few minutes before six, she brought down her suitcases and put them in the car. Too quickly everything was packed with the exception of her purse and camera for the front seat. Slowly she walked back up the porch steps to Grand sitting in one of the rocking chairs. *She looks so small sitting there. Please don't let me start crying now!*

Taking her granddaughter into her arms, Grand prayed for her safety. *It's always hard to say goodbye after long visits, and this was the longest visit in ten years.* "Call me when you get there. Don't be a stranger."

Squeezing her tight, Viviane said, "I will. Don't worry. I love you."

Each could see the tears in the other's eyes, but neither could say more. As Viviane walked to her car, Grand thought, *I'm grateful the plan is working well, but until she has a wedding ring on her finger I won't give up getting her back here permanently.* Waving as Viviane pulled out of the drive, she went back inside her heart already missing her girl.

Over an hour later, Viviane pushed open her front door and took her bags to her bedroom. *I really want to go to bed and not think about anything.* As she walked past the kitchen, she noticed a note on her fridge. It was from Daphne and said she left food in the freezer with directions to heat it up. She then ordered Viviane to call her and Erica to set up a time for dinner later in the week.

Viviane hugged the note to her chest, grateful she had given the girls a key to her apartment after the Chinese takeout night. She pulled out a casserole and put it in the stove, before deciding to call Cole.

"Hello?"

"Hi Cole. I wanted to let you know I made it home."

"Good. How was the drive?"

"It was fine." She hated the strain between them. *Is this because of the awkward moment this afternoon, or will it always be this way, now I'm back in Atlanta?*

"Well, I'm glad you made it okay. I'll let you unpack... Viviane?"

"Yes?"

"I... um... I'll keep an eye on Grand for you."

"... Thanks. I guess I'll let you go."

"Okay. Bye, Vee."

That was depressing. Part of me wants to analyze that phone call and go over every detail, but I gave this all to God. I'm going to unpack instead. I hate unpacking, but it's better than thinking about Cole.

Cole was sitting in his favorite recliner with Moses' head in his lap. He hung up the phone, staring off into space. *I can't believe the conversation was so bad on my end. I've wanted to talk to her all evening, because I haven't been able to get our almost kiss out of my head.*

He looked down at Moses, "I shouldn't lie to you. I want to start dating Viviane and should've said something before she left. I don't know if we're meant to be anything more than friends, but I want to try if Viviane's willing." Scratching Moses ears, Cole kept speaking, "I've never met anyone who made me as happy as she did and I'm tired of looking. I need to see if God brought me the right woman seventeen years ago."

Moses looked at him, she didn't care what he wanted to do as long as he kept scratching her head. Knowing he was talking more to himself, he said, "I'll say something when she gets back to town. Asking a girl on a first date shouldn't be done over the phone, not with the history between us.

Satisfied with his plan, he thought of how great it would be to date now that they knew themselves and each other better. He stopped petting Moses to ask, "Want to go for a run, girl?"

Moses leaped up, practically turning over the recliner as she raced to get her leash on the counter. That was the best thing he said all day.

Chapter Nineteen

Viviane woke up Tuesday morning with a terrible feeling in the pit of her stomach. She grabbed the blanket she kept at the foot of her bed, even though January had been unusually warm this year and curled up in the sitting area of her bedroom that consisted of a green recliner with a side table and a small bookcase, where she often sat for her devotion time. She loved being surrounded by her favorite books and a picture of Grand could be seen sitting on the little table.

Glancing at the bedside clock she saw it was a little after six and opened her Bible to Psalms. *Please God lead me in what to pray about this morning that's so urgent. I've had this feeling before and know it means You want me to pray about something specific. You've always shown me later how I was praying for someone in desperate need of help.*

As she spent a few minutes reading and praying for guidance, she came across Psalm 121. Puzzled, she thought, *I usually read this before going on a mission trip.* The last two verses jumped out at her, "The Lord will keep you from all harm - he will watch over your life; the Lord will watch over your coming and going both now and forevermore." *Lord what are you trying to tell me?*

She sent up a quick prayer for Grand, *I've not seen her since New Year's when I made a quick trip home. Work has kept me really busy on the weekends and most of my trips to Cartersville have been short. I wasn't able to spend any time with Cole, because he was with his family for Thanksgiving and Christmas. Between the holidays and his church duties, he had only visited once and that was months ago. We never talked about the almost kiss, but thankfully the awkward phone call was never repeated.*

Keeping her head bowed, she focused on resting in God's presence waiting on direction, when a voice spoke quietly to her heart, "Go to Cartersville. Leave now."

Lifting her head, she knew it was from the Lord. *I've learned over the years to trust Your prompting, I just pray this isn't because Grand's sick, or even worse.* She dressed quickly and threw a few things in an overnight bag. She was on the interstate by seven.

The radio station talk pertained to the crazy warm weather, a high of 73 today and tomorrow warm with possible thunderstorms. *Even living here my whole life, Georgia weather can be strange. I can't believe it's the end of January and I'm wearing a t-shirt and jeans.* Driving as fast as she could, she prayed for both no cops and for Grand's health. *I don't want to worry her by calling if she isn't in trouble.* She was constantly eyeing her phone to see if she missed any calls.

Only thirty minutes from Cartersville, she almost ran off the road when her phone started to ring, but when she glanced down she didn't recognize the number. *Lord please don't let it be the hospital.* She strangled out, "Hello?"

"Viviane, it's Mike... Mike Hollister, Cole's friend."

"Hi Mike. Is something wrong?"

Taken back that it was Mike, she wasn't sure how he even got her number. *He was friendly enough over the holidays, but distant. I know he was wary of my friendship with Cole, and while I think it's sweet he's protective, it's silly of him to be worried. We're only friends, four months of just friends Lord.*

"I know it's weird for me to be calling you, but I felt you should know Moses is missing. Cole's going a little crazy with worry. We've spent all morning looking and can't find her anywhere. I don't know what to do."

"Oh, that's awful. I know how much Cole loves that dog. How did she get out?"

"We're not completely sure, but when Cole woke up this morning she wasn't in the house and the front door was open. We think she got scared and ran. You know she's scared of everything."

"I remember Christmas when I came over to watch the game with you two, and she freaked over a car backfiring." *The silly dog took a long time to warm up to me and it wasn't until she jumped in my lap terrified that she started to like me after I petted her for ten minutes to calm her down.*

Mike made a strange noise, and said, "It's all my fault! I came over last night to watch the game and Cole went on to bed early, but I stayed for the end." Mike explained, "He has a few sports channels I don't and told me to lock up when I left, but I think I forgot to lock the door, because I left in a hurry."

Viviane could tell even over the phone how upset Mike was and tried to calm him, "It's an accident, Mike. Cole knows that."

"Maybe so, but I'm afraid Cole might think I wasn't joking when I said he needed to get a better dog." Choking back a sob he said, "I care for that dumb dog, too."

Worried, Viviane said, "I'm almost at the Cartersville exit. Are you at Cole's?"

"Yeah," the relief evident in his voice, "We called his parents to help us, because we're worried it will start raining. It's so cloudy and you know how Moses reacts to the rain."

"I know it's bad. I saw her stuck outside in a downpour and she howled for hours even when she was inside."

"And she was only outside for ten minutes."

"Don't worry, Mike. I'll be there soon."

"I don't know how, but I'm glad. I didn't know what to do. He's so upset and I just thought you could help us look... and help him, too. You know?"

"Yeah, I know. It's a God thing I'm coming and I'll be glad to help."

After Mike hung up, she said a prayer of thanks that God sent her to help and a special prayer for Moses to be found safe. *People might say God doesn't care about such things, but if it's important to us, it's important to God. He gave dogs' human-like personalities and individuality, a sign that God has a heart for dogs, too!*

Remembering the Psalm from this morning, *help comes from the Lord. He watches over us day and night. If God cares for the birds of the air, and lilies of the valley, then He cares about a crazy chocolate lab named Moses.*

Comforted, she took the exit for Cole's house without conscious thought. *I've always loved visiting the West family and Cole's place had been turned into a stunning home by his mother. Lynn did an excellent job, but the thought of him cooking in a kitchen with granite countertops and a professional stove makes me laugh. He's no cook.*

When she arrived, she saw several cars in the driveway, but no one around as she got out of the car. She pulled out her cell phone to call, when she heard a noise and saw two men striding through the trees. Even from a distance she could see it was Cole and his dad, Carson. Almost a carbon copy of his son, Carson West had the same build and easy smile. The only difference was his graying hair, but both were tall, handsome men.

They aren't smiling, so they haven't found Moses yet.

Cole came out of the woods in deep conversation with his dad, but once he saw Viviane, a smile lit up his whole face. He broke into a run and his quick strides covered the distance to grab her in a big hug before swinging her around. "What are you doing here, Vee?"

Viviane held on tightly, it was the first hug they had in weeks. "It's a God thing. He woke me up and said go to Cartersville. Mike called while I was on my way to say Moses was missing."

Cole didn't want to let go, *I don't care what brought her, I'm just glad she's here.*

Viviane finally stepped back, "Hello, Mr. Carson."

Carson shook her hand, smiling broadly. *I've been worried about Cole, but this is a good sign.*

She turned back to Cole, "Mike's really upset... he feels terrible."

He ran his hand through his hair. "I know and I don't blame him. He should know that."

"Cole and I were about to drive his usual running route he takes with Mo. If Viviane doesn't mind, why doesn't she drive and the rest of us will split up and search further out. It's time we expand the search," Carson said with his hand on Cole's shoulder.

"Yeah, Dad, that sounds like a good plan."

Everyone agreed to keep in touch and moved to expand the search. As Viviane and Cole drove off, Carson prayed they would find Moses soon. *Viviane showing up is a good sign for finding Mo, and a better sign about my son's relationship with Viviane. Just friends my left foot,* he thought.

Chapter Twenty

Cole directed Viviane down the road past all his favorite running trails. They drove in near silence with the occasional shout of Moses' name out of the rolled down windows. *The tension in the car is high, but I know it's from worry over Moses and can use it to motivate me to pray harder.*

"Moses, here girl!" Cole shouted as they drove. Viviane echoed it with her own, "Come Moses. Come here girl."

They drove around for several miles, but with no signs she turned to Cole, "Is there anywhere else you take her? Any other places you run?"

Cole thought for a moment, *I take Mo lots of places, because she's good with both kids and adults.* Quite abruptly he turned to her and shouted, "We sometimes go to the park by the elementary school. Mo likes to watch the kids play. She loves kids."

"Then we'll go to her favorite park," Viviane said already turning the car in that direction. Familiar with Hamilton Crossing's park because Cole's family often used the fields, she needed no directions. The West family's flag football game was legendary, and she had participated many times growing up.

Viviane parked near the edge of the park and suggested they walk around. It was a large park with areas a car couldn't drive and walking would allow them to cover more ground. They started at the ball fields and moved inward past the tennis courts and playgrounds. Since it was a school day, the park was empty without a soul around to ask if anyone had seen a chocolate lab. They kept calling for Moses but heard no happy barking replies.

Viviane kept praying for God to lead them to the dog, because she felt He had brought her here for a reason. *Please don't let it be to help comfort Cole over losing his dog.*

They had almost walked the entire park when she noticed a new fence. "When did they put this up?"

"It's been years, Vee," Cole looked at Viviane, then back to the fence. Viviane could see the sadness in his eyes, when he continued, "I guess I didn't realize how long it's been since you were here."

"I guess it has been a long time." The two stood staring at the fence and what it represented. *This awkward moment isn't about Moses being gone, but me. I don't like to think about how we both needed time away from each other to grow up. It's hard to swallow.*

As Cole started to walk back to the car, Viviane paused near the fence standing absolutely still listening. *I thought I heard something, but I'm not sure what the noise was exactly. It definitely wasn't a bark, but it wasn't a bird either.* "Cole," she reached out to grab his arm, but he had already moved too far away, "Cole did you hear that?"

As he paused to listen, she heard the noise again and she grew excited. *That's definitely an animal trying to get our attention.* "Moses?" She called, moving toward the noise.

"Vee, that isn't Moses." *I don't know what she heard, but it wasn't a sound my dog would make. I know that much.* "It's not her bark." He started marching back to the car not waiting for her to follow. *We need to look somewhere else. This is a dead end.*

She ignored him and kept walking toward the senior center behind the park. She saw a chained metal fence and at the far end a large dark shape. As she got closer, she could see Moses caught in the fence. Relief coursing through her, she yelled back, "It's Moses, Cole. She's here."

She didn't even turn to see if he followed but took off in a run to Moses who was visibly shaking with excitement over being found. "Cole, I think she's caught on the fence. Help me get her free."

I can't believe she found my dog, Cole thought running after her. When he rounded the building, he saw Moses' collar had been caught on a loose piece of wire. When Moses saw him, she struggled desperately to get free, but was strangling herself in the process. Cole stooped down to calmly pet her to keep her from injuring herself more. He began to work to free her, but her collar was too shredded from trying to get loose.

It's cutting off her air. That's why she couldn't bark and alert anyone. His hand slick with blood, he rested his head on hers, "I'm so sorry, Mo. We'll get the collar off you and then you can bark up a storm okay?"

He turned to Viviane and could see by the tears in her eyes, she had seen the blood. *I'm glad she didn't say I told you so for not listening earlier.* Tears in his own eyes, he asked, "I don't have anything to cut off her collar. Do you have something in your car?"

She fumbled for her keys, "Here, I've got a Swiss army knife on my keychain."

He took the small knife and cut Moses' collar off. Excited she had something to help, he said, "I love you, Vee."

After Moses was free from the fence, Moses tackled him and covered him in wet, sloppy dog kisses. Completely focused on Moses, he didn't see Viviane's face when he told her he loved her. Shocked by his unexpected words, she felt hot and cold running up her body. *I want him to say it to my face and take me in his arms, not Moses. Does he even realize what he said? Was it just an automatic reply for saving his dog?* Watching him hug Mo, she realized, *now's not the time.*

Moses finally moved away from Cole and came slowly padding over to her and licked her hand. The big chocolate lab was covered in mud, dirt and leaves, but none of that mattered as Viviane bent down to gently hug Moses, carefully not to hurt her neck. Moses leapt up to lick her face. She wasn't stupid. She knew who saved her life.

"We need to get her to a vet. That place on her neck should be looked at."

Cole only nodded, he didn't think he could speak he was so happy Moses was okay. *I've been seeing images all morning of her dead on the side of the road. If we hadn't found her when we did, Moses would've choked to death. It's a miracle she hadn't already.*

Viviane touched his arm, "Why don't you get Moses and we'll go to the car."

Cole called Moses and he picked her up with a grunt, "Mo, you're going on a diet when we get home."

"It's impolite to tell a lady she's fat. I think she's fine and you," she said pointing and laughing, "should start lifting weights." Viviane smiled at Moses, gently scratching behind her ears.

Moses wagged her tail which conveniently hit Cole in the face. Moses decided she liked Viviane a whole lot, especially when she pulled out a warm blanket from the trunk of her car. Wrapping Moses up, Cole said, "Thanks for the blanket. It's going to get dirty, and your car, too."

"It's okay. Everything will wash. You should call your family and the vet to let them know we're coming."

He got in the backseat with Moses and pulled out his phone. Viviane drove, while he made quick phone calls to everyone and soothed Moses. When they arrived at the vet's office, he carefully carried Mo inside where the office staff was waiting to rush her back. Viviane started walking to the waiting room when Cole asked, "Aren't you coming, Vee?"

Seeing the expression on his face and Moses' liquid brown eyes had her saying, "Of course, if you two want me."

Following behind she watched Cole gently lay Moses on the exam table to find the doctor already waiting. As Cole told him about the exciting morning, the doctor examined Moses neck and checked the rest of her body for injuries.

"Her neck looks bad, but I don't think there's any permanent damage. I'll need to take some x-rays to be sure, but she'll need stitches. Neck wounds tend to bleed a lot." The vet kept petting Moses while he spoke, "I'll get some medicine for you to put on her neck and something for all the scratches, too."

After the doctor led Moses through the back door to the x-ray machine, Viviane sat down. Cole knelt in front of her, speaking so quietly she had to lean forward to hear him. "Vee, I want to thank you for this morning, driving me around town, and for..." He paused, it was extremely hard for him to continue, "For hearing my dog when I couldn't."

He had taken both her hands and was rubbing his thumb across her fingers. She felt herself relaxing, leaning forward to rest her head on his chest and promptly burst into tears. "I was so worried we wouldn't find her." She sobbed, "I didn't like seeing you hurting, missing her. I was afraid I wouldn't be able to help you, but I'm glad you thought I was helpful."

Holding her while she cried, he thought, *I'm so thankful God sent her to me. I'm not sure we would've found Mo without her. When I said I loved her it was automatic, but I realized during the car ride it's true. I want to stop being only friends.*

When she stopped crying she was embarrassed about blubbering all over his shirt. Cole didn't seem to mind, because when she sat up, he kept holding her hands. She wanted to apologize but once she looked into his eyes, she lost all ability to speak. *Don't let the doctor walk in, please God.*

Time seemed to stand still as he slowly lowered his head and kissed her. Closing her eyes, she thought, *finally.* It was her last thought for several moments.

Cole knew he was going to kiss her as soon as she started crying in his arms. All he could think was she's mine and I've been waiting for a long time. He promised himself, *I'm never letting go again.*

After the kiss, they stayed in each other's arms smiling. No words spoken as they both enjoyed the moment. When the doctor walked in a while later, he told them good news. "Moses will be fine. Neck wounds can be messy, but her throat wasn't seriously damaged. She won't be doing any barking for a bit. It'll be sore for a while, but she'll recover quickly."

"Thank you, doctor." Cole and Viviane said together. Smiling at each other, Cole turned to the doctor, "Is there any special care for Moses?"

The doctor said, "No, keep the area clean when you give her a bath and be careful of the stitches."

After the doctor left, Viviane asked, "Why didn't he offer to bathe her?"

"Oh, well... um," Cole replied avoiding her eyes, "they refuse, because the first time I brought her for grooming, Moses practically drowned the woman trying to give her a bath. She ended up spraining her ankle wrestling her. You know because of her fear of water." Cole laughed remembering being confronted by an angry teenager soaked to the bone and on crutches. "Now I'm the only one she'll let bathe her. It's a nightmare let me tell you. We both end up pretty wet."

Viviane laughed as she pictured the wet dog and wet owner. As Moses led them out of the room, Viviane said, "The things we do for love."

Cole smiled, "Yes, for love."

Chapter Twenty-One

They didn't talk as they drove back to his house, but Cole held her hand as they both kept an eye on Moses in the back seat sprawled out asleep. She seemed content after her morning adventure. Viviane drove on automatic pilot thinking about what happened in the exam room. *The kiss was perfect and felt like a first kiss. I hope this begins a new phase with Cole. Dating him will be better than before, because I'm a healthier, happier person. Having a personal relationship with God will help us both.*

Cole couldn't wait to talk to Viviane about moving their relationship forward but didn't think it was a conversation for the car. When they pulled into his driveway, he was surprised to see his parents still there. He opened the back door for Moses to charge up the front porch, flying to find his parents in the kitchen preparing a late lunch.

"Hi, Mom and Dad. The vet said Moses is okay, spoiled rotten but okay."

Moses sauntered to Carson and Lynn wagging her tail as she begged for attention. Carson bent over to pet her when Lynn fussed at him, "Carson West you better wash your hands before you continue to help me with lunch."

Carson chuckled while petting Moses, "Yes, dear."

After a thorough greeting to the dog, Carson stood up to wash his hands. Lynn turned to Viviane and said, "I'm glad you were here to help us. Dad told me you felt prompted by God to come up." She wiped her hands on a towel and walked to Moses. "I never grow tired of hearing how God takes special care of our needs. Cole told us you were the one who found Mo and he made it clear we would have lost her if it hadn't been for you."

Viviane watched her bend over to pet Moses whose tail wagged furiously. She noticed Lynn hadn't changed much over the years, almost matching her husband's six-foot height with her own 5'9". Her light brown hair was sprinkled with some gray that looked elegant on her. Still pretty trim from an active family life, Viviane wasn't surprised to see she was still a strong, formidable woman. *She has to be with three active men in her life.*

Moses was elated when Lynn started petting her. Lynn might seem tough to everyone else, but she often snuck her food from the table. Moses knew this woman didn't know the meaning of scraps, because she always ate very well when Lynn visited.

"Thank you, I'm glad I could help." Viviane walked further into the kitchen and smelled something wonderful cooking on the stove. "Is there something I can do to help?"

"No dear, Dad and I are almost done with a chicken pasta salad." Lynn moved to wash her hands. "Cole, why don't you and Viviane give Moses a bath? Lunch will be done by then." She started to chop spinach for the salad. "We knew you'd be hungry. It's almost one. I bet you two didn't have breakfast."

"Right as always." Cole said as he kissed her on the cheek. He turned to grab his phone, "I need to call work and let them know what's going on. I left a message, but didn't realize it would take all day to care for Mo."

"Don't worry, son. Your mom called Mrs. Owens." Carson said washing vegetables.

Lynn chimed in, "I called to let Misty know you found her and were going to the vet. She said not to worry about coming in but take care of Moses. It seems everyone loves our Mo, phobias and all."

Carson chuckled, "And that means a lot considering how tough Mrs. Owens can be. She was practically in tears worried about Moses."

"Mo has a way about her that's for sure." Cole said pulling out her medicine. He turned to ask Viviane, "Do you want to help me bathe her? It might be easier with two of us."

"Sure. We'll need to cover her neck wound. The doctor said not to get the area wet." She turned around, "Where do you bathe her?"

"My bathroom is the only one large enough for my big girl."

"Cole, I told you don't insult a lady's weight. We're a sensitive species."

Lynn laughed, "She's right. We women have to stick together. It doesn't matter how many legs we have!"

Carson nodded in agreement, *being a happily married man for thirty-four years, I know better than to make fun of a woman's weight, no matter the species.*

Cole pointed for Moses to scoot, and with her head hanging low she slowly pawed her way to the master bathroom. She felt grimy enough to submit to a short bath.

Following Moses, he said, "I'll get you an extra t-shirt and sweats for you. You'll ruin your clothes with mud. I'm warning you, she thinks if she has to get wet, everyone should." Tossing clothes to her, he pointed past the kitchen, "You can change in the half bath."

Thankful to wear dry clothes when they ate, Viviane heard Lynn call out, "Hurry you two. Lunch will be ready in twenty-five minutes. That's plenty of time to wash the dog and both of you."

Lynn waited for Viviane to join Cole, before she raised an eyebrow at her husband. Carson didn't respond but shrugged continuing to chop vegetables. Finishing the meal prep, she thought, *I've been wanting to see Cole and Viviane together, since she came back in September. I know they're friends now but want to see if they've started dating.*

Moving to stir the pasta, she frowned thinking, *it's time Cole settled down. His younger brother is happily married with two adorable little girls. I love my son, but I think all the gossip is wrong about Viviane breaking Cole's heart. Cole has a tendency to sabotage things and I can admit that about him and pray for his stubbornness to give way to common sense. Viviane's a sweet woman who would be perfect for him. She was a wonderful first girlfriend, even though sometimes she looked like a wounded animal. Her eyes used to be full of pain, but I've noticed a change since she came back.*

As Lynn finished up the salad, she prayed Viviane had found peace in her time away and asked if it was God's will to bring them together, He would do it soon.

Hearing laughter coming from the master bath she smiled, *that's a wonderful sound to hear. Cole doesn't laugh enough.*

Carson saw his wife's smile and said quietly, "Sounds like Mo isn't the only thing Cole's taken with."

Murmuring an agreement, Lynn finished cutting the last of the vegetables. After being married thirty-five years, her husband off by one, she thought, *Viviane's good for Cole and he needs to marry her while he can.*

They finished setting the large dining table, as two soaked people and one dry dog stepped into the living room. "Cole, I thought having two people would make it easier to bathe Moses." His mom said arching her eyebrow.

Cole ran a towel through his wet hair grunting, "That was the theory, but once the water hit her, she practically leapt out of the tub before we could grab her. It took two of us to hold her down!"

Viviane soaked to the skin said, "Yeah, I think that's the craziest thing I've ever done. I would've been drier going over Niagara Falls."

Carson and Lynn laughed seeing Moses with her short coat already dry. "Clean up and then I'll allow you to come eat at the table." Lynn said smiling as she sat down.

"Gladly," Cole said already moving back to his bathroom. He called back to Viviane, "Aren't you glad now you changed?"

She threw a towel at him, before ducking into the powder room. *I should've drowned him when his dog tried to drown me.*

Cole chuckled as he dressed, *I don't want to admit I liked her helping me bathe Moses. She looked adorable in my big marathon t-shirt and sweat pants, especially with them rolled up several times. I left the bathroom door open, because my large master bath felt very tiny with Viviane in there with me, which let Mo think she had a chance to escape.*

When he came back out everyone was seated waiting on him. *Maybe I was daydreaming a little too long. I'll have to be careful so no one knows how love sick I really am.*

His mother made a request for him to say the blessing, but he caught the satisfied smile that passed between his parents. He reached for his father's and Viviane's hand, before he prayed, "Thank you Lord for family, both the two legged and four-legged kind. Thank you we're all here together, healthy and mostly dry. Bless the food and the hands that prepared it. Amen."

During the prayer, he squeezed Viviane's hand thinking of her as family. He would have smiled to know his mother squeezed her other hand on the word family, too. A chorus of amens accompanied the sound of people filling their plates while talking and laughing. It was a celebration meal that Moses enjoyed most of all with Lynn sneaking her bits of food, along with Carson, Cole and Viviane.

Chapter Twenty-Two

After lunch, everyone helped clean up. The men cleared the table, while Viviane wiped off the counters, and Lynn put dishes in the dishwasher. There wasn't much talk until Carson asked, "Who turned down the lights?"

Everyone looked up and noticed how dark it had gotten. Viviane looked at her watch to see it was only three-thirty, but the view outside looked much later. Viviane glanced out the window and said, "It looks like it's going to rain."

Lynn walked over to the big bay windows, "More like it's going to pour! Honey, we need to get home and check on the animals, and batten down the house."

"Viviane, you're not planning on driving back to Atlanta in this are you?" Carson saw the concern on his wife's face and immediately thought of Viviane's long drive home.

"No, if I went back to Atlanta without seeing Grand, she'd kill me." She tried to be light hearted, but the sky looked bad.

Seeing the storm clouds rolling in, she was grateful when she called Kathie to say she was driving up to Cartersville, and Kathie told her to stay through Monday, because it would be their only break for the next few weeks. As she told Cole's parents, she tried catching Cole's eye so he understood what she was saying. *If he wants to have a date before I go back, he needs to move fast.*

"I'll walk everyone out. It's best if I don't leave Moses alone, if it's going to storm." Cole moved to the front door, praying for everyone's safety and his sanity stuck in a storm with Moses.

"Bye, dear." Lynn hugged her son, "Call us later and let us know how Mo is." She bent over to pet Moses still safely inside the door. The dog wasn't going outside, she wasn't stupid.

"Goodbye, son." Carson waved, and walked over to Viviane. "Take care, Viv. We'll see you Sunday, if not sooner." He winked before he walked to his car.

Viviane waved goodbye, before turning to Lynn. Reaching out to hug her, Lynn whispered, "I can see honey, you're doing well. The peace in your eyes warms my heart. Don't let my silly son lose you this time, okay?"

Hugging the woman tightly, Viviane thought, *I've always loved this family, even longer than I've loved Cole. I've always thought my Mom would've been a lot like Lynn and that's why she and Grand were so close.* "Thank you, Mrs. Lynn. I do believe I've found true peace."

Lynn squeezed her one more time before getting in the car. Viviane waved as they drove off, and felt Cole move closer to where she was standing. *I should rush home to Grand, but I don't want to leave, not yet. It turned out to be a wonderful day, even with how it started. I don't want it to end, terrible weather or not.*

Cole reached for her hand, "Vee, do you have plans for Friday night?" He was so close he could smell the wildflower scent of her shampoo.

"Friday, well let me see..." She paused, watching him frown. "I guess I can turn Grand down for one evening to spend time with you."

Cole bumped her hip with his, "You crazy woman. I know you were dropping hints earlier when my parents were here. You can't fool me." He turned his head toward the driveway. "I bet we didn't fool them either."

Viviane laughed, "No we didn't, because your Mom said I'd better run for the hills. I was too good for you." *I know he's wondering what his mom said to me.*

Cole reached out to grab her, but she saw his arm coming and turned to run down the porch steps. "Sorry, Cole," she sang out, "I need to get home, before it starts to rain. You should go in and take care of Moses."

Cole gave chase, and Moses caught up in the excitement followed. She caught up with Viviane before Cole did, and Viviane rewarded her with a belly rub. "Good girl, Mo. You're not scared of a silly old storm, are you?"

Moses understood, because she yelped and ran back into the house. Cole forgot about his chase as they both bent over laughing at the silly lab. When the laughter stopped, he grabbed her hand and said, "Call me when you get home."

"I'm only twenty minutes away." She was pleased he cared and walked slowly to the car.

"Fifteen with the way you drive, so call me please."

Viviane lifted her chin, smiling as she said, "Okay. I'll call like always."

Her smile got bigger as he leaned down to kiss her goodbye. She carried the feel of his kiss and the one from the vet's office with her. It took her the full twenty minutes to get home, because she forgot to speed she was so happy.

Cole walked into the house and watched Moses pace from room to room, looking out the windows. "It's okay, Moses." He said to her when she walked by. "Everyone will get home safe and we'll stay here to wait it out."

Moses ignored him and kept pacing.

When his parents called to say they locked up and everything was fine, he wished them goodnight and ignored their remarks about how nice it was to see him with Viviane. *I know they'll be overjoyed I'm planning our date for Friday. I want to sweep her off her feet and top my seventeen-year-old self.*

When Viviane called she quizzed him about his plans, but he teased her by keeping it a surprise. She guessed correctly he didn't know himself, yet. He couldn't plan their first date without remembering how badly he botched things the first time around. *I almost ended our friendship, because I was mad at myself for not recognizing my best friend had turned into a beautiful woman.*

Homecoming week our senior year, I was sitting in the cafeteria talking to some of the guys on the track team when she came running up to him all excited. "Cole, guess what?" She didn't even pause, but continued, "Brad asked me out! We're going to homecoming. Isn't that great?"

Cole started to speak, but she didn't let him get a word in obsessing about what to wear. He couldn't believe his best friend was acting like a girl! Viviane didn't care about that stuff, she spent her time reading, or playing sports with him and his brother doing guy stuff.

Over the next few days, he told himself she would get over it, and come to her senses. He barely paid attention to her talk about Brad the Jerk, and what color dress she should wear. It's Viviane after all, his Viviane, not Brad's. *I should've known then I was in trouble, but it wasn't until they were sitting in the lunchroom the day before the dance that I completely lost it, yelling at her to be quiet.*

"Good grief! You've been talking my ears off for days about this dance. It's not a big deal so cut it out, okay." *Trying to act like it wasn't bothering me, I completely missed the upset look on her face. Tears welled up in her eyes, but I didn't notice or I'd known I went too far.* "If you must talk to someone, go find one of your girlfriends." *Only now, I realize how upset she must have been with that thoughtless comment.*

"Cole Mason West," her tone of voice was low, scaring him, "you know I don't have girlfriends. You're my best friend or you were until this minute."

What an idiot I was, he thought remembering her tear streaked face. *That wasn't the last idiotic thing I did either. So afraid to face my feelings, I walked up to the first attractive girl I saw and asked her to homecoming. I thought I'd show Viviane, girls wanted me and she would be jealous when I danced with a pretty girl.*

They didn't see each other the rest of the week. At the dance, Cole and his date arrived and immediately went to mingle with the other kids. *Funny, I can't even remember my date's name anymore. Maybe that's part of the reason the night didn't go well. I can't blame time for my forgetfulness, because I know the trouble was I didn't remember anything about her that night, either.*

He began to look for Viviane and Brad the Jerk as soon as they arrived. *I wanted to gloat and show off my beautiful date, but once I saw Vee on the dance floor, I finally admitted I'd been lying to myself.*

It had been fifteen years, but he still remembered every detail. She wore a midnight blue dress that caught the light and seemed to shine. The dress had an empire waist and went to the floor in long, flowing lines. He frowned at the time, because he only knew that because she talked about the dress so much.

Anguish washed over him standing off to the side of the dance floor as he watched her dance with Brad the Jerk. He smiled, *to this day I can't think of Brad without calling him a jerk and the guy's happily married living in Ohio.*

Cole spent the night staring at Viviane, completely ignoring his date, who eventually started to dance with other guys. He thought he was going to just watch from the sidelines all night, but when he noticed Brad leave, he realized this was his chance to prove to himself Viviane didn't mean anything, it was only a pretty dress. *I should've known the way my palms were sweating and how I had trouble breathing, holding her close wasn't going to help at all.*

When he asked her to dance, he was afraid she would say no, but was elated when she nodded yes. He put his arms around her just as the DJ put on a slow song. It was a Faith Hill ballad he still couldn't listen to without thinking of their first dance. *I couldn't help but think the whole time, it should've been me who took her, not Brad the Jerk.*

He didn't want to stop dancing, but once the song ended he knew he had to walk away. *It's one of the hardest things I've ever done, even harder than breaking up, because then I was lying to myself. I can still see the hurt look in her eyes, as I said,* "Thank you for the dance, Vee. I really enjoyed it."

She looked at him strangely, because it was the first time he called her Vee. Brad came back, taking Viviane in his arms to whirl her away, and Cole's had date stormed out when she saw him dancing with Viviane. When he was sure his date had a ride home, Cole left. He couldn't stand to watch Viviane dance with anyone else. The drive home was horrible, because all he could see was his girl dancing with Brad the Jerk. It was when he put his car in park at home, he realized Viviane wasn't his girlfriend, possibly not even his friend anymore.

His dad saw him pull up and came over to see what was wrong. *The look on my face told him it was bad, and Carson West being a smart father and smarter man, knew I finally figured out I'd taken the wrong girl.*

"Cole," he said, "You're going to have to apologize to Viviane."

He had started to interrupt to say he knew that, but his dad continued, "You also need to apologize to your date with flowers."

Flowers! Cole thought at the time, *they're so expensive, and I already got her flowers for her corsage.* He had hung his head on the steering wheel defeated, as his dad explained, "Being a man means being accountable, even when you're stupid." He patted his son on the shoulder, before walking away. "Just ask your mother," he said with a grin.

He sent his date yellow roses, because his dad said it would be appropriate. He knew she was mad, but once the roses arrived with an apology note, she quickly moved on. She told everyone she knew all along he and Viviane were meant for each other.

Cole had gone to Viviane's house with a handwritten apology note to ask for forgiveness and a date for next Friday. When she called to say yes, he had been so excited, he did extra chores to make up for the money he spent on apology flowers for his date.

On their special first date, they had dined at the nicest restaurant in downtown Cartersville and strolled the square where he kissed her. *I told myself I planned on never stopping, Viviane was the one. How did I get it so wrong?*

Cole came back to the present with the first loud clap of thunder and Moses landed in his lap, shaking. Taking pity on his dog, he moved to the recliner where they could curl up together and ride out the stormy night. He spent the rest of the evening planning a special date for his second favorite girl. After all, Moses felt she was the first.

Chapter Twenty-Three

Viviane could hear the wind moaning outside her window. It was still dark outside; the sun couldn't seem to rise through the heavy clouds; the rain was too much for it. It didn't bother her, because she liked the rain. It made her think of lazy days reading a book in Grand's parlor. She curled deeper under the covers, glad she didn't have to be up early. It had rained all night, the wind constantly bending the trees to the ground. The town was in for bad weather, and she prayed for protection remembering Bartow County had been hit by some nasty storms a few years ago.

Lying in bed, she remembered coming home yesterday to surprise Grand pulling up in the driveway unannounced. Grand heard the car and came out to see her grabbing her bag and rushing up the porch steps moments before it started pouring.

Viviane smiled a Cheshire grin as she thought of how she slowly dangled the information of a date with Cole on Friday. The woman had practically danced in the living room with ecstatic joy. Delighted to make Grand happy over her reunion with Cole, she felt pretty happy, too!

It wasn't until she was getting ready for bed, she realized she had a tiny problem. She brought nothing to wear on the special first date she knew Cole was planning. She felt like crying and laughing all at the same time. When she had driven to Cartersville, she hadn't been worried about clothes, because she kept several spare outfits in her closet, but nothing special enough for Friday. Thankfully, Viviane carried her camera bag with her, and kept an emergency makeup kit for clients for touch ups. The bit of makeup in her bag would be fine, she didn't wear much, anyway. *A vain part of me wants to look spectacular Friday night, really knock his socks off so to speak.*

Cole's always well dressed, and she had liked that about him, even though he was more of a clothes horse than she would ever be. She decided to pray about an outfit before bed last night and was able to sleep peacefully. She thought it was because of Cole's kiss, because she realized it didn't matter what she wore- it would be wonderful night. Their first date was magical, eating in the square and walking around talking and laughing for hours. It made her wish she knew what he was planning for this second, first date.

As she continued listening to the rain, she prayed about the day and remembered the cute shops in the square. It had been so long since she had been in Cartersville, she sometimes forgot how much downtown had grown. *I'll drive over there tomorrow when it isn't storming and shop a little. Grand's birthday isn't too far away and I'll do a little window shopping.*

A quiet knock startled Viviane from her thoughts, "Yes?"

Grand poked her head around the door, "Sorry, I didn't mean to disturb you. The storm sounds awful... I saw your light and wanted to see if you're okay."

"I'm fine. Just daydreaming while I'm snuggled under the covers."

Grand could see the smile on her face even from the darkened hallway. *It's good to see my girl blissfully in love.* "I'm going to do my Bible study in the kitchen and then make breakfast. It seems like a good day for pancakes. Want some?"

Viviane knew Grand's pancakes were worth getting up for. "Yes, I'll be down soon. I want to read my Bible, and then I'll even come help. We'll make breakfast and enjoy some time together."

"I'd like that." Grand watched Viviane reach for her Bible on the nightstand and told her, "I'll even stay in pajamas, so don't change!"

Viviane loved Grand in this playful, happy mood. *Apparently being in love was contagious.* "Deal! Pajamas it is."

Viviane watched Grand close the door and move down the hall, before the noise from the rain hid the sound of her footsteps. Before she started her devotion, she tried to remember the last time Grand had been in PJs, just for fun. Not since college, when she brought Erica home for a girl's weekend. It was actually only a few weeks before she and Cole broke up.

The next few hours were spent in the kitchen cooking breakfast together while laughing and singing to the music on the radio. Viviane felt energized to see how well Grand was feeling, because she didn't sit until breakfast was ready.

Grand placed the syrup dispenser that matched her favorite blue glass dishes on the table, a wedding gift from her parents. "This surprise visit from my favorite girl deserves the good dishes. Thankfully I put new flowers on the table yesterday." Looking out the window to the pouring rain, she laughed, "It's been so warm my flowers have been blooming."

After finishing breakfast, they straightened the kitchen and went to the living room to keep an eye on the weather through the big windows. Grand set a large flashlight on the coffee table, while Viviane turned the television to the weather channel.

The weatherman warned of possible tornados, but neither of them were worried. An hour later, they turned their attention to the television for updates about the weather and discovered a tornado had touched down in Adairsville, close to Cole's family home.

Viviane reached for her cell phone to call him as her phone began to ring, when her hand closed around it. Relieved to see his name on her caller ID, she said quickly, "Cole? How are you? How's your parents and Moses?"

"I'm ok, I'm at church. I've talked to my parents and they've checked on Moses. Everything's fine. She tackled my parents, but she's okay. What about you two? Any damage?"

"No, we're fine." Viviane sighed with relief. She turned to Grand to let her know, but in the short time she had been on the phone, Grand had received a call.

Viviane could hear her telling someone she would help with food on Saturday but didn't know what was going on. She thought it was Jill, because she mentioned a granddaughter named Maddy. Cole started speaking to her, and since she couldn't listen to both conversations at once, she moved outside to the front porch.

Cole continued speaking, "They've cancelled church services around Cartersville. I've been in the office all morning as people have called to check in. There's lots of property damage. We'll know more as the day goes by."

"I'm glad it isn't too bad, and that your family's okay. Poor Moses alone during the storm! I hate that, poor thing."

"Yeah me, too! I've got a feeling I'm going to find a shredded pillow or two when I get home, which is how Mo deals with stress. When she wouldn't run with me this morning, I should've known something was wrong."

"You ran in this!?! There's been lightening all morning!"

He chuckled, teasing her, "I didn't run, Vee. I just asked Mo if she wanted to. I think she actually rolled her eyes at me."

"She should've, you're nuts!" Viviane moved to sit in a rocker as she talked to Cole.

"They're plans in the works for a cleanup on Saturday in Adairsville. A lot of churches along with SPLASH are organizing, and our church plans to put a group together. Want to help?"

"Okay, I can clear debris with the best of them. Grand might be helping with lunch. I think she's on the phone with Jill Adams." The white rocker continued to glide slowly back and forth. She closed her eyes listening to the steady rain and Cole's calming deep voice.

"Jill's helping gather a group of ladies to organize food for the workers. They're planning for at least 1,000 volunteers on Saturday."

"It's wonderful our county is ready to lend a hand and really practice being the hands and feet of Christ." She could hear some strange noise coming through the phone, "What are you doing? What's that noise?"

"I'm on the computer checking something for our date on Friday." Viviane could tell he was smiling.

"You mean the date you won't tell me about? Don't you know girls need to know what to wear...?" Viviane quickly continued, knowing his typical male reply, "Don't you dare say, 'it doesn't matter, you always look nice.' That isn't the point!"

He laughed, *It's crazy she can still read my mind. A clue would be fun.* "Dress in layers, because warmth will be very important for a part of our date! It'll be cold by Friday."

She grinned even though he couldn't see. *I enjoy sparing with him as much as he does with me.* "Well, thanks for giving a girl a heads up at least."

"Oh, when I talked to Mom earlier she was making a big pot of chili and wanted me to ask if you and Grand would like to come over for dinner tonight. Can you?" He tried to be cool, but he really wanted to see her before Friday. *I really need to see her smile. The church is getting reports of terrible devastation and I could use a smile that wasn't over the phone. Friday's too far away to see Vee.*

"Let me ask Grand and I'll call you back."

"Okay. Talk to you soon."

She hung up, before going inside to see if Grand had plans for that evening. She found her sitting on the sofa, the TV back on the weather with every channel covering the after effects of the tornado.

"Grand?"

Grand turned down the volume as she walked over. "Cole called to check on us. Church is cancelled tonight. SPLASH is getting volunteers together for a cleanup on Saturday."

She didn't want Grand to cancel any plans she made, just so she could spend time with her boyfriend. Viviane smiled, *I love the thought of Cole as my boyfriend.*

"Yes, Jill called and I volunteered to help."

When Grand didn't mention any other plans, Viviane causally brought up Lynn's offer for chili.

"Really? I haven't seen Lynn in ages. They traveled a lot over the holidays. It'd be great to see them," Grand said smiling.

"Good. I'll call Cole and let him know. Seven work for you?"

"Yes, honey. Seven works. Tell Cole we'll bring fresh baked bread. I can make some by then, if I hurry.

Viviane kissed Grand as she moved to the kitchen to start baking. Staying on the sofa to call Cole to confirm dinner, she dialed the number thinking, *what a day!*

Chapter Twenty-Four

It was almost six forty-five, and Viviane knew she needed to hurry. Thankfully, she was almost done with her hair, because at the last minute she decided to curl the ends to wear it down. Cole wasn't due until seven, which gave her time to fuss for a few minutes.

"Perfect," she said after a final primp. With one last look in the mirror, she gave herself an approving nod before she grabbed her purse. *I've got just enough time to say goodbye to Grand.*

As she walked down the back stairs, she heard Grand moving around the kitchen, and only reached the middle landing when the doorbell rang. She checked her watch and thought, *ten minutes early... hmmm...Cole was never early for dates before.* She pondered this fact; *a new maturity seems to have given him punctuality.*

Grand never saw Viviane as she greeted Cole at the front door. She said something about how handsome he looked, but Viviane was unable to hear Cole's reply. Moving quickly, she turned the corner as Grand exclaimed, "Viviane, you look lovely."

After a moment of staring, Cole walked up to Viviane and tenderly handed her a bouquet of beautiful flowers, never taking his eyes off her. She brought the delicate blossoms close to smell the lovely fragrance, and saw he went to a florist because of the label. Touched by his extra effort, she started to thank him when he leaned over to whisper, "You take my breath away and the evening's just beginning."

Viviane was pleased by his sweet comment, and felt her nerves give away to excitement. She spent all yesterday shopping in the cute little stores that opened up in recent years. When she realized what a gold mine downtown Cartersville had become in fun and unique gifts, she bought presents for all of her friends and family for the rest of the year. For the first time in her life, she was done with her Christmas shopping and it was only February.

All she had brought were t-shirts, and she needed something warm since the storm brought the bitter cold this season had been lacking. She found a lovely outfit that started with a gorgeous coat in a used clothing boutique on a clearance rack. She fell in love with the dark teal coat and its long lines that when cinched at the waist belled out like a skirt. It was marked down, because of a tear along the seam someone hadn't sewn very well. She could fix it easily and it was detailed enough to be a dress itself. Pairing it with a white sweater and black pencil skirt, she wore a long necklace of teal, and nude pumps she discovered in the back of her closet. To satisfy the artsy part of her personality, she found decorative hose in magenta that went perfectly with the coat.

The look on Cole's face was a definite sign she had done well. Holding the flowers stilled the butterflies doing jumping jacks in her stomach. Realizing she had been staring a long time, she quickly spoke up, "Thank you, they're lovely. I've always loved calla lilies."

Cole never took his eyes off Viviane, his only reply was a simple, "I remember."

Viviane could see the sparkle in his eyes, and thought he looked handsome with his dark gray pants and collared shirt under a light gray dress jacket. His shoes told her they were going somewhere nice, because he was wearing shiny, black loafers with no socks. *Cole never wore socks, unless he was running. He always hated them and it's nice that detail hadn't changed over the years.*

"Viviane, dear," Grand said taking the flowers from her. "I'll put these in water." *I've got to say something or they'll stare at each other all night.* "Cole probably has reservations and you need to get going." Still not moving, she gently pushed Viviane, "Go on you two. Dinner reservations, right Cole?"

Cole shook his head coming out of a trance, but finally answered, "Yes, Grand. You're right as always." He held out his hand and Viviane intertwined her fingers as he held the door open. He noticed Grand didn't move from the entry way, "We won't be out too late." About to shut the front door, he said, "Tomorrow morning, we're meeting at eight to drive to Adairsville for the big clean up."

"I wasn't worried," Grand said with a smile on her face. She walked slowly to the kitchen to put the flowers in water. *They make quite the picture.* Singing while she got the pretty cut glass vase her husband had given her years ago, she imagined them at their wedding. *They'll look even lovelier on that special day.*

Neither Cole nor Viviane were aware of Grand's plans for an imminent wedding. The young couple was only thinking it was a beautiful evening to spend together.

"You still haven't told me the plans for tonight, expect to prepare for the cold," Viviane hinted as Cole helped her to the car, "and telling Grand we'd be home at a reasonable time."

Once she was tucked inside, he walked around grinning at her, "We're going to dinner, and that's all I'm saying." He turned on the CD player and she was momentarily distracted when she heard Frank Sinatra's duet with Ella Fitzgerald. She knew this was one of Sinatra's classic duets, because it was one of her favorite CDs.

Very touched by his thoughtfulness, she relaxed in the seat and asked, "Is where we're eating a surprise, too?" She decided, *if he wants playful banter, I can play along.*

"Yes, I think you'll like it. I don't know if you've been there before, but I've always want to go and want my first time to be with you."

She smiled, "I'd like that."

Traffic going south on I-75 was heavy, but thankfully moved quickly. They talked about their week, the tornado recovery, and members of the church who were affected by the storm. They never ran out of things to discuss and the drive went quickly.

When the duet CD finished, Cole suggested she pick something from his CD case in the back seat. She discovered it was filled with CDs from every era beginning with the 1930s to more current jazz. She didn't remember him being so eclectic in his musical tastes. Curiosity filling her she finally asked, "What's with the music? I don't remember you listening to such a variety before."

Cole hesitated, *I might as well come clean and fess up.* "All those years you made me listen to jazz and stuff...well... it seems to have rubbed off on me. I found myself listening to it when I was alone. It's my secret vice that no one knows. I've got another case of music I keep out for others. I thought tonight you'd appreciate listening to this."

She didn't know what to say, the thought of her taste in music rubbing off on him made her happy. She gently squeezed his hand, "I appreciate it, thank you."

"Good." He said turning to a lighter subject, "We're almost there. Are you hungry?"

She told him yes, and Cole smiled before he became preoccupied with navigating through downtown. He seemed to know where he was going, but Viviane asked anyway, "Need any help? I happen to be very familiar with this area."

Cole chuckled, but politely replied, "No Vee, I'm fine. I know exactly where I'm going."

Viviane shrugged, *a girl has to try.* She spent the next few minutes thinking of possible restaurants, but she gave up with too many options.

"Have you guessed yet? We're about to arrive."

She could hear the excitement in his voice, and knew they were close. She looked out the window and saw the Westin hotel. The restaurant at the top was well known, because it revolved as you dined. She had never been before, because it was fancy.

When he pulled into the valet station, she exclaimed in disbelief, "Here, Cole? I've never been before." She clapped her hands together, *I can't believe I'm going to see Atlanta from above seventy stories.*

He turned off the engine as a parking attendant helped her out and took the keys from Cole who led her inside to the elevator. "I'm glad you haven't been here before." He gently pulled her closer while they waited in line.

"Cole," Viviane whispered, "I don't want to seem ungrateful, but this place can be expensive. Plus, you mentioned this was the first thing we're doing tonight... and I..."

He saw her wringing her hands, and pulled her off to the side, "Vee, I don't want to you to worry about anything tonight. Fifteen years ago, I had to mow lawns to earn money and it was only enough for dinner." He took her hands in his, "I make a good living and have saved money for the day I would get to date a wonderful woman and have her consider marrying me and start a family. I can afford this treat."

He makes me feel treasured, and we haven't even been seated yet. She leaned forward to kiss him on the cheek. "Cole, our first date in Cartersville was very special, but I understand your need to top it." She gave him a sly look, "Of course, you'll have to do something amazing to achieve that. It's always been my favorite."

Hand in hand, the two of them quietly moved back in line and were soon riding up 73 stories in the glass elevator. The sun set for the evening, and the lights in Atlanta were out in stunning glory. She felt breathless with his arms around her as she enjoyed the dazzling view.

He was also out of breath, but not because of the view of the city. Her reply about topping their amazing first date humbled him. When he thought of the date with only dinner and a walk around town, it didn't seem worthy of her, and now she said it was her favorite which made him very glad for the choices he made for tonight. *More and more I'm starting to realize how much Viviane deserves. When I mentioned saving to provide for a future wife and family to have a nice life, I want that with her.*

Once they were seated, she noticed the live jazz band and pointed, "Did you know about the band?"

"Yes, it was the deciding factor."

After their waiter left with the orders, she looked up to see him watching her, "You seem in deep thought," she said.

"I was just watching you."

She felt herself beginning to blush and steered the conversation to a variety of topics, which carried them through appetizers, the main course and dessert. It was almost nine-thirty when he said as she sighed over her last bite of dessert, "We've got to be somewhere in fifteen minutes. Are you almost ready?"

"Let me run to the ladies' room first."

He helped her rise from her chair and watched her walk away. It had been a wonderful evening and he had something else planned to wow her. It would mimic their first date that he knew she would enjoy. He paid for the meal knowing Viviane was worth it. When he saw her walking back toward him, he thought, *she's beautiful. I'm the luckiest guy in the room.*

"Ready?" He asked holding out her coat.

"Yes, it was a lovely dinner," she said buttoning up snuggly. *He put his coat on so I assume the chilly part of the evening is approaching. I wonder if we're going walking like we did on our first date.*

"We're to meet someone downstairs," he said placing his hand on the small of her back to lead her to the elevator.

Viviane pulled out gloves, "I'm looking forward to it."

As they walked out the front lobby, she saw a horse drawn carriage pulled up to the curb and an older gentleman in a top hat stood calling out, "Cole West?"

"That's us." Cole called to him as he waved, leading her to the carriage. He helped her sit and covered her with a blanket before climbing in to wrap his arms around her. It was a cold, but clear night and she could barely contain her excitement, never having been on a carriage ride before.

Viviane spent much of the ride dividing her time between looking at him and the city shining clearly around them. She loved everything about this magical night. *I would've had fun eating a cheeseburger in Cartersville, but this... well it's a dream.*

Cole loved having her in his arms and was right in thinking it would be worth the cold to have her snuggled up against him. *I wanted an over the top date, not just to make up for my stupid mistake, but because she deserves something unique from the city she calls home.*

Thirty minutes later, Viviane couldn't feel her nose, but still considered it a fantastic night. While Cole tipped the driver back at the hotel, she knew this date would always be special, because it was the first date she was sure she was with the man she would marry. When his car arrived, they got in and turned the heat up full blast. They drove back in quiet, only instrumental jazz playing in the background. No talking was needed after such a perfect evening, a little hand holding was all that was required.

When Cole pulled into Grand's driveway, Viviane could see the lights were still on, even though it was a little after eleven. *Even if it had been three in the morning, Grand would've stayed up to hear about my date. She stayed up to hear about it fifteen years ago, too!*

Walking her to the front door, Cole said quietly, "I won't come in. I know Grand's anxiously waiting to hear about the evening. I'll see you tomorrow morning around 7:30 to drive to church. We're taking the van to transport teens whose parents can't drive them to Adairsville."

Viviane nodded, "I'll be ready."

Cole leaned forward and gently pulled Viviane into his arms, "It was a perfect first date and I can't wait for a second."

As he kissed her, she felt the cold air sizzle around her. *He's a great kisser, slow and sweet.*

"Night, Vee. I'll see you in the morning. Sweet dreams."

"Good night Cole, thank you for a lovely evening and well... everything."

Viviane unlocked the front door but turned to watch him walk back to his car. She waved and turned to find Grand standing in her robe a few feet in front of her. "Cole gone?"

"Yes, he's picking me up tomorrow around seven thirty."

"Well, come into the living room and tell me all about your date. Was it fun?" Grand thought she knew the answer, *it's a silly question by the stars in Viviane's eyes. I can see them even in the dim entryway.*

"It's was a fairytale evening. I'll tell you all about it after I put on my PJs. Give me a few minutes, and I'll be right down."

Viviane ran upstairs, before Grand had a chance to reply, causing her to chuckle. *I'm watching my granddaughter fall head over heels in love and it's a beautiful sight.* She went into the kitchen to fix the two of them a cup of tea. *We'll have a quick chat, I want all the details and then scoot to bed. I've got to be up early, too. Jill will be here to pick me up at eight to help make lunches for the volunteers. Now I'll need to get up earlier to fix breakfast for those two. Cole won't eat anything good and hot, and that won't do at all. My future grandson-in-law will need sustenance to get through a long day of hard labor. The plan was working perfectly!*

Chapter Twenty-Five

"Thanks for breakfast, Grand. It was wonderful." Cole said wiping up the last bit of gravy with a bite of biscuit.

"No problem, dear. The two of you needed a big breakfast, since you're going to be working really hard. Lunch's a long way off."

When Grand answered the doorbell, Cole told her he already eaten, but once she put a plate in front of him, his protests faded away. Grand had a sneaking suspicion he came hoping for hot food, since he was twenty minutes early. *The boy loved his Southern breakfast.*

"Thanks, Grand. We've got to get going, Cole's driving the church van to the check-in site. We'll see you at lunch. Don't do too much." Viviane grabbed Cole's arm to drag him away from the table as he was going for his third helping. "Let's go. We were supposed to be there five minutes ago."

When he looked at his watch to see how late it was, he grabbed another slice of ham. "For the road," he said with a wink at Grand.

Grand laughed as she listened to them arguing over who made whom late. *Just like old times*, she thought as she cleaned up. She heard Viviane say, "I'll drive. I'm faster." As he protested, Grand wondered who would win the old argument this time.

He won, because his car was blocking hers. As he drove, Viviane chided him for going slow. When they finally arrived, the church parking lot was full of people trying to organize equipment and vehicles. Cole stepped out of the car and was immediately surrounded by several parents. Over the mild roar, he answered questions about when the kids would be back, where to meet, and if he was leaving soon, the whole time moving toward the church van where the teens were waiting.

"Cole, it's so good of you to join us. We thought we might need to get someone else to drive. You seem to be having a lot of trouble being on time lately." Viviane turned to see Lauren Blake walking up. The woman was dressed as if she was going to a cocktail party, not a disaster clean up. *I can't believe she's actually wearing three-inch heels.*

"Mrs. Blake, I'm sorry about being late." Cole ignored the comment about it becoming a habit. *I've learned over the years to pick my battles. The woman's determined not to be happy unless she's in control of everything.* "We'll be leaving in just a few minutes. I've got to grab some water from my office. We don't want to have anyone get sick from not re-hydrating."

Viviane hid a smile as Cole ignored Lauren's ruffled feathers. *He does it in a way that seems like he's a big goofy kid. It's very impressive to watch*, Viviane thought, *a skill I'd love to have.*

"Well, get Hillary to help. She's been looking for you, because I told her to ride with you as another chaperone." Lauren said pointedly, ignoring Viviane standing right behind her.

"Sorry, but Viviane already volunteered and since I brought her, I'm responsible for her." Cole leaned around Lauren and said to Viviane, winking so only she could see, "If you'll unlock my office, I'll meet you there after I tell the kids we're leaving in a few minutes."

Catching the keys, he tossed, Viviane moved to the church side entrance, but still heard Mrs. Blake start to mutter, "Well, I never..."

Viviane sped up, *It's best if I don't know what Mrs. Blake's going to say.* She knew the woman pushed her daughter toward every available bachelor in Cartersville since Hillary was sixteen. *Poor Hillary, she's a sweet girl, completely unlike her mother in every way.* Viviane said a quick prayer for God to intervene in the young woman's life to get her away from her controlling mother, adding thanks Grand wasn't manipulating her life.

A few moments later, Cole caught up with her as she unlocked his office. He grabbed a case of water, while she held the door open. As he walked past her, he said, "Thanks, love."

Viviane only grinned, thinking as she followed him, *It's going to be a fun day.*

When they reached the van, the seats were almost full with nine teenagers packed inside. *It's great to see them giving up a Saturday to help out the community.* It wasn't until she was closer that she saw a pretty blonde head in the front passenger seat, happily waving at them.

"Cole are you coming?" Hillary called from the passenger side window. "Mother said you volunteered to give me a ride, since she's helping with the food." She turned to Viviane without pausing, "Hi, Viviane. Do you want to sit up front? I can move to the back."

Viviane chuckled when she heard Cole groan next to her, "Stay where you are Hillary, I'll hop in the back. You already look comfortable."

Turning to Cole, she said quietly, "Keep your hands to yourself, no hand holding with the teens watching."

Cole knew she was teasing him. *Oh Lord*, he prayed, *please give me strength for these three women out to get me. The best way to handle this is to get to Adairsville as quickly as possible.*

With that goal in mind, he gathered a few stragglers, while Viviane grabbed her camera bag out of his car and got in next to a pretty, dark haired girl. She looked very familiar, but Viviane couldn't place her. The skinny girl turned and said, "Hi, I'm Maddy Adams."

"Oh," Viviane said, "You're Jill Adams' granddaughter."

"Yes, that's my grandma." Recognition flashed in the girl's eyes, "You're Mrs. Delia Anne's granddaughter. I've seen pictures of you. Are you coming with us?" Before Viviane could answer, Maddy pointed to her camera bag and asked, "Did you take the picture at the auction everyone's talking about?"

Viviane had forgotten how fast teens could jump from one subject to another. "Yes, I did. Do you like photography?"

"Yes, I'd like to take lessons, but they don't offer it at my school. I go to Excel, the private school. You've heard of it, right?"

Nodding, Viviane said, "Are there classes offered through a non-school program?"

"If there is, my family couldn't afford it now. Dad lost his job with the economy stuff. Money's tight and they really want me to stay at Excel." She sighed, "So we're making sacrifices as Mom says."

That must be hard. "I brought one of my smaller cameras and can show you some things. It's cloudy, which is good for pictures outside. I'll even let you use the camera when we break for lunch, okay?"

Maddy's face glowed with happiness, and Viviane was glad she sat next to the girl, because she learned a lot about her in the short ride. Maddy came from a large family, the oldest of three. *No wonder the family had to tighten their belt with three kids in private school.* Maddy was a junior and worked part time at the daycare next to the school.

"With two younger siblings, I know my stuff. I work in the nursery with the babies, which I love. They're so sweet and I'm able to watch them grow and learn. It makes up for all the stinky diapers."

Viviane enjoyed Maddy's stories about the babies she took care of. When the group arrived, everyone signed in and split up into two groups with their assignments.

Viviane saw there were over fifty adults and kids from their church alone and was told at check-in over eighteen hundred volunteers had shown up. She sent up a prayer of thanks and strength for the ladies making lunch.

Cole, Hillary, and a few other parents along with Maddy made up Viviane's group. They spent the next three hours picking up limbs and branches, gathering trash and putting everything in large garbage bags. They had a big area to clean up and it took a long time to cover it. She worked steadily, spending hardly any time alone with anyone, but Maddy who followed her like a shadow. She didn't mind, Maddy told funny stories about people she knew, places she wanted to go, and things she wanted to see. *The girl would make a wonderful writer*, Viviane thought, *she has such a natural flair for storytelling.*

Occasionally, the sun poked its head between the clouds, but most of the morning it looked like rain. Even with the cold temperatures, Viviane felt hot and sweaty. She grabbed a bottle of water from her bag and sat down a minute to watch the others. The devastation was horrible, and the people of Adairsville were grateful for the help, which made the sweaty work worth it.

One older lady cried when she saw the group walk up in orange vests offering to help without asking for anything in return. It was for that reason alone, Viviane was glad to help, and decided to volunteer with SPLASH next summer. *It'd be rewarding to use my love of photography for both ministry and helping Bartow County. It's rare for a large and diverse community to share a common vision of helping others.*

She had shown Maddy a few pointers about taking photos, when they took a break an hour ago. Maddy was a quick study with a good eye for framing shots. Viviane looked around for the girl helping take down some fences destroyed by the storm and saw her standing next to another teen from Cole's youth group. Continuing to watch while sipping her water, she noticed Maddy sway for a moment. Grabbing a second bottle of water, Viviane rushed over, pulling her away from the fence.

"Here Maddy," she said pushing the water into the girl's shaking hands. "Drink some water, slowly." Even though it's cold outside, you still get hot from all the exertion."

Maddy smiled thanks and took several long sips looking hot and tired. Viviane said, "Sit a moment. I'll help Sara with the fence. You rest, okay?"

Maddy nodded and Viviane went to help Sara Mallow finish tearing down the fence, before Viviane sent her to take a break. Maddy had almost finished drinking the water by the time Viviane sat down next to her. "Are you okay?"

"Yes."

Viviane smiled, "Grace Cartwright told me a funny story about passing out in awkward places. Apparently, it happens to her a lot. So much that her Mom doesn't panic anymore but waits for her to wake up and then feed her."

Maddy laughed a little, "I heard she passed out at one of the big church productions years ago and they carried her outside in only her slip because she got so hot. She was the angel and they called her the fallen angel for years afterward, because the only exit off stage was through Hell."

Viviane laughed, "I remember that. It would be mortifying, but sweet Grace laughed it off."

"Thanks for the water, Miss Viviane. I got a bit dizzy, but I'm fine now."

"Good." Looking up because she saw movement, Viviane said, "I think that's Cole coming over. I hope it's about lunch. I'm starving."

"Everyone's headed back to check in for lunch. Sara will you please go tell the others?" Extending his arms, he asked Viviane and Maddy, "Can I escort you, ladies?"

Maddy giggled, but Viviane only smiled and said, "Thank you, kind sir." Both ladies took an arm and trekked back to the church.

I didn't realize how much we'd done, Viviane thought walking back seeing all their progress.

By the time they got in line, Viviane saw Grand and other ladies from church handing out sandwiches. Maddy ran off to join her friends when Cole remarked quietly, "She seems quite taken with you."

"She's a great kid. I've enjoyed spending time with her."

Viviane said hello to Grand and Jill serving at the front of the line. Grand smiled at them and asked, "How's it going?"

"Great." Viviane said taking a sandwich. Turning to Jill she said, "I've spent the morning with your granddaughter, Maddy. She's a gem."

Jill beamed with grandmotherly pride. "We love her. She's been a tremendous help since my Michael lost his job. Construction was one of the first things to be hit by this batty economy. I know they'll be okay. Maddy's mom, Noelle went to work at the daycare. Every little bit helps, and God takes care of the rest."

After saying a quick goodbye, Viviane moved to sit with Cole and some of the other volunteers. She was ravenous from all the work, her meal quickly gone. She was thinking of getting more water when Maddy came to ask her to show her more about photography. "You've eaten already?"

The girl nodded her head, batting her eyes in exaggerated pleading, "PLLLEEAASSE before we go back to work."

"Okay." She laughed, pulling out her camera. The two of them spent the next twenty minutes discussing photo techniques and then she let Maddy take a few shots around the church.

"You have talent."

Excited, Maddy asked, "Are you going on the winter break trip? We could take pictures then."

Viviane shook her head, "I can't, I have a big wedding that weekend, but we'll work something out."

Maddy dropped her head dejected, *the trip to Alabama would've been more fun with Viviane along.*

Shortly, the group returned to finish the cleanup with only a few hours left. The afternoon went quickly and before long it was time to go home. Thankfully, it didn't start to rain until everyone was back in their cars. Viviane put her bag in the van and was surprised to bump into someone standing right behind her. "Oh, sorry. I didn't see you behind me, Cole."

Cole grabbed her hand, squeezing it gently while he whispered, "I've missed talking to you today. It's been hard seeing you and not being able to kiss you, especially with all my male students watching you with equal fascination."

"Funny!" She said, gently pushing him away. *The only guy I want fascinated with me is currently looking smug.* "Seriously though, you've got some great kids."

He beamed with pride watching the teens load the van, "Yeah, they're really great. I don't know if I'd been so quick to give up a Saturday to help cleanup."

Smiling, Viviane thought, *He would have, it's his nature, but I understand what he means.*

"Hey, Maddy you did great out there today." Cole had a soft spot for the girl with a lot on her shoulders.

When the last of the students loaded the van, Cole waved Hillary over. *I don't know about anyone else, but I'm tired.* Shortly into the drive he noticed the van was silent and looked in the rearview mirror to see most everyone was asleep. Catching Viviane's eye, he winked as she put a finger to her smiling lips.

At the church, the kids slowly got off the bus and Cole waved goodbye stifling a yawn himself. Viviane hugged Hillary, before telling her, "I enjoyed working with you today." Viviane couldn't help but think, *she's nothing like her mother. She's a sweaty mess from all her hard work.*

After everyone was gone, Cole got in his car to take Viviane home. Neither talked as he drove to Grand's house. When they arrived, Viviane unbuckled her seat belt, but Cole stopped her. "I'm too tired to come in, but I wanted to say I really liked seeing you today. Even though we barely talked, I still had the best day knowing you were close by."

Viviane settled back in her seat, "I did, too! I enjoyed getting to know your kids and work with them. I'd forgotten how much I loved this town. I liked looking up to see you nearby, too!"

He smiled as he leaned forward to kiss her, a slow kiss that made them both forget for a moment how tired they were. Too soon he leaned back, "I'll see you at church tomorrow. Lunch with you and Grand?"

Viviane smiled, "I think she'd like that. I'll be busy for the next few weeks, and I know you have your trip, but..."

Cole brushed a stray hair back from her face and said, "Don't worry, Vee. I'll keep in touch. You're not getting away from me that easily."

She kissed him lightly one more time, before she went inside. She waved goodbye, pretty sure she had never been happier. Deciding a shower followed by a nap was needed, she went to check on Grand and tell her the plan for Sunday. Cole drove home happy with the way things were going. Like Grand, he too hoped for a future with Viviane Stanton-Mays.

Chapter Twenty-Six

"What do you mean your uncle wants to take your wedding photos, Rebecca?!?"

Viviane thought, *I've got a feeling this is going to be dreadful.* Trying to keep her voice calm, she couldn't hide her utter disbelief over the woman's crazy plan. *I shouldn't have come in today.*

Usually, Wendy took care of the office, since Kathie and Viviane weren't organized, but her daughter was sick, and Kathie had an appointment.

Which is why I'm listening to Rebecca give a long explanation about some uncle taking photos as a wedding gift and the foolish bride explain why she's canceling the contract for THIS Saturday.

"Miss White, you're telling me you don't want us this Saturday? You're going to depend solely on your uncle the full-time plumber, part time budding photographer?" *Kathie's going to love this!* Sighing, she said, "It's really nice of your uncle, but I think it would be a good idea to have a backup photographer. We have a contract and would be happy to take pictures of your special day."

Rebecca ignored her, "Don't worry about the contract. I'm prepared to pay the cancellation fee. I really want my Uncle to take the photos. I've always been impressed with his work. Sorry about the late notice, but I've talked to my fiancé and he agrees. The check's in the mail."

"Well, if there's nothing I can say to change your mind... I hope you have a beautiful wedding."

Hanging up, Viviane shook her head thinking, *I'm glad I'm not that Uncle, because if he doesn't do her wedding justice, Rebecca won't let it go. She's one of the most difficult brides we've ever had and I can't say I'm upset she cancelled.*

Hearing the front door open, Viviane looked up to see Kathie walking through the front door, "You're never going to believe what Rebecca White called to say!"

Not looking up from the mail she was sorting, Kathie asked, "Is it about the stupid doves again? I've never seen a bride so obsessed with doves before?"

"I think she's finally topped finding doves to carry her train down the aisle like a fairytale princess. She's having her uncle the plumber be the sole photographer at her wedding!"

"She's what?!?" Kathie looked up, dropping the mail on the floor. Running her hands through her dark pixie haircut, she said, "She's out of her ever-loving mind."

Viviane considered Kathie more like an older sister, than her boss. The two women looked similar with the dark hair and thin builds, though Kathie would be considered plain skinny. She was the one who taught her the most about the photography business and brought her in after she graduated. They met when Viviane was in the eating disorder program, because Kathie volunteered after her older sister died from anorexia. The two bonded instantly over their love of photography and a growing friendship bloomed.

"I can't believe she's letting some unprofessional..." Kathie struggled with the right word. "I mean the thought of letting someone with no experience is crazy. Too many things can go wrong and does go wrong," she said while walking to her office.

"Now Kathie, it's probably for the best. Rebecca's difficult to please and her engagement photo shoot was a nightmare. You've complained more about her and her family than anyone else, ever." Viviane thought, *I know losing a client can be hard, but time and time again God has a reason.*

Kathie mumbled, "Crazy people! I regret having had anything to do with them." She yelled out from her office, "Mark my words, she'll be on a court TV show suing her plumber uncle."

Viviane only chuckled to herself, *better him, than us.* She heard her cell ringing and grabbed it out of her purse. "Hello?"

"Vee, it's Cole. How are you?"

Something's wrong, Viviane thought. *I've known him to long, not to know when he's upset.*

"Cole, I can tell somethings wrong. Tell me."

He sighed into the phone, "I just talked with two of my chaperones who have the flu. It's Wednesday! Where am I going to find another female chaperone? I've got enough guys, but I'm short a female and we leave this Friday."

Viviane smiled, *I should be brightening his day very soon.* "Cole hold on a second." She didn't wait for his answer, but set the phone down calling out, "Kat?"

Kathie poked her head out the door, "You called?"

"Since the wedding's cancelled, can I go out of town this weekend?"

Kathie shrugged, "I don't see why not? We've been working non-stop for weeks. I haven't seen this office so much, since I first started all by myself."

Viviane laughed, "Today has made me even more grateful for Wendy. She's so good at her job."

She unmuted her cell phone as she heard Kathie say amen. "Cole would you take me as a chaperone? I recently got off the phone with a client who's letting Uncle Bob take photos of her big day and I'm free this weekend."

"Uncle Bob, what Vee? Are you saying you can help?"

"Yes, if you want me, I'm yours for the weekend."

He didn't answer, and Viviane wondered, *has my phone disconnected? Sometimes my cell doesn't work in the office.* "Cole are you there?"

"Yes, sorry. I'd love for you to come this weekend. We leave the church Friday at four."

"I'll be there. I can leave my car at the church?"

"Yes. Thanks, Vee. I really appreciate this."

"Not a problem. See you Friday."

After they hung up, she sat a few moments, *he seemed distant. I thought he'd be more excited, but he must be worked up about the trip, responsible for all those teens.*

Kathie walked back in, "When are you leaving?"

Viviane looked up, "Not until Friday at noon. That should give Wendy's daughter time to get well and save you from answering the phones."

"Sound good to me." Kathie shuddered, *I hate being tied to a desk. It's why I became a photographer, I like constantly moving.*

"Lunch? My treat for working the phone until Wendy's back."

While Kathie went to pick up food, Viviane stayed behind to get all her editing finished. Every once in a while, her mind strayed to think about Cole and their strange conversation. *We talk all the time on the phone, we've both been so busy and I find myself looking forward to his calls, telling each other about our days. Most nights, we talk for hours like teenagers. It's given us a chance to learn all of the little details we missed the first time we dated.* Shaking her head, she said sternly to the empty office, "Enough reminiscing, get back to work."

While she worked to clear her weekend, Cole sat at his desk staring off into space. He was stuck, unable to function repeating what Viviane said, "If you want me, I'm yours."

I wish she was talking about more than chaperoning for the weekend. What have I gotten myself into? Inviting the woman, I love to spend a weekend together where I can't hold her or kiss her, because teenagers will be watching our every move.

"Torture." Cole said to his empty office, "that's what I'm in for." *For the first time ever, I don't want to go on the trip.*

Chapter Twenty-Seven

"Chloe, you can't take seven bags of luggage. You've got to leave most of that here." Cole explained to a weeping teenage girl. "The trip isn't even a full week long! Take some of that back to your parents." Walking away, he thought, *and be grateful I'm ignoring the fact you're in heels and have more makeup on than anyone under the age of forty should ever wear.*

He walked over to deal with the next crisis popping up. He looked at his watch, *only fifteen minutes more and I can load the kids on the bus. Once the kids were away from their parents, things should settle down.*

Ten minutes later, he had handled every crisis, but still no sign of Viviane. He tried calling several times, but she didn't answer. *I want to make sure everything's ok. When we spoke last night, she planned on being here early to help.* As he turned to start gathering the kids, he saw a gray car whip into the parking lot. Cole felt his spirits rise, *finally.* He ran over, just as she was getting out.

"Sorry, I'm late. Wendy's daughter is still sick, so I manned the phones until two when Kathie could come in and on top of that traffic was horrendous." Viviane talked a mile a minute, *I was afraid I wouldn't make it.*

Cole grabbed her luggage, *I'm grateful she packed light. I'd hate to have to tell her to leave something.* He put her luggage in the underneath storage compartment of the bus to give him time to remind himself he couldn't pull her into his arms while surrounded by the thirty-seven spectators going on the trip. "We're going to have prayer and then load the kids, if you want to go save yourself a seat."

"Sounds good to me." Viviane said taking her camera bag, but not before he grabbed her hand, "I'm glad you made it, Vee."

Before she could respond, she heard "Miss Viviane, you're here!" It was the only warning she got before a blue blur tackled her in a big hug. "I'm so glad you're coming!"

Viviane caught Cole's eye, winking as she mouthed, "Me, too!"

"Hi, Maddy. It's good to see you."

Smiling Maddy asked, "Will you sit with me?"

"Sure, why don't you put my bag with yours on the bus and then come back quickly so Cole can pray."

Viviane watched her run off as Cole walked to the parents gathering around. After he prayed for a safe trip, and God to change lives, she could feel the kid's excitement as they shouted to load the bus. Cole warned the chaperones, "It's going to be fun, be prepared for anything."

Twenty minutes later, the group was on the interstate and Viviane could hardly contain her own excitement. She hadn't been on a mission trip in several years and had forgotten how crazy it could be. The talking, laughing and singing was already at an unbelievable level, when Cole told her there would be a lot of hard work, but the kids always made it fun.

She caught a glimpse of that as Maddy talked nonstop, "We always cross over into Alabama before we stop for dinner. We won't get to the host church until nine. I saw you brought your camera. Will you teach me more this weekend?"

Maddy's glee was contagious and Viviane promised to teach her more as the trip went along. The two of them talked until the bus quieted down and Cole put in a DVD once the winter sun set. There was little talking to disrupt the movie the kids voted on last week.

As Cole walked back to his seat behind Viviane, he leaned forward to confess putting up a little extra money for a DVD player. "We'll stop in another hour to eat and you can meet the other chaperones. I think you'll like everyone."

Viviane settled down next to Maddy who offered to share her blanket and pillow. The two women snuggled up to watch the funny comedy and time on the bus passed quickly.

Sometime later, she felt Cole tapping her shoulder, "Hungry, yet? We're pulling off the interstate to eat soon."

Viviane turned slightly, trying not to disturb Maddy watching the movie. "I could eat, but I really want to meet the other adults."

"Soon." Cole said as he got up and moved to the front. After he stopped the movie to a chorus of groans, he called over the roar, "I'll start it again after we eat."

The mention of food sent up shouts as students stretched and slowly got off the bus. Viviane waited next to Cole, who stood by the bus to make sure everyone exited.

He led her to the food line where everyone was hurrying to eat, because of the tight schedule. The five chaperones were sitting at a table and left room in the middle for Cole and Viviane to join them.

Cole moved to sit across from her and as she sat down, a tall black man extended his hand as he scooted his tray over to make room. Viviane thought he looked a lot like Cole's best friend, when the man smiled and said, "Hi, I'm Malcolm, Mike's younger and cooler brother."

Extending her hand, she said, "It's nice to meet you. I didn't know Mike had a brother, much less a cooler one."

Several adults laughed, and a man in his forties said, "Ignore Malcolm, he's just so excited to be around adults, he doesn't know how to act. I'm Remy Turner and this is my wife Patty." He pointed to the blonde woman sitting next to him, who looked like his sister with their matching Georgia Tech sweatshirts. "We're glad you could help us at the last minute."

"Yes, sweetie. Cole told us the Madisons had to cancel and we're grateful for reinforcements. That's how we got stuck with Malcolm. He took a few days off from college." Patty told Viviane, after winking at Malcolm.

It's great everyone's kidding the young man. That's a good sign, Viviane thought.

"You're all awful. We're supposed to be the adults on this trip."

Viviane turned to the last female chaperone who spoke up. She had steel gray hair, and wire rimmed glasses framing intelligent green eyes. She had finished eating and was reading a book.

"Hello, I'm Rhonda Wells," she said putting the book down, "the only serious person on this trip. Oh, and you're sitting next to Wilson."

Viviane extended her hand, but Rhonda had already stuck her nose back in her book. She turned instead to speak to the older gentleman seated next to her. He was adorable in dark khakis, a maroon sweater vest, and matching striped bow tie. His belly made his vest buttons look ready to burst open, but his cherub smiling face had Viviane smiling back.

Wilson leaned forward motioning for Viviane to move closer. He whispered, "Don't let her fool you. She's a cut up, probably worse than anyone here, and that includes the teenagers. Check your sleeping bag before you get in." He winked at her as he straightened up beaming, "I should know, I married her."

Viviane motioned for him to lean forward again and then whispered, "Thanks for the warning. My Grand always said beware of the quiet ones," she glanced around to make sure no one was watching and then continued, "They're planning to take over the world you know."

The white-haired man bellowed loudly, and everyone stopped talking to look at them. He slapped his hand on the table and said, "I like this woman, Cole. She's entertaining."

The group finished eating, talking quietly as they told Viviane more about themselves. Malcolm was a sophomore at Georgia State, while Mrs. Wells was a retired high school English teacher, she and her husband were a second set of parents to a lot of the kids. According to Malcolm, Mrs. Wells had been around as long as he could remember. He told her later, she was strict but fair. "She'll make the kids behave, but she's fun. Really knows how to make you laugh."

The Turners were a married couple that had been helping Cole every year since the trip started. They worked in real estate and took time off to help since they owned their own business. She found out later from Cole the couple couldn't have kids and adopted everyone in the youth group.

After the meal was done, Cole quickly went over the trip agenda and rules. "Not much has changed, and the kids will be sleeping at opposite ends of the hall, boys on one end, girls the other. We're working at the elementary school on Saturday and a few homes the rest of the week."

Cole passed out a few papers, "Starting Sunday in the afternoons, we're doing a Backyard Bible Club at the church. The host church is providing breakfast and lunch. We'll eat out for dinner except Sunday night when the community's hosting a thank you dinner for us."

Viviane knew they had been there three years ago and Cole laid everything out very well. Looking over the handouts, she had no questions, and neither did the other chaperones when Cole asked.

"Good. Let's round everyone up and move out." Cole gave everyone twenty minutes to finish up and load the bus. After threatening to leave anyone who was late, and pick them up on their way home, Viviane finished the last of her fries before taking her tray.

Maddy offered to throw Viviane's away, and she moved Maddy's cups to add her own. When she was ready to get on the bus, she looked for the girl in line and found her wrapped in her blue blanket. Wishing she had brought a heavier coat, Viviane thought, *the weather turned really cold after the tornado a month ago and Maddy must've brought her blanket inside.*

"Hey Maddy, when we get back on the bus, please share your blanket with me. It's freezing and will take time for the bus to warm up."

Maddy nodded, "Everyone makes fun of me for having a blanket, because I'm always cold, but they love when I share."

Viviane laughed, "It's smart with this weather. I always like taking a blanket from home on trips. It's comforting."

After Cole counted heads, he started the movie to loud cheers. It was quiet even after the movie ended an hour later. The kids were tired after putting in a long day at school, many up before six. When they arrived at the church, the kids gathered their belongings and got ready for bed knowing they would be up before seven to put in a day of painting and hard labor.

It seemed like hours later when Viviane was finally able to lay her head down on her pillow. After the kids arrived, it had taken them a bit to wind down. She thought, *Mrs. Wells is the smart one, she brought an air mattress, face mask, and ear plugs!*

Before the lights were out, Mrs. Wells was snoring at the door entrance. Maddy, who put her sleeping bag next to Viviane's giggled whispering, "No one sleeps close to her, because her snoring gets louder through the night."

Viviane didn't know how that was possible with the noise already at deafening levels. She told herself to fall asleep quickly, it would be an early morning, and a long day. *What have I gotten myself into? I don't know how I'm going to sleep on a hard floor with a loud bull frog blaring intermittently, but I'm determined to try.* She began to pray, *Lord, thank you for allowing me to spend time with Cole's teens. Please show me how to glorify You on this trip. I believe I'm here for a reason!*

Chapter Twenty-Eight

Startled, Viviane woke up when someone roughly shook her awake. "Miss Viviane, you've got to wake up if you want breakfast."

Her first thought was to shove the person away and roll back over. She hadn't fallen asleep until very late, but remembered she was on a church trip and had to set a good example. Opening one eye, she saw Maddy hovering over her. "Morning Maddy. I see you're very chipper this early hour." She knew she wasn't hiding her grumpy tone very well. *I'm not a morning person.*

Maddy only grinned, *Most of my family aren't morning people either.* "I've brought you some coffee. Pastor Cole told me you take cream and sugar. Here you go!"

Handing the steaming cup of coffee to Viviane's outstretched hands, she watched her sit up to drink it. *Adults need their coffee before they can function. My parents are the same way. The smile on Miss Viviane's face says I've done the right thing. It's amazing, she slept through everyone getting ready, and talking loudly before going to breakfast.*

"Oh, I've got a note from Pastor Cole. He said to only give it to you if you sat up. Otherwise, I was to get Mrs. Wells to wake you." Maddy leaned forward, handing the note to Viviane and whispered, "You DON'T want Mrs. Wells waking you."

Viviane placed the note beside her, too intent on her coffee. "Thanks for the coffee and saving me from being humiliated by Mrs. Wells. I couldn't fall asleep last night, but I'm fine now."

"Ok. See you in a bit."

Viviane waved her off and continued savoring her coffee. *It's excellent,* she thought closing her eyes as it warmed her up.

Suddenly her eyes flew open, as she comprehended Cole sent her a note. She frantically looked around until she spied it on her pillow. She thought, *You're not acting like a chaperone, but one of the teens, but I can't deny how excited I am to get a note from Cole.*

> Morning Love,
> I know you're probably having a hard time getting up, so I sent Maddy to wake you. You were never a morning person, which makes you volunteering for this trip even more special to me. I can't wait to see you when you join me for breakfast.
>
> Love, Cole

Viviane smiled reading the note a second time. *He still knows me so well. I was always the last one to get up on trips in high school. How sweet of him to send Maddy with coffee.* Warmed by Cole's love, she thought, *what a great way to start the busy day.*

Motivated to quickly get dressed, she hurried to the loud noise coming from the fellowship hall. Arriving to find everyone being seated, Cole came up to her while she was getting food. "You missed the prayer, but I couldn't keep the hungry horde waiting any longer."

Viviane turned to Cole and whispered, "Thank you for the coffee and the note. It wasn't until Maddy woke me this morning that I remembered how much I hate early mornings."

Cole laughed, "I remembered for both of us. Sit with me at breakfast?"

Nodding, Viviane filled her plate, and went to sit down. She saw Maddy sitting with some other teens who had already eaten, laughing and talking. *I'll apologize for my grumpy mood later, but I still don't understand how anyone can be that happy this early in the morning.*

After everyone finished, Cole quieted them down to explain the day's agenda. "We're going to the elementary school to paint several rooms and put together a playground for the kids. Their old one was deemed unsafe last year and the kids only look at it from a roped off area."

Cole paused a moment to answer a question, but Viviane couldn't hear. Cole then said loudly, "We'll be rotating throughout the day, so everyone will get a chance to paint and work outside. Anything else?"

With no more questions, Cole told everyone to be on the bus in ten minutes. Viviane finished her breakfast and went to thank the church ladies who fed them, before grabbing her camera bag. She found it buried under a shirt. *I must've covered it up when I was hurrying to get dressed.* Checking for charged batteries, she ran to catch the bus.

Cole saw her standing in line and said, "I'm glad you've got your camera. I need someone to document the trip, since the woman who got sick was our photographer."

The two of them moved off to the side as he explained, "We have a slideshow during our youth program on the last Sunday of February when the teens takeover the entire service. I'm preaching and the kids are in charge of worship. We show pictures of all the youth activities during the year to interest new families and showcase the youth."

"Sounds fun."

"It is, and not only because yours truly preaches a mean sermon." Cole grinned smugly as he said, "Will you be able to make it?" Seeing everyone waiting for them, he gestured for her to move to the bus.

Viviane nodded, "Sure. I want to see my pictures on the big screen, don't I?"

Everyone cheered when they finally boarded. She and Cole sat together to talk about the service, and a few specific photos Cole wanted. He seemed really excited as he talked about the kids practicing to lead worship and one of the kids who wrote a skit about tithing. Everyone had been practicing for months.

Pulling into the school parking lot, Viviane thought, *I know why this is considered a poor community. The school looks rundown with lots of dirt and grime. I'm glad to know we're providing playground equipment.* The youth group voted to make this their big money project for the trip, and a portion of the silent auction money went to buy equipment and paint.

The kids were split into three groups to build the playground, paint the gym and two classrooms. The chaperones were divided up, and Viviane was in the cafeteria with Mrs. Turner. Cole stayed to show them what to do, before he went outside to help with playground.

Viviane spent the morning painting the walls in the cafeteria, leaving for short breaks to take pictures of the different groups working. She found herself impressed by how the kids had been laughing and joking at breakfast, but once they got to the school they went to work. There was still joking and laughing, but the teens were doing an amazing amount of hard labor.

By lunch time significant progress had been made painting and getting the playground put together. As she walked around, she felt the Holy Spirit impress upon her to pray. *It's the same feeling I experienced last night that kept me awake so late.* She prayed for protection and guidance but didn't know what specifically to pray about. *I'll have to cover everyone in prayer until I do.*

Now that she spent more time with the youth group, she felt she knew them better. More than just their names, but also their friends, and their backgrounds. She was beginning to care for them in a similar way Cole felt for them. Many of the teens called to her as she walked by, stopping to ask her to take their picture or show off their work. It made her feel connected, and she spent time thanking God for bringing her and making her a part of something special.

While she was outside taking pictures, Cole told her it was time for lunch. "Some of the ladies from the school came to make us lunch as a thank you."

Viviane picked up her camera bag, "That's sweet."

Cole held the bag up while Viviane slid her lens into their protective compartments and said, "Thanks for taking pictures. I've seen you shooting stuff all morning."

"I don't mind, it's what I love to do. Plus, it lets me keep an eye on everything."

She hesitated, *Should I tell him the burden I've felt to pray for the kids? I don't want Cole to think I'm having doubts about the trip, especially since I'm not sure why I'm covering everyone in prayer. I don't want to worry Cole.* She decided not to say anything until God gave her a clear idea what she was praying about.

She moved to get in the quickly forming line. While they waited, some kids rushed over to say the two classrooms were complete and could help in the cafeteria. Moving to the front of the line, she smelled the food being set out. "It smells heavenly, nothing like cafeteria food."

Cole sniffed, "Good, because I'm starving."

As she made her way through the food line, she was offered several homemade choices of chicken soup or chili with homemade cornbread and sides. Once everyone was seated, Cole prayed over the meal and the lunch ladies who prepared it.

Viviane enjoyed the food so much she went back for a second helping and made sure to thank them for the fantastic meal. The ladies were pleased, and she chatted with them a few more minutes before rushing back to eat.

Lifting her spoon to her lips, Viviane caught Maddy slide in next to her, "Miss Viviane could I use your camera while you're eating? Please? I'll be really careful with your camera. Promise."

Viviane nodded, "I trust you, Maddy. You've always shown great care with my equipment."

The girl hugged Viviane before carefully pulling the camera out of its bag and was soon busy taking photos. Viviane watched her take several shots of the lunch ladies with some of the teens. *Glad that's one picture off my list.* She finished her meal while talking to Mr. Turner and Malcolm about the work on the playground.

"Everything should be finished this afternoon. Those kids work really hard and fast." Mr. Turner said in between bites of chili, but Viviane could hear the distinct pride in his voice. Malcolm nodded, but didn't contribute much until his plate was clean.

When it was time to get back to work, she looked for Maddy and saw her bringing the camera back. Placing in back in the bag, Viviane asked, "Where are you working this afternoon?"

"Outside, I helped paint most of the morning."

"I'm helping in the cafeteria, but I'll see you when I take a break and shoot a few more pictures."

Maddy waved to her before following some kids outside, and noticed she was still wearing her blanket over her coat. *It's cold inside, but it will be freezing outside.*

The work went faster with two large groups and by three the school was finished. The kids were ready to go back to the church to clean up and have some free time before dinner. The church had several showers in the gym, and the girls were warned only quick showers. Under much grumbling and protesting, everyone was soon clean and in non-paint covered clothes.

The adults took turns showering, and when Viviane finally got to shower, she tried not to moan in enjoyment. *It feels good to wash all of the paint out of my hair.* When she went back to the room, she pulled out her hair dryer. *It's too cold to leave it wet like I normally do.*

As she dried her hair, she thought of Cole. *It's amazing to see him in his element teaching the kids about being Christ-like servants.* Thanking God for letting her see this part of Cole, and share this experience with him, she prayed for the kids again. *Please Lord, show me why I'm praying so I can be more specific. I know You have a reason and just wish I knew what it is.*

With her hair finally dry, Viviane joined the girls going to the bus for dinner. It meant a lot when they asked her to sit with them and she was honored to be accepted. Tonight, after dinner they would break into groups to spend the evening playing games and bonding. Everyone including the adults would get to act crazy and have fun. Cole told her each night they would focus on a specific goal and the first night was to learn more about each other.

The second night on Sunday would be more reflective for the deep questions about your relationship with God. *I'm most excited about the last night, because it will allow the teens to open up and pray together. At least, that's what Cole said he was praying would happen. I pray God will guide everyone and have His way in each session.*

Chapter Twenty-Nine

Cole couldn't believe it was already Monday afternoon, the trip had flown by. He watched the youth playing with a group of local kids teaching them Bible stories with puppets they made. *I never cease to be amazed by these kids. Many of them come from a rough home life and are facing challenges I didn't face until I was much older.*

Viviane passed by busily taking pictures. He had seen some of them and was impressed by the emotions she was able to get on her camera. All of the kids were very taken with her. They begged to sit next to her, talk to her, and simply spend time in her presence. *I'm a little jealous the teens have spent more time with her than I have on this trip.* He spent much of his time telling himself not to pull her aside and kiss her. *I have to keep reminding myself I'm the youth pastor and not a teenage boy, so I can't act like one.*

Each evening he made a point to talk to all the chaperones to see how the day went and discuss any problems or concerns. It was the only time he got to talk to Viviane alone, but the conversations were too short and no more than a minute to hold hands. Last night, they talked for a bit longer after he led a discussion about the personal relationship you can have with God that doesn't depend on your age or your experience. God would meet you right where you are, you just have to follow where He leads. They talked for over an hour about the kids, the trip, and their own experience with a personable God. *I felt we learned a lot more about each other by talking about our relationship with God.*

The plan for tonight had the kids spending an evening encouraging each other, and Cole prayed God would really bind them together as a group. He worked it out for the chaperones to watch the kids for an hour before dinner so he could pray without any distractions. *I'm praying for everyone to get something out of the evening, especially Viviane who feels accepted by the group.*

"Thanks for all of your help, Malcolm. I'm glad you could come at the last minute."

"Not a problem, Pastor West. I'm glad I could help."

Viviane watched the two men shake hands before Malcolm walked to the boy's room. Viviane waved as he walked by and he said, "See you in the morning, Miss Viv. It's been great to work with you this week."

After Malcolm was out of sight, Cole came to sit beside her on the couch in the lobby. He reached for her hand and savoring the quiet moment together. Viviane couldn't help but think about tonight, *the youth were reluctant to engage at first, and she could see Cole was worried.*

He started off by taking a huge ball of yarn and holding the end, he tossed the rest of the ball to one of the kids. His name was Sam Zane and he was new to the youth group, quiet and shy. He came from a family with a lot of kids, and no father figure. She noticed he struggled to fit in. Cole called out his name as he threw the ball, and then said, "Sam works harder than anyone I've seen. He was the best with the kids teaching them a song while we waited for the puppet show to start. I'm glad Sam came on the trip."

Cole told Sam to hold onto a part of the yarn and throw the ball to someone else and say something encouraging until the yarn ran out. Sam sent it to one of the other quiet kids, and the string ended up going around the group multiple times. It took time for the kids to be comfortable and honest, but it was amazing to watch as the night unfolded.

Even the adults were included, and Viviane felt privileged to have several students say sweet things to her. Maddy talked about her genuine acceptance of everyone and other kids mentioned her skills as a photographer with her way of including everyone in the pictures.

Leaning against Cole, Viviane said, "Tonight was touching. It was a great way to end the trip with the kids building each other up. When one of the kids spoke of how fun Mrs. Wells turned out to be, I nearly cried."

He sighed, "It went better than I hoped." *It was a great way to end the week, but the best part was sharing it with Vee.*

"I loved at the end everyone was connected by a web of love." Sighing with contentment, she thought, *the church is quiet with everyone gone to bed. Tomorrow's the last day and it will be busy, building a ramp in the morning and the last Backyard Bible Club.* Glancing at Cole, she smiled, *I've loved every minute of it, even though I hate getting up early. Maddy's been a sweetheart bringing me coffee and a note from Cole each morning.*

"Vee, I have to tell you this trip has been really hard for me."

She pulled back to look him in the eye, "Why?"

"Because I haven't been able to kiss you this whole trip!"

Softly laughing, she thought, *I'm glad he hates that part, too!*

Bumping his arm, she said, "I expect you to kiss me once the last kid goes home."

He laughed as he said, "Deal!"

Knowing it was getting late, each of them were reluctant to go to bed. Cole stalling said, "Maddy sure is taken with you. She could benefit from someone befriending her. She's liked by everyone, but she can be shy and she's not as outgoing. I've noticed her sitting in the group, but she doesn't seem to really be engaged anymore. I know it has to do with the family rough patch, and it doesn't help her carrying that security blanket around all the time..."

Viviane didn't hear a word he said after security blanket but flashed back to the outpatient eating disorder program of a girl with anorexia weighing under a hundred pounds. She was cold all the time and so thin she carried a blanket with her everywhere. In group sessions she called it her security blanket, because she wanted to hide all the time from people, hating the way she looked and felt.

As she remembered all of this, Viviane thought back to all the time she spent with Maddy. *I can't remember ever seeing her eat anything. Maddy always says she's full or she had just finished eating. Is she anorexic, Lord?*

Praying, she remembered the first day she met Maddy at the tornado cleanup when she passed out. *I thought then it was from all the hard work.* Feeling she was right, Viviane needed to talk to Maddy. *Lord, do I talk to her now?*

Feeling a strong need to see her, she felt God saying, Go, go now. Standing up, Viviane said, "Cole, I've got to go talk to someone... to Maddy. Please pray for me to say what God wants."

Cole didn't move or question her, but only said, "I trust you, Vee. I'll pray for both of you."

She started to walk away but came back to hug him. Walking to the girl's sleeping room, she thought, *I don't want to outright accuse the girl, or wake her up to pull her from the room. Lord, am I crazy? Help me! If this is what you want me to do.*

Rounding the corner as she finished her prayer, she reached for the door to peek inside, but before she could turn the knob, someone plowed into her.

Putting her hands out, Maddy whispered, "Oomph. Sorry Miss Viviane. I'm getting some water."

Viviane sent up a silent prayer of thanks, "That's okay, Maddy. I was coming to see if you were still up."

"Oh, did you need help with something?" Eagerness evident in her voice.

"Go get some water and then we'll talk."

"That's okay. We can talk instead."

Lord, give me the words. "Let's go to the sanctuary."

The two women walked to the front of the church and Viviane made sure to avoid the lobby area where Cole was still sitting. She held the door for Maddy to walk through. "Let's sit here in the back."

"Okay." Maddy sat down in a pew and look at Viviane expectantly.

I don't know what to say, so I guess I'll just start with my story. "I wanted to tell you a bit about myself. My parents died when I was nine in a car crash. I went to live with Grand, and she was great. I was in therapy and things slowly got better until I got into high school. It was an awful time. I didn't have my mom to talk to about things like boys, makeup, and other girly stuff. My Grand tried, but she was a reminder my mom was gone."

Watching Maddy's face while she talked, she could see the girl was curious about where the story was going, "I was angry at God for taking my mom and started not eating, unless I was surrounded by people. Then I went home and took laxatives to lose whatever I'd eaten."

She noticed a change in Maddy when she reached this part. The girl lowered her head looking at her clenched hands as Viviane continued, "I did this for years. On the outside I looked like I had it all together, but on the inside, I was hurting, angry, and very sad. It wasn't until I was a junior in college and Cole broke up with me that I hit rock bottom. He said some hurtful things that I didn't handle well. I went back to school completely depressed. I stopped eating, quit going to class, and eventually didn't even get out of bed."

Maddy looked up at her when she mentioned the break up, and Viviane could see the tears shining in her eyes. Reaching out to take Maddy's hand she continued, "I spent a lot of years angry at God and decided to control my eating, since I felt I couldn't control my life."

She could feel the sobs start to rock Maddy's small frame, and she leaned forward to hold her, gently rocking her, "It's okay, Maddy, but I need to know... do you have an eating disorder?"

Maddy nodded her head as the tears flowed freely, "Yes, I've been starving myself for months. It started small, just skipping a meal or two, but the harder things got at home the more I stopped eating. I used to be pudgy," wiping her tears she sniffed, "everyone called it baby fat, and thought I was just maturing, but now I can't stop... not eating."

"I know your dad lost his job..." Viviane said, but Maddy interrupted her.

Pulling back, she began to gush out the secret fears she had been holding inside. "Yeah, Mom and Dad are worried about money. They talk about it all the time and I hear them at night worried and arguing. I hate it, and it's my fault. Dad lost his job because of me. He took time off, because I got sick. Mom was visiting Grandpa out of town, and Dad missed a whole week of work all because I had the flu. It's all my fault."

Maddy's sobs shook her entire body as Viviane held her. "It's okay sweetheart. It's not your fault. The economy is bad right now, but none of that's because of you. It's going to be okay."

Through the sobs, Maddy said, "I don't know what to do anymore. I can't talk to my family and ask for help because that will cost money we don't have!"

Viviane took Maddy by the shoulders to look her in the eye, "Maddy, your parents love you and they'll want you to get the help you need. I know money is tight, but God will help your parents. He's in control and can help all of you, but honey, you need to get help now."

Maddy nodded her head, *I know I need help and I'm relieved I don't have to hide my secret anymore. It helps to know Viviane's gone through this, too!* She sat with Viviane still holding her until she slowly stopped crying.

"What do we do now, Miss Viviane?" Maddy asked in a quiet voice. "Do we have to tell the others in the youth group?"

"No, we don't have to tell the group. We do need to talk to your parents so you can get the help you need."

"I don't know what to say to them. I don't know if I can..." Her voice cracking.

Viviane afraid she might start crying again said quickly, "If you would like, I can talk to Pastor West. He knows your parents and can meet with all of you to talk about this."

Maddy gave a slight smile, "I'd like that. Do we have to tell my parents... tonight?"

"No, it can wait until you're home. We don't need to rush you back. Just promise, you'll come to me if you need to talk before we get home."

"Promise." Maddy smiled through watery tears. "Will you talk to Pastor West tonight?"

"Yes. I told him I needed to talk to you, but he doesn't know what it was about. He's probably worried by now. I'll tell him and mention you'd like him to talk with your parents. Head on to bed and get some sleep. We've got a busy day tomorrow."

Maddy started to get up and leave, when she asked softly, "You don't think I'm a bad person do you, Miss Viviane?"

"Of course not. We're friends and friends don't judge. I'm glad I could help you."

The two hugged before Viviane sent the worn-out girl to bed. When Maddy was gone, she went in search of Cole. In the front lobby, she spied him on the couch fast asleep. "Cole?"

When she reached out to shake him, he lunged forward yelling, "I'm awake." His phone hit the floor with a clatter, and he looked all around trying to orient himself.

Giggling, Viviane sat down next to him holding out the phone she scooped up. Cole took it, fully awake and asked, "What happened, Vee? You left rather abruptly?" He looked sheepish as he said, "I was praying. I only fell asleep a moment ago. Promise."

"It's okay. I didn't realize how long Maddy and I talked until I saw the time on your phone."

"Can I ask what the two of you talked about?" He smiled as he put his arm around her.

"First, I need to tell you I've felt a burden all week to pray. I wasn't sure why until tonight." Viviane scooted closer, taking his hand.

"I know I said something and then you stopped listening." He turned to face her.

"Something you said about Maddy triggered a memory of when I was in the outpatient program. I started thinking of different things about Maddy, such as the blanket, almost fainting on me at the tornado cleanup, and Sunday afternoon playing with the kids. I realized I've never seen her eat."

Cole thought for a moment, "Yeah, I've never seen her eat either."

Viviane nodded, "It all started to add up, so I went to talk to her. I wasn't sure and didn't want to accuse her, so I told her my story."

He leaned forward and asked, "Vee are you saying Maddy has an eating disorder?"

Tears in her eyes, she nodded, "Yes, she started crying and told me she feels like she's to blame for her dad losing her job." She buried her head in his shoulder, "Oh, Cole, it was heartbreaking."

He pulled her closer to put his head next to hers, "I can't believe it. I missed the signs, again."

She pulled back to look him in the eye, speaking in a clear but authoritative voice, "Cole, you can't do that to yourself. This was something she worked at hiding, and so did I. Eating disorders are hard to recognize. Look at me, I had one and was in a program surrounded by girls with eating disorders with all kinds of symptoms and didn't recognize it until I was hit over the head."

Seeing he was hurting, she leaned closer to put her arms around him, "You've got to understand you can't know everything, let alone be everything to everyone. That's not your job, but God's. He's the only one who can take care of everyone all the time."

Cole held on tight as he kissed her gently on the lips. After a moment, he leaned back to look her in the eye. "I was very blessed when you came back into my life. I'm sorry you went through the pain of having an eating disorder, but I'm glad God is using it for His glory and to help heal others."

They stayed in each other's arms for a few minutes, enjoying the stolen kiss. Viviane knew it would be the last until they were back in Cartersville and the kids had all gone home. *Cole told me he wouldn't feel right about any public displays of affection, since we weren't married and he wanted to be a good example to the teens. I understand and will treasure this entire experience.*

Neither of them saw Chloe Green peering behind the doors of the sanctuary. She had seen Maddy come back and decided to investigate. When she saw the youth pastor kissing Viviane she was surprised. *Everyone thought they were dating, but no one had seen them acting like a couple on this trip. I can't wait to tell my friends what I saw, but Cole* mentioning Viviane has an eating disorder, well that's BIGGER news than them kissing. She snuck back to the room, glad Mrs. Wells hadn't caught her. *I'll have to decide who to tell first. This is too juicy to keep to myself!*

Chapter Thirty

A particularly loud snore from Mrs. Wells woke Viviane with a start. She lay very still, trying to think what happened last night for the small amount of sleep she got and Maddy flashed in her mind. Not seeing any sunlight, she moved to check her watch, and realized Maddy was holding her hand. *She must have grabbed it during the night after I finally crawled into bed. Cole and I talked for thirty minutes after our kiss.*

Gently pulling her hand out of Maddy's grip, she saw it was 6:40, which meant she had time before the girls started getting up. Deciding to get ready early and go pray in the sanctuary, she quietly sat up and groped for her things in the dark.

Twenty minutes later, she was sitting in one of the pews and immediately felt she was in God's presence. Falling to her knees she began to pray quietly, knowing she wouldn't be disturbed. "Oh Lord," she said, tears falling. "Thank You for working everything out to bring me on this trip. Thank You for opening my eyes to see Maddy's pain, and for using something which was a shameful part of my past to restore Your daughter. She's an exceptional girl who has a special place in my heart."

Viviane spent the next few minutes praying for God to bring the right people into Maddy's life to help her and her family. She prayed for Cole to find the right words when he talked to the Adams family and for God to work out the finances.

When they talked last night, she told him Maddy was afraid to talk to her parents, confessing she already said he would talk to them when they got back.

"I don't mind, but do we need to get her home tonight?" Worry had pierced his voice.

"No, she's not in any immediate danger, and it'd be better if she didn't get pulled away early from the trip and have the kids talk. I'll keep an eye on her and you can meet with her parents later this week."

When he agreed to trust her judgement, she was elated. They talked a bit about what to say to her parents, and places Maddy could go for help."

Viviane's watched beeped, and she knew it was time for breakfast. When she arrived in the fellowship hall, she saw she was one of the first along with some hungry teenage boys. Grabbing a doughnut and coffee, she sat with them when they called her over.

"Can't believe you're up this early Miss V." Tommy, a ninth-grade boy said when she sat down. "Aren't you always the last one up?" Laughter erupted from the four boys.

"I know, it surprised me too!" She said before taking a bite of a chocolate frosted doughnut.

Viviane was well liked by the group, guys and girls alike. They weren't stupid; everyone knew Cole and Viviane liked each other. Tommy, along with most of the other kids thought it was great Pastor Cole had a girlfriend, even though no one had seen them acting like a couple. Most of the talk was about when they would admit they liked each other and get married already.

The boys and Viviane spent time talking about the plans for the day and how much everyone enjoyed the trip. She was excited about this morning, because they would finish building a ramp for a local church member's grandfather. He moved in when he became wheelchair bound and the family couldn't afford to finish the ramp for him to go in and out of the house. The kids would help finish it this morning, and then have the last Backyard Bible Club before they went home. *We'll be in Cartersville by ten, and I'm looking forward to sleeping in my own bed.* She was staying through Thursday before a wedding shoot this weekend.

By the time everyone arrived for breakfast, Viviane had already put away her trash. She decided to put away her bath stuff and check on Maddy, because she hadn't seen her yet. *It would be fun to wake Maddy up for a change.* Waving hello to several stragglers, Viviane was surprised to find the sleep room deserted except for Maddy sound asleep with her head covered to block out the light.

"Maddy, honey wake up." Viviane gently shook her. "Come on sleepy head, it's time for breakfast."

"Five more minutes, Miss V. I'm tired."

"Come on, get up. You know the drill with waking me up all week." *Is Maddy still upset from last night?*

"Did you bring me coffee?" A sleepy voice asked from underneath a pile of blankets.

"Maddy, you don't like coffee."

The girl poked her head from under the covers, a huge grin lighting up her face, "Oh, yeah!"

Laughing as she pulled the blanket off Maddy, Viviane was glad to see the girl was only tired. *I understand the feeling, it's been a long, active week even before our late-night talk.* "Get dressed sleepyhead. Breakfast's waiting."

Maddy slowly got out from the mound of blankets, "Just give me a second."

Viviane packed up some of her things while she waited, not knowing if she would get a chance later, since she would help load the bus. When Maddy came back into the room, chipper and wide awake, she offered to carry Viviane's camera bag. The two women arrived to see everyone seated and almost finished eating. "Maddy get something to eat. I've eaten already."

Maddy hesitated, and moved closer to Viviane to ask quietly, "Will you sit with me while I... um... eat?"

Viviane hugged the thin girl, and said, "Yes," before gently pushing her to the table. She watched her put the smallest doughnut on her plate and sighed knowing the girl had a long road ahead.

"How's our girl doing?"

Cole had snuck up behind her after watching them walk in.

"Fine, she's only tired this morning." Viviane said, pointing her finger at her chest, "I had to wake her up."

Cole chuckled, "And who woke you up?"

Viviane smiled sweetly, "God."

His eyes twinkled with laughter, "Touché."

When Maddy came back, Cole waved them off to a table while he went to make sure supplies would be at the morning building project location. After Maddy and Viviane prayed, they talked about the remaining photos she needed, when one of the teenage girls walked up to their table.

"Aren't you going to eat Miss Viviane?" The girl asked in a sing-song voice, loudly interrupting the conversation.

Viviane looked up to see Chloe standing there, pushing her long brown hair back out of her blue eyes. Viviane knew she was one of the more popular girls, usually always surrounded by a group of teens. "Hi, Chloe. No, I was up early this morning for a change and had breakfast."

"Oh... well," she played with her hair a moment, then gushed, "I guess I'll see you later with your camera."

"Yes, you will."

She waved as the girl walked off, but Maddy looked at her from a half empty plate, pieces of doughnut crumbled up, "She's acting strange."

"What do you mean?"

Maddy shrugged, "I don't know, but she's a little too concerned." Eyes widening, she whispered, "Do you think she knows something?"

"No, Maddy." Viviane patted her hand, "It's okay, sweetie. She knows nothing. Don't worry. Finished?"

Maddy nodded, *it's hard for me to eat in front of people, but it helped Viviane didn't look at me and talked about other things besides last night. I wonder how she knew that.* Throwing her plate away, she wondered, *How will my parents handle all of this? I usually make dinner for the family, and then go to bed after homework, because I'm so tired between school and work. My parents are so busy, they never know if I eat or not. I'm not looking forward to this trip ending and my parents talking with Pastor Cole.*

Last night she had laid in her sleeping bag praying about her talk with Viviane. She was scared, wondering about her parents, if she could get better, would her friends find out, and a thousand other things. She tried to stay awake until Viviane came back but fell asleep because the next time she woke up it was really late and Viviane was asleep next to her. At one point, when she felt anxious and overwhelmed she grabbed Viviane's hand.

The rest of the morning, she saw Viviane and Pastor Cole occasionally watching her, but didn't think anyone noticed. She couldn't believe how fast the morning was flying by. The ramp was finished by noon and everyone was proud how the project turned out. The older man cried when he was able to wheel himself out of the house without help for the first time in two years. He thanked each person by shaking their hands at least twice, the whole time saying how great it looked. Viviane lined everyone up for a final picture with the smiling grandfather and his family. Maddy could see the tears in Viviane's eyes when she snapped the picture. *I'm glad we were here to help*, Maddy thought.

Chapter Thirty-One

"No, miiinnneee."

Viviane sighed at the small two-year-old girl she held in her arms. The little blonde girl had a firm grip on a cuddly stuffed unicorn and refused to give it back. She was trying to give the child to her mom, but the little girl wouldn't give the toy back and it wasn't hers to give away.

"Sweetie that toy belongs to the nice lady. Come to Mommy and let's go home."

"NOOOO!" The toddler yelled, knowing if she went to her mom, she would have to give back the unicorn.

Cole walked over to help, sensing a situation he needed to diffuse. "Katlynn, don't you want to go back to your Mommy?" The little girl grew quiet but didn't move out of Viviane's arms.

Viviane was grateful for any help, the last few hours with the little kids wore her out. *I'm tired and hungry, which means very soon this baby is about to see a grown woman break down and cry.*

Abruptly, the child lost interest and went to her mother. Under her breath, Viviane muttered, "Thank you, Jesus."

When the last family took their kids home, the Backyard Bible Club was officially over. In a few short hours, she would be sleeping in a real bed. Deciding she wouldn't break down after all, she turned to Cole, "Thanks for trying."

"That girl was really attached to you."

He had been watching her with the child in her arms most of the afternoon. *The picture of the two of them tugged at my heart. Even with the child gone, I can't get the idea of her one day holding our kids out of my head.*

"She was more devoted to the necklace I was wearing, I think." Viviane said readjusting the simple chain around her neck "I should've taken it off, but once I saw she was attached I couldn't or she would have spent the past three hours crying." *The other teens refused to spend the afternoon with the screaming little girl, so I volunteered to keep her quiet.* "I'm glad that's over."

"Yes, babies can be difficult." He said, bending down to pick up toys scattered all over the floor.

As she cleaned up, Viviane didn't see Cole's face as she said, "It's easier when they're yours, because they love you and you love them, unconditionally."

Cole thought, *This isn't the time to talk about our future children, but I plan to have that discussion with her soon.* Instead he continued to pick up, while changing the subject. "Are you packed? We leave soon and I need someone to help direct the loading of the bus." He was grabbing armloads of toys to avoid looking at her, afraid he might grab her in his arms. "I've got other chaperones helping elsewhere and need some help outside." He thought, *far away from me.*

"Just tell me where you need me." She put the last of the toys in plastic containers before standing up to stretch.

After Cole left, Viviane didn't have a chance to analyze his inability to look at her, because she went outside to find the kids already loading the luggage. Sometime later someone came up and tapped her on the shoulder, "Miss Viviane, do you want me to put our stuff on the bus?"

Wiping her forehead, she turned to see Maddy with her suitcase. "Thanks, Maddy. Yes, please. We're almost done and should be leaving soon."

Maddy grabbed Viviane's camera bag and went to save a seat on the bus. She hoped to have a chance to talk to Viviane before her parents picked her up tonight. *I really want to thank her again for reaching out and thank Pastor Cole for talking to my parents later.*

Before Viviane knew it, they were driving on the interstate for home. The drive home went fast, especially after dinner when the kids became silent. Looking behind her, she saw many had fallen asleep and wasn't surprised with how hard everyone had worked all week.

A little after ten, the bus pulled into a busy parking lot filled with anxious parents waiting to pick up their kids. The teens woke up and talking broke out as they met their parents and got their belongings. After the parents hugged their teens, many came up to Cole to say thanks before heading home.

Cole spent most of his time making sure the kids got all their luggage and shaking hands with sleepy parents. Tessa Green and her husband walked up to say thanks, when Chloe came running with Sara a few steps behind her. "Mom is Sara still staying the rest of the week?"

"Yes, since your school is out the entire week I worked it out with Sara's mom. Grab all of your things and get in the car."

The girls squealed, jumping up and down before they went to get their luggage. Tessa pulled at her husband's shirt, thinking, *He needs to stop talking to Cole. I'm tired and want to go home.*

Cole waved goodbye, starting to feel the long week catching up with him. *My eyes feel like lead! I'm ready to go to bed.*

Viviane was putting her camera bag in her car, when she saw Maddy rolling over her bags. "Thanks. Are your parents here?"

Maddy nodded, helping Viviane load the bags in the trunk. "Yeah, Pastor Cole's talking to them."

Viviane noticed her hesitation and put her arm around the girl as they walked over to her parents. She heard the end of Cole's conversation, "... tomorrow afternoon works for me."

Maddy's mother Noelle reached out to hug her daughter, "We've realized while Maddy was gone how much she's been doing. We thought to let her take tomorrow off from the childcare and let her relax. I know she's tired from all the work she did on the trip."

Viviane could see the tears in Maddy's eyes and sent up a prayer of thanks God was already working things out for the whole family. Her parents realizing how much Maddy does will go a long way to help her begin to heal. Maddy introduced Viviane before everyone waved goodbye.

In the silent parking lot, Cole put his arm around Viviane to walk her to her car, both enjoying the silence of each other's company. Realizing it was after eleven, he said reluctantly, "I probably won't see you until later this week. I know you have a wedding this weekend. How soon can you get me the photos for the slideshow for Sunday?"

"Thursday, before I go back to Atlanta so you can look through them." Viviane turned toward him, and he hugged her tightly, thanking her for this week.

Feeling shy, Viviane ducked her head when she said, "I truly loved every minute."

Glad to hear, he kissed her with complete assurance things would work out. He sent her on her way with a promise to call when she made it to Grand's house. He watched her pull out of the parking lot thinking, *I want to talk to her soon about our future. We've waited long enough.*

Chloe and Sara talked quietly in the back seat of the Green's four-wheel drive. The adults were grateful because they were tired, but Tessa was surprised to hear the girls talking at all. Last year, Chloe slept the whole ride home and most of the next day. *Maybe*, she thought, *it's because Sara's staying the rest of the week that has them hyped up.*

When the family arrived home, she and her husband, Danny, sent the girls upstairs to Chloe's room. Tessa put on her housecoat before going to say goodnight. When she reached the closed bedroom door, she heard them giggling and talking, "I can't believe Pastor Cole and Viviane were kissing outside the sanctuary like that."

Tessa recognized her daughter's voice and paused to listen to her continue, "But what really surprised me was she has an eating disorder. Can you imagine? She's skinny, but not that skinny! How can Pastor Cole date her knowing she's sick?"

Tessa grabbed the door knob with white knuckles, shocked by what her daughter said. *I can't decide if I'm more upset about the Pastor kissing Viviane on a youth trip or Viviane has an eating disorder.* She moved her body closer to hear more.

"... I saw Pastor Cole kissing Viviane several times. I walked around a corner to find them making out in some hidden spot." This comment came from Sara, jealous her best friend learned so much about Pastor Cole's girlfriend. She made up a story about seeing them kiss, not wanting to be left out, since Chloe had already told some other girls. Everyone had been talking all week about how much they thought Pastor Cole liked Viviane. Most of the kids were happy about it, but after Chloe mentioned the eating disorder, some of the talk began to change.

Tessa didn't know the girls were trying to outdo one another's story as she thought, *I don't like what I'm hearing and feel it's my duty as a youth parent to stop it.* She knocked on the door, startling the girls who immediately quieted down. Chloe caught Sara's eye, but when her Mom didn't say anything, they assumed their secret was safe. Both girls said goodnight, promising to sleep.

Turning out the lights, Tessa paused in the hallway to think about what she needed to do. Checking her watch, she saw it was late, *but it's my duty to let others know about the woman Pastor Cole's obviously dating and hiding from everyone. It's one thing to be dating the woman who broke his heart, but now, I know Viviane isn't worthy of him at all.*

She began to mentally count the women who might still be up and planned to call one, maybe two of them tonight about this issue. *It's best to put a stop to the whole mess, before someone gets hurt.*

Chapter Thirty-Two

When Lauren Blake woke up to her phone ringing early Wednesday morning, she was surprised at the hour. She answered the phone with her usual dramatic flair, but once fully informed of the Viviane situation, she became livid. *To think*, she angrily thought, *Viviane's wormed her way back into Cole's life using him. He's only spending time with her to help with her eating disorder. Cole's confused and not really in love with this sick woman.*

Forty minutes later, after talking with different church members to find out all the sordid details, she realized she would need to hurry to get ready for a busy day. As one of the ladies said over the phone, even though she didn't have a child in the youth group, she was very involved and the mothers decided she was the best person to deal with this situation. Going over several scenarios in her head while she dressed, she decided to talk with Viviane directly. *She'll be home alone, Delia Anne has a Bible study on Wednesday mornings, and then the ladies go out for a late lunch.*

Viviane woke up thanking God she was back in her own bed. She prayed for Maddy and her family, knowing they would meet with Cole this afternoon to discuss getting help for Maddy after they deal with finding out about the problem. *I pray God's wisdom and strength for Cole and Maddy. Please give peace to the entire family long after the meeting is over.*

She decided to sleep in as late as she could, which is why she was surprised when she rolled over to see it wasn't very late. *Grand said she'd be gone all day and I'm staying in pjs for breakfast. I want to do my Bible study over coffee and scrambled eggs. I've eaten enough doughnuts for months.*

Humming as she went downstairs, Viviane didn't see the little black car in Grand's driveway on her way to the kitchen. Making herself a cup of coffee, she heard the doorbell and pulled her robe tight around her. *Thankfully I put it on to ward off the February chill, at least I won't feel indecent opening the door. I hope it's only the UPS guy because I'm starving and those eggs are calling my name.*

As she rounded the entry way, she saw Mrs. Blake standing outside tapping her purse against her arm while looking at her platinum watch. "Oh Lord," she prayed grabbing the wall for support, "Please don't let her be here to upset Grand." Taking a deep breath, she steadied herself before facing a furious Lauren Blake.

"Good Morning, Mrs. Blake," Viviane said opening the door, "What brings you over so early?"

"Aren't you going to invite me in? It's cold and looks like rain." Lauren didn't wait but marched directly into the living room. She never looked back, expecting Viviane to follow.

Pulling her blue robe tighter, Viviane suddenly wished she had gotten dressed. *Lauren Blake seeing me in pjs is a nightmare I'm sure I've had before.*

She followed after Lauren already sitting in the formal chair Grand only used to throw her knitting bag on. Sitting on the sofa, Viviane thought, *I've got a feeling I need to be seated for this conversation.*

She turned to Lauren and waited, noticing the woman's immaculate dove gray business suit against the cream Queen Anne chair she was regally sitting on. *I can't help but feel like she's perfectly poised for an attack.*

"I came to speak to you Viviane and I want to get straight to the point." Mrs. Blake cleared her throat and continued without looking Viviane in the eye, "But first, I must say I've not been pleased with all the time you've been spending with Cole. I know you broke his heart ten years ago, and apparently he decided not to learn his lesson." Pausing to brush imaginary lint from the chair, she continued, "I'm not family, but care for him like a son. I felt it wasn't my place to tell him who he should or shouldn't see, but the call this morning changed my thinking about having you around."

Red flooding Viviane's face at the harsh words, she fumed. *How dare this woman have the audacity to tell me I'm not good enough for Cole?*

About to speak her mind, when Lauren raised her hand and continued, "I understand you're angry, but you should understand the church knows. More importantly the youth group knows," she paused, licking her lips, relishing as she added, "they ALL know about your eating disorder."

Viviane's mouth snapped shut. On the verge of giving Mrs. Blake more than just a piece of her mind, but the entire cake, the last comment stopped her in her tracks.

Stunned, she fell back against the sofa listening as Mrs. Blake continued with a large Cheshire grin.

"I don't want to say we're judging you, but children are impressionable, and in this day and age we must protect them more diligently." She waved her hands back and forth to emphasize her point.

Viviane thought, *she looks like a spider crafting her web to catch prey.*

"Your life's in Atlanta and the entire church agrees with me that it's time for you to go back and leave Cole and his youth group alone. None of them need your damaging influence." When she finished Lauren sat back, rigid and unmoving with her ice blue eyes focused on Viviane.

Mustering up every bit of courage and dignity available, Viviane said quietly but firmly, "Mrs. Blake my relationship with Cole is none of your business. My eating disorder isn't something for you to discuss with anyone. Cole and I are..." but she was unable to finish.

Lauren interrupted with a dismissive flip of her hand, "Normally, I'd say your relationship's your own business, but for two things. The most important is you're dating OUR youth pastor, and second until this trip where you were watched by nosey teens constantly, NO ONE knew you were dating. Cole's keeping it a secret. Doesn't that tell you something?"

I thought this conversation couldn't get any worse, but I was wrong. Cole hasn't told anyone we're dating?!? I know he said his reputation was important and cared what the kids think. Is Mrs. Blake, right? Was I supposed to be a secret until he thought I was good enough to bring it out into the open?

Lauren could see the tears in Viviane's eyes and told herself, *I hate to hurt the girl, but sometimes the truth hurts. It's best if the relationship ends now, before people become too involved.*

Abruptly, Viviane stood and said, "Thank you for stopping by, but I think you need to leave. Now."

She didn't wait but walked to the front door forcing herself to stand tall and look Mrs. Blake in the eye as she held the door open. Lauren wisely said nothing, walking out quickly. As soon as she cleared the threshold, Viviane closed and locked the door. *I want to slam it shut but can't because Grand's training is too well ingrained.*

She went to the kitchen to pour herself a cup of coffee and put the eggs back in the fridge. *I don't think I can eat without being sick.*

Slowly sitting down, she saw tears falling into her mug. *I don't know if I'm crying because the church's decided I'm not good enough for Cole or because Cole still doesn't think I'm good enough.*

Giving into her pain, she buried her face and sobbed on the table. Her whole body shook until finally she could cry no more. Grabbing a few napkins to wipe her nose, she made plans for what to do next. *It's time to go back to Atlanta for good. Grand's health* isn't a concern anymore and I'm happy in Atlanta or I will be again. She looked at her watch, *It's almost eleven and Grand won't be home until three. I need to leave quickly before she gets back. I can't face her, she wouldn't understand why I've kept this a secret for so long. Now she's going to find out through the church gossip, and I can't stop it.*

I don't know what else to do but run.

Her heart breaking, she prayed, "Lord, please don't let Grand hear the horrible gossip about me until I'm back in Atlanta." Wiping her eyes as the tears started falling again, she said out loud, "Go pack. It's over."

Chapter Thirty-Three

It took Viviane less than fifteen minutes to pack, because thankfully she only unpacked a few items last night. *I don't want to take the chance of Grand catching me sneaking out. I'm ashamed to be running but feel it's better to talk to her later when the wounds aren't so raw and freshly reopened.*

Zipping up the last bag, she made the bed before moving her luggage downstairs. *I don't want her to know I left in a rush. I'll leave a note saying I was called back to work early. A little lie won't hurt, not if it's to protect someone I care about.*

She reached the last stair when she heard a car door slam. *Oh Lord, please don't let that be Grand, but the UPS guy for once.*

Her prayer request was denied when Grand came walking through the front door to see her standing in the entryway looking guilty.

"Viviane," Grand cried seeing the bags in her hands, "are you leaving already? I thought we had until tomorrow."

Suddenly feeling like a young girl with her hand caught in the proverbial cookie jar, she shifted from foot to foot, stalling because she was unable to think of a valid excuse on the spot. "You're home early. I thought you'd be gone until three."

"Elizabeth Viviane Stanton-Mays are you running out on me?" Grand raised her voice to a near screeching level.

"Not really..." Viviane said quietly hanging her head.

"I felt I was supposed to rush home after the Bible study and now I know why." Putting her hands on her hips, Grand stared while asking, "What's wrong? Tell me the truth! All of it!"

Feeling cornered, Viviane knew it was time to spit it all out. She turned toward the living room, "Fine, but let's sit down." She didn't wait, but went to sit on the sofa, barely able to walk because her knees were shaking. She felt a wave of déjà vu, *except this time I'll be telling the bad news.*

Grand sat across from Viviane and saw the tear stains on her cheeks and her red-rimmed eyes. "Please tell me why you've been crying, baby?"

Viviane took a deep breath, her words barely above a whisper, "I've several things to tell you, and the first is really hard to admit. It's a secret I've kept from you for a long time, because I didn't want to hurt you." She went on to tell the entire story of her eating disorder, starting in high school and how the break up with Cole triggered her break down.

As she spoke, she closed her eyes, because she couldn't stand to see the tears running down Grand's cheeks. *I hate knowing I'm hurting someone I love very much, my only family.* She felt Grand's arms wrap around her, giving her strength to end with how God's restoring grace helped put her life back together better than ever. The two of them locked arms and cried when Viviane finished.

Grand held onto Viviane, rocking her back and forth, tears streaming down her face, as she prayed, *Lord, how could I have missed something so important? Why didn't I see my girl was struggling? Why couldn't she tell me? I thought we were so much closer than that. Guide me to help her now.*

It was some time before they calmed down and Grand looked her in the eyes to ask, "Sweetheart, why are you telling me this now? Don't misunderstand, I'm thankful you've finally told me, but I don't understand why you're so upset now." *I'm not going to let her see how hurt I am right now, I need to be strong for her, and do what's best for Viviane for once.*

Grand's eyes flashed, "Is Cole mad? Did he find out and doesn't want to see you anymore?" She thought, *If Cole's mad about Viviane's past, I'll tie a knot in his tail and straighten him out. It wouldn't take long either, I've been working out.*

Viviane gave a half smile over Grand's protective instincts, before she told about Cole hiding their relationship, because he felt the youth group shouldn't see him acting like a teenage boy on the trip.

She began to cry in earnest, tears streaming down her face, as she told about the feeling she had to pray and how she discovered one of the girls had an eating disorder. *I can't reveal who, it's not my place, but I can tell how I talked to Cole and our kiss must've been seen by one of the teens.*

"It's all over the church that I still have an eating disorder and I've been told," omitting it was Lauren Blake, "it would be better if I didn't see Cole anymore. He needs someone better for a pastor's wife."

Grand watched Viviane bury her face in her hands as Viviane collapsed against her. Putting her arms around her, she stroked her back like when Viviane was a child thinking, *how dare the people in my church decide my granddaughter isn't good enough for Cole? If anything, she's too good for the whole lot of them. I can't decide who I'm madder at, Cole who let this whole mess happen or the busybodies at church who are spreading vicious gossip.*

"Sweetie, Cole doesn't feel that way. He cares about you, he loves you. I know he does." Grand rocked her adding to herself, *if I'm wrong about that boy, God help him.*

Viviane sniffed, and mumbled, "But Grand, I've thought about what Mrs. Blake said and she's right about Cole hiding our relationship. He broke up with me the first time, because he said I wasn't cut out to be a pastor's wife. It seems he still feels that way, because he's been hiding me from everyone."

"He said what?!? That's why you broke up?" *I can't believe my ears,* she thought, *the arrogant up start hurt my girl by saying she wasn't good enough.* Grand felt tears well up as she watched Viviane sob harder. Grand asked herself, *Lord what have I done? All of this is because I didn't know Cole said my baby wasn't good enough. My meddling caused Viviane even more pain, because of my selfishness.*

As sobs racked Viviane's body, Grand held onto her praying for God to help her baby. Viviane didn't realize she mentioned Lauren Blake's name, and Grand was having a hard time controlling her anger. Piecing some things together, Grand said, "Now, I understand why you've stayed away all these years. You plan to go back for good this time, don't you?"

Viviane straightened up, unable to speak as she wiped her eyes with the back of her hand, nodding her head. Reminding Grand of when she was a little girl, hating to cry because she cried so much at a young age. Reaching over to grab tissues, Grand sighed, *since Viviane's done some confessing, it's time for me to do the same.*

Swallowing a lot of pride, Grand said, "Baby girl, I'm afraid I'd better do some confessing, too. This is ALL my fault. I brought you home and started this whole mess with my selfishness. Please forgive me," she cried, reaching for Viviane's hand. "I wouldn't have done this if I'd known the pain it would cause you. Really honey, I've never wanted to hurt you like this... I really thought I was helping you."

"What do you mean?" Viviane asked, looking into her pained face.

"Last summer after a sermon by Pastor Winston, I came up with a plan to get you home to fix things with Cole and settle your differences. I've always felt the two of you were made for each other, and if you both talked you would be able to work everything out and get married." She averted her eyes, "So I pretended to be sick and started dropping hints to get you to come home." Tears began to fall down her lined cheeks as she struggled to finish, "I was thinking of my great grandkids instead of your happiness."

When Grand finished, she broke down crying earnestly. *I can't believe the pain my plan caused with not only heartache but shame my girl didn't deserve.*

Seeing Grand so upset, Viviane reached out to wrap her arms around the sobbing woman. "Grand, it's okay. Please don't cry. I've known for a while you weren't as sick as you claimed to be. It's okay."

Grand stopped crying, gasping a bit, "What do you mean? I've been working hard to keep this a secret." *I can't believe this, Viviane's only trying to make me feel better.*

Viviane laughed for the first time all day, "Grand, if you want someone to believe you're sick, don't get a two-year gym membership."

Grand looked sheepish, "Oh? I don't know... what you're talking about." She did have the grace to crack a smile when she said it.

"I picked up your mail almost every day in September, because you said it was too much of a walk. That's when I saw the bill arrive. Next time, have the gym bill you automatically and then it's only on your bank statement. I finally put two and two together when you got so much better after I started dating Cole."

Bowing her head, Grand thought, *I can't believe I was so careless after working so hard. I was so sure I was fooling her completely.*

"Plus, every morning I could smell the sausage you got up early to cook, which was why you were never hungry when I offered to make breakfast. You tried to cover the smell with spray, but that made it more noticeable."

Grand laughed loudly, "Well, I've got to have my morning sausage. It isn't breakfast without it."

Viviane burst out laughing, hugging her grandmother tightly. After a few minutes of childish laughter, they settled back down and remembered how this conversation started. Sobering up, Grand understood Viviane needed to leave, *and this time I'm determined to let her.* "It's almost noon, let me make you lunch. You'll still be in time to miss traffic."

Touched Grand was letting her leave without a fuss, Viviane quickly agreed. The two ladies went to the kitchen, since after the crying and confessing, Viviane was starving. They only talked of happy things, letting the past remain in the past for the meal. Later when Viviane hugged Grand goodbye, she told her, "I'm glad you know, even though it hurt you deeply."

Grand hugged her back fiercely, "Me too, honey. You can tell me anything even when it hurts, because I love you, okay? You're my baby girl." *It's going to be awhile before the hurt over the secret Viviane's been keeping from me goes away.*

With hugs and kisses, she sent her granddaughter back to Atlanta. Once she was hidden from view by the magnolia trees lining her yard, Grand closed the front door and slowly made her way up the stairs to her bedroom. *I have a strong desire to pray for the first time since June for God's direction about my little girl, since I hatched my plan for Viviane's future.*

Chapter Thirty-Four

"I'm glad you were able to come in." Cole said to the three family members standing inside his door. The Adams family had finished their meeting and were getting ready to leave.

"Oh, no Pastor Cole, thank you. We're just sorry it's taken so long. We've been in your office for over three hours." Noelle Adams said while extending her hand, standing at only five feet she had to crane her neck to smile up at Cole.

"Not a problem, Mrs. Adams. I'm just glad Maddy will get the help she needs. You and your husband have been wonderful," Cole said. *I was nervous how this would go, praying constantly, and when I think of God's amazing faithfulness in this delicate situation, I could burst with happiness.*

Maddy's parents agreed to meet with him after lunch and pulled Maddy out of school early when Cole strongly hinted it was important for all four of them to talk. He sat next to Maddy as the brave girl poured out her heart with her fears and secret eating habits to her parents. After the shock, they all discussed how to help Maddy get better.

Noelle said, "I knew something was off, because Maddy's been withdrawn and quiet." Brushing a stray gray hair out of her face, she hugged her daughter, "I'm glad you told us." Grateful this was coming out, Noelle thought, *Lord, I'm going gray with all the stress, but I trust you to work this out. You knew when Michael lost his job months ago this would happen. I trust You have a plan.*

Tomorrow, they would see a doctor to find a program that would let her stay in school and still get the help she needed. Now late in the afternoon, the Adams family would spend some family time together.

Michael Adams held out his large hand to Cole, "Please tell Viviane thank you for us. We'll be extending thanks ourselves but want her to know how grateful we are for her help."

Shaking Michael's hand, Cole remembered he was a former college football player, but admired his devotion to his family. Neither parent condemned Maddy but told her they loved her. When Maddy cried it was her fault, Michael scooped her up in his big arms, telling her it wasn't and he loved her more than any job in the world.

Everyone moved to the front office area where Mrs. Owens was manning the phones. Cole stopped at her desk to see if he missed any messages. *I'm hoping to hear I missed a call from Viviane, and we can go out for a late dinner.*

About to ask for his messages, he heard in the midst of chatter Grand's authoritative voice, "Cole, we need to talk."

He turned to see an immaculately dressed Grand, but with red rimmed eyes that couldn't be hidden with makeup. As he walked over, Mrs. Misty bluntly said, "I've told Mrs. Delia Anne you have a very important meeting at four and don't have time to speak with her, but she's insisting."

Misty was cold toward Delia Anne, because she heard the gossip about Viviane. She spent the entire morning thinking, *Poor Cole taken in by a girl with so many problems. It's sad. Maybe Hillary would make a better wife, at least she ate.*

Cole didn't understand why Grand was upset or why Mrs. Misty was taking her bad mood out on Grand. *Something's very wrong.* "I canceled my 4 o'clock when I realized my meeting would be longer than expected." He waved for Grand to follow him to his office, ignoring Mrs. Misty's shocked look.

Misty snapped her mouth shut, *I can't believe he cancelled his appointment without telling me. I don't understand what's happening with that young man*, she thought blatantly staring as he walked past, shrugging his shoulders.

Grand didn't speak, the only noise came from her heeled footsteps clipping softly on the floor. Her silence worried him, but he held his curiosity until they reached the privacy of his office. He motioned for her to sit down in a comfortable chair, shutting the door before he sat down opposite her.

When she continued to stare, he cleared his throat, "I had... uh... a family meeting, and I haven't had a chance to put the chairs back in order. I should mention to Pastor Winston I need a bigger office." He expected her to comment or at least smile, but she only stared at her shoes.

Grand putting two and two together thinking, *it's probably Maddy with the eating disorder. Please God help heal them during the difficult road ahead.*

Unable to wait any longer, worried Viviane had been in a horrible accident, Cole asked, "What's happened? Is Viviane okay?" He was almost afraid of the answer, because at the mention Viviane's name, Grand closed her eyes as a tear slipped down her cheek.

Taking a deep breath, she finally spoke, "Cole, I want you to know I've always thought of you like a son. I felt the two of you had something special, and if forced to spend some time together you'd work out your differences."

A little thrown off by her speech, he blurted out, "Is Viviane hurt? Was there an accident?"

Realizing he was in anguish worried about Viviane's safety, she quickly reassured him. "No, she's fine. She called ten minutes ago to tell me she arrived home safely." She patted his knee, but quickly pulled her hand back.

After much prayer and begging God for forgiveness, her anger at him had finally melted away. Anger at Lauren was a different story, but she had several days before she had face her. *Now my only focus is what's best for Viviane. Cole needs to know what's going on and that she won't be coming back.*

"This afternoon Viviane told me about her eating disorder. We spent several hours talking and I confessed about my plan to get you two back together."

Relief coursed through Cole, *Obviously she's upset learning about Viviane's eating disorder after so long.* "I'm glad she finally told you. I know what a shock it can be finding out such a big secret."

"I don't think you understand," Grand said shaking her head, "There's a lot more I need to tell you." She told Cole about coming home early to find Viviane in a rush to leave, because the church found out about her eating disorder and rumors of them making out on the trip.

Cole rashly spoke out, interrupting, "But that isn't true. We weren't making out on the trip. We kissed once after Viviane told me about the girl with the eating disorder, because I was so proud God used her pain to help one of my kids. We've done absolutely nothing to be ashamed of."

A little glimmer of hope blossomed in Grand's chest, and she thought, *I've placed this whole situation in God's hands. I've learned my lesson and God's the only one who can fix this.* "Lauren Blake confronted her at my home and told her the church wanted her to walk away from you and that you've been hiding your relationship."

Anger burned in Cole's chest, clenching his fists he thought, *I can't believe the gall of that woman! She has no right.* Unclenching his fist, he felt shame was over him, *have I been hiding our relationship? Am I still questioning whether Vee would make a good pastor's wife?*

Looking at Grand, he knew his answer, *no. I love Vee, Lord. Please show me how to fix this, because only You can.* "I can see why Viviane thought the worst. I don't deserve her forgiveness." He had tears in his eyes when he said, "I want you to know I love your granddaughter. I'm ashamed for what I said all those years ago and I want to make it up to her."

Thrilled to hear him say that Grand was unsure where he was going, but still held onto a bit of hope. *Please let Viviane be wrong about him, Lord.*

He continued, "I let fear of what people would say about me dating at my age keep me from treating her the way she deserves to be treated. Maybe if I had been more open about our relationship, the gossip about her eating disorder wouldn't be so bad."

Grand laid her hand gently on his knee, "Cole from what I've been able to discover, most of the gossip implies she's still actively fighting an eating disorder. I understand people not wanting you to marry someone who hasn't dealt with it, but this gossip is all lies."

Cole reached for Grand's hand squeezing it gently, "I feel the church needs a reminder about God's unconditional love and restoring grace." He was thoughtful for a moment, *Lord, show me what to do. Viviane doesn't deserve the mean, vindictive gossip going around.*

The door to Cole's office opened slightly as Pastor Winston poked his head through, "I knocked, but don't think you heard me." He saw Delia Anne, and quickly said, "Sorry, I didn't know you were in a meeting. I wanted to let you know I'd be in my office the rest of the afternoon if you wanted to talk about Sunday's sermon."

Cole smiled, *God answered my prayer with Pastor Winston's timely reminder. With everything going on, I forgot this Sunday was youth takeover day. I was planning something different for my sermon, but I seem to have some new ideas based on recent events.*

"Thank you, Pastor Winston. I'll stop by soon. We've got several things to discuss."

Pastor Winston nodded, *I'm not sure what's going on. Delia Anne looks upset, but Cole's smile makes me think everything will be okay, because when Cole spoke with such authority, Delia Anne looked up with a slow smile. Maybe things are looking up for my single youth minister?* He thought, *only God knows.*

Cole turned to Grand after the pastor left, "Do you think you could convince Viviane to come Sunday? I'd really like for her to be there."

Grand shook her head, *I pray you've got a plan that's truly inspired by God, unlike mine.* "I don't know. What are you up to?"

"Lots of things Grand, but don't worry. I believe God's given me a great idea for Sunday's sermon. It would mean a lot to the kids, especially Maddy if Vee came. I know those kids care for her, eating disorder or not. I don't care what the gossips say, those kids care."

"I'll try. Just pray God helps me convince her."

"Oh believe me, I will." Cole stood up and helped Grand to her feet, before hugging her goodbye. He sat down at his desk to make some notes for his new sermon, feeling peace steal over his heart. Furiously scribbling on a yellow legal pad, he prayed out loud, "Lord, show me what to do. I don't want to make a mess of this, not with Viviane, the youth group, or the congregation." He needed a clear idea before he met with Pastor Winston.

Chapter Thirty-Five

Viviane riffled through her camera bag looking for an extra memory card. The wedding shoot was almost over, but her card needed to be changed, before the couple moved to the limo on the way to their honeymoon. "Finally," she said under her breath, quickly flipping over her camera. *I can't mess this up.*

Kathie was taking pictures as well, and between them, they had taken over four thousand shots since five am. A morning wedding, the couple said their vows at eleven and the reception was held at one. The wedding party was the largest she had ever shot with ten bridesmaids and matching groomsmen. The bride had a large, extended family and all were expected to be involved.

Viviane had been thinking of her own wedding day the past few months, deciding a small outdoor wedding would be perfect, since her family was so small. There would be no sides, everyone would sit where they could have the best view of the couple. Tears started sliding down her cheeks, she moved to brush them away quickly. *I'm afraid if I start crying I won't stop. Remember it's over with Cole for good this time. I'm not a naïve teenager anymore.*

"Ready Viviane? They'll come down the stairs in three minutes." Kathie said walking up cautiously. She watched Viviane from across the ballroom, upset and shaken and knew it was because of Cole.

Viviane didn't answer but put her camera around her neck to follow Kathie to the front of the large plantation house. As Kathie moved to the front stairway, Viviane volunteered to shoot outside where the guests were waiting for the newlyweds. She didn't wait for a reply but positioned herself near the limo decorated with cans and streamers. Seeing the guests lined up, excited to throw rose petals at the happy couple, made her want to sit down and cry. *I've never had so much trouble shooting a wedding before and it doesn't help the groom looks a little like Cole with his brown hair streaked with blonde from the sun.*

Viviane sent up another prayer for strength to get through this last part for at least the millionth time. She pleaded with God to heal the wound she felt growing at the thought she would never walk down the aisle to Cole. *This ending's so much worse, because now I know what I'm missing.*

A loud cheer brought her attention to the beautiful bride arm in arm with her new husband. She spent the next thirty minutes doing justice to their special day with stunning photos for them to cherish in the album she and Kathie would make. Taking the final shot, she quietly snuck inside to the spare bedroom to pack up.

The party was still in full swing downstairs, but Viviane closed off her mind to focus solely putting away the cameras, computer, and other equipment. She was so intent on her work, she didn't hear Kathie until she felt a comforting hand on her shoulder. "Are you okay, Viv?"

Viviane jumped, almost dropping the lens she carried. "I'm fine Kat, just focused on putting this up." She tried to sound calm but was pretty sure she failed.

Kathie didn't reply, *I know her too well not to know she's really upset.*

When Viviane came into the office Thursday, she confided about the horrible ending with Cole and the gossip going around the church. They talked for hours as Viviane cried in her arms over losing the man she loved. *I understand why she ran and think it all stinks!* As she comforted her, Kathie thought, *those church ladies should be horsewhipped!*

Finishing the last of the packing, Kathie knew now wasn't the best time and prayed God would intervene. "Are you headed back to Atlanta?" Kathie asked, struggling to carry several heavy bags to her SUV. *I don't want Viv holed up alone in her apartment and become even more depressed.*

Viviane ducked her head, and said quickly, "No, I'm actually leaving for Cartersville."

"Cartersville!" Kathie shouted, dropping an equipment bag, thankfully it was heavily padded. "I don't understand. I thought you weren't going back and that Grand understood your need to stay away?"

Viviane carefully set down the bags she carried, "I got a call from Maddy late last night. The youth have a special service Sunday and she wants me to be there." *I couldn't say no after she begged. I couldn't bear to disappoint her.* "Her family's invited Grand and I for lunch after the church service. Her grandmother and mine are best friends and I couldn't say no."

Kathie heard the plea for understanding, and sat her bags next to Viviane, before she reached out to hug her, "Honey, I understand, but what about the church gossip and seeing Cole?"

Viviane sighed, but said with firmness in her voice, "I told Grand when she asked the same thing that I'm going with my head held high." *I really hope I'll be able to pull it off by Sunday.* "I don't have anything to be ashamed of, not my past or my relationship with Cole. We did nothing wrong," Viviane's voice faltered when she added, "whether Cole agrees or not."

Grand was excited when Viviane told her she would be going to both church and the picnic, almost going overboard, and Grand seemed to realize it too, because she quickly changed the subject to how the rehearsal dinner went. *I thought Grand might've forgotten Cole and I are really over, but she agreed I didn't need to be with someone who was ashamed of me.*

"I'll keep all of this in my prayers as always. I care for you, so don't forget I'm here."

The two women hugged, and then Viviane picked up her bags, trudging over to her car. She stowed her equipment in the trunk before leaving for the interstate. *It's mid-afternoon, but I'm tired since I was up early after getting in late last night from the rehearsal dinner. That's why I want nothing more than to crawl into my bed at Grand's, and it has nothing to do with being depressed*, she told herself. *I'm just taking a nap.*

She drove listening to a local radio station, unable to listen to her usual music which only reminded her of the perfect date with Cole. For the first time in Viviane's life, she knew the top five songs playing on the radio. Viviane frowned the whole drive, she hated every single one of them.

Grand kneaded dough, covered in flour up to her elbows thinking she should let it rise another thirty minutes. Even though it was cool outside, she had the windows open in the kitchen, because it was so warm from baking all afternoon. When Viviane pulled up a little after five, the poor girl practically asleep on her feet when she walked through the front door carrying thirty pounds of equipment.

Wiping off some perspiration mixed with a little flour, Grand moved the dough into baking pans, before walking to the sink to wash dishes. After she called Cole to let him know Viviane was upstairs and would be there tomorrow, she hoped he would tell her more of his plan. *Truth be told, I'm not exactly sure he plans to get Viviane back. All he said was he loved her and she didn't deserve to be treated badly over her past.*

Grand paused washing the dishes to wipe a stray tear, *learning about Viviane's eating disorder still hurts. To think of my baby girl hurting all these years in an effort to keep from hurting me. That's what really upsets me,* Grand thought clenching a towel, *knowing how long Viviane's hurt alone, feeling she couldn't tell me.*

She sent up a prayer of thanks Viviane had been able to help Maddy. The main reason they were going over for lunch was for the Adams family to personally thank Viviane. When Jill called Thursday with the invitation, Grand mentioned it casually to Viviane, but she was understandably reluctant and didn't want to pressure her. *I put it in God's hands and He worked it out so I didn't even have to ask again. I know she's hurting, but I know God loves her even more than I do and that's a whole lot.*

Cole hung up the phone with Grand while seated in his favorite chair where he spent most of the day praying and prepping for his sermon tomorrow. He felt momentary triumph, followed quickly by fear. *I can't tell myself it's just another Sunday, because this one's more important than all of the others.*

Moses came up to him with her leash and dropped it in his lap. Cole smiled at his dog wagging her tail in anticipation of a run. He walked her quickly this morning and promised her a run later. He didn't know if she understood or if she was just tired of waiting, but either way Cole decided to keep his promise.

"Okay, girl. Let me get my shoes and we'll go running," he said scratching her ears.

Ready to go a moment later, Cole put the leash on a jumping Moses and opened the front door. She jerked him outside, and he yelled, "Slow down a second, Mo. Wait for me to get down the porch."

Gripping the leash tighter, Cole locked the front door and set off on a slow jog toward his parents' place. He hadn't talked to them about everything that had happened this week. Twenty minutes into his run, he cut through his parent's backyard to see them sitting on the screened porch eating dinner.

When his mom looked up to see him, she waved before moving inside. By the time she was back with another plate, Cole was walking up the porch steps. "Hi honey. I thought you'd show up eventually. Want some dinner?"

Cole produced a huge grin as he plopped on the comfortable porch chair, "Thanks Mom. I'm hungry, I haven't eaten much today."

Carson laughed at his son, and offered to get Moses water, since this wasn't the first time he had run over around a meal time. As the family settled back down, Cole started to eat, while his parents lingered over coffee. They talked about the youth trip in greater detail than what Cole mentioned briefly on the phone late Tuesday night.

As Cole talked about how much work the kids did and how well Viviane fit in with everyone, Lynn became quiet listening to him say Viviane's name every other word. *I'm glad the trip went well, but I want to hear what happened after the trip.*

Lynn glanced at her husband, catching his eye with a see-I-told-you look he knew very well. *I've been getting phone calls from several concerned church ladies to discuss Viviane and Cole. I've wanted to take out most of the church for hurting Viviane and my son.*

Carson told her to politely tell the callers to mind their own business, and she spent the past few days praying she wouldn't have to throttle her son for being an idiot, along with certain meddling church ladies.

Cole cleared his throat when he noticed his parents sharing a look that both he and his brother knew very well. "I assume you've heard the gossip about Viviane."

Carson nodded, but Lynn muttered, "Yes, we have." She continued in her head, *and we want to know what you're going to do about it?!?*

Cole told them Viviane's whole story and couldn't help seeing the concern on his dad's face or tears in his mom's eyes. *I'm grateful my parents care about her almost as much as I do.*

"I found out about the gossip when Grand came to me Wednesday to say Lauren Blake went to Grand's house to confront Viviane and tell her to leave Cartersville and me alone."

Lynn dropped her coffee mug, and as it spilled coffee all over the table, she angrily pounded a napkin down to clean up. Cole smiled, "Glad to know we're all of the same opinion. Viviane will be in church tomorrow and I hope to resolve this once and for all."

"Good." Lynn said, wiping up the last of the coffee. "I've always loved that girl, and I'm glad you've finally come to your senses and are going to do what you should've done years ago."

Carson put his hand on Lynn to calm her down, and said to Cole, "What your Mom's trying to say is we both agree the church has treated her unfairly for years. We support you both, whatever your decision."

"Carson West that's not what I meant..." Lynn spewed, pausing she blushed, "not completely anyway." *I can't let my temper get the best of me.*

Cole laughed, *I love these people dearly. They've set a wonderful example of what a loving, caring marriage should look like. Not easy, but worth the effort you put in.*

"I understand what you mean Mom. I've been planning for several days and praying for God's guidance. I guess the reason I'm here is to ask for your blessing and prayers for tomorrow."

Lynn stopped glaring at her husband to look at Cole and missed the wink he sent his son. "Of course, Cole. We support you on this."

Carson reached across the table to grab his son's hand, "We always pray for you, but will pray especially hard about tomorrow."

The three of them prayed, before Cole finished his meal, and Cole felt peace fill him once again. The talk turned to more general topics for which Cole was thankful. He still needed to finalize his sermon and look through the pictures Viviane sent for the slideshow of the youth trip. *I haven't been able to look at them until I knew whether or not she'd be there tomorrow.* Later when Cole left his parents place and took Moses home, he thought, *I've got a busy evening planned, and a lot of prep for tomorrow's big day.*

Chapter Thirty-Six

Viviane woke up early but didn't know if it was because she went to bed so early yesterday or was nervous about today. When she couldn't fall back asleep, she pulled her Bible off the nightstand for her devotion from the book of Joshua, chapter one verses 7-9: "Be strong and very courageous. Be careful to obey all the law my servant Moses gave you; do not turn from it to the right or to the left, that you may be successful wherever you go. Keep this Book of the Law always on your lips; meditate on it day and night, so that you may be careful to do everything written in it. Then you will be prosperous and successful. Have I not commanded you? Be strong and courageous. Do not be afraid; do not be discouraged for the Lord your God will be with you wherever you go."

Feeling more at peace, Viviane thought, *as long as I follow God's commands, no one will succeed against the plans God has for me. God's prepared a path for me to follow and my only job is to walk it out to the best of my ability. God will give me strength as I go along.* As she prayed, she was grateful for Godly timed devotions when you needed them most.

Turning on the Christian radio station, she took her time getting ready, spending more time singing than actually getting dressed. Wearing one of her favorite artsy outfits, a dark green turtleneck paired with a soft, tan leather skirt and riding boots, she rushed downstairs to beat Grand in making breakfast.

She wasn't too surprised to find Grand already in the kitchen preparing a simple meal after she spent most of yesterday baking bread and a complicated dessert to take to the Adams' lunch. A habit her mother ingrained in her from an early age.

Finished with breakfast much too soon, Viviane found herself driving them to church, her palms sweaty on the steering wheel. She walked into class holding onto Grand, forcing herself to hold her head up high. Grand timed it so they would be a few minutes late, running back into the house to grab her Bible at the last minute.

Viviane wondered if Grace heard the gossip about her and regretted she would learn about it that way. *I pray she understands and gives me a chance to explain.*

Barely clearing the door, Viviane saw everyone in her class standing in a circle waiting for them. Each of the ladies had big smiles on their faces and all moved in to hug her. Tears in Viviane's eyes, Grace was the first to walk up and hug her, while she said, "Welcome my friend. I'm glad you're here today."

She stepped back to allow Sharon, Zoe and other ladies a chance to hug her. Grand stood near beaming, *I'm glad I joined this class of wonderful ladies. They've really banded together to help someone in need of grace and love.*

When Grace called early Saturday to ask if Viviane would be here, Grand was nervous, knowing Grace must have heard the gossip. Grace only asked if she needed to be praying for Viviane to get help, not once condemning her. Grand happily told her Viviane conquered the eating disorder with God's help years ago and it was only mean gossip being spread to keep Viviane away from Cole. Grace didn't say anything more, and Grand thought she knew who led the angry mob.

Laughing, one of the women said, "Let Viviane sit."

After everyone was seated, Grace said, "Let's pray ladies." Bowing her head, Grace prayed, "Lord, thank you for bring us together this morning. Thank you for the sweet friend we've found in Viviane and for the caring ladies in this class, who when they heard the gossip called to ask how to help. Each of them chose to believe in Viviane and rally around her in a united front. Show us how to continue to lift one another up. Amen."

Viviane was touched by Grace's prayer and these special ladies who were supporting her, quickly wiping away tears, as Grace looked up at Viviane to say, "The ladies and I wanted to let you know we love you, support you, and are glad you're a part of our class."

The other ladies nodded as Grace continued, "Everyone chipped in for a special gift to remind you how special you are to us and more importantly to God." Reaching down, she pulled out a large, beautifully wrapped box from behind her chair and held it out to Viviane.

Viviane grabbed it, smiling at the ladies, "You didn't have to do anything."

Sharon smiled, "Think of it as a very long overdue welcome to our class gift."

Viviane opened the card to find it signed by everyone with notes of love and encouragement. Tears began to fall down her cheeks as she continued opening the gift. Pulling the wrapping off, she found a canvas print of one of her sunset photos from the field near Grand's house with a quote in elegant script. One of the ladies piped up, "Read it out loud. We debated long and hard, almost starting a fist fight." The ladies giggled, because it was partly true.

Viviane smiled through her tears, and read, "Hardships often prepare ordinary people for extraordinary destiny. C.S. Lewis."

Viviane set the canvas in her lap as Grand handed her tissue to wipe her eyes.

Zoe smiled at her and said, "The idea was Sharon's and we got together to select a photo and quote." Smiling broadly, Zoe told Viviane, "But I found the quote everyone finally agreed on, and Grace put it together."

Viviane couldn't ever remember being so touched by a gift. *In a very sweet gesture, the ladies not only showed support, but also affirmed God's in control of my life. I've prayed God would use my pain to help others. I saw a glimpse of that last week, but it touches my heart these special women thought the same thing.*

"Thank you everyone for this thoughtful gift! I promise it will always be with me, and I'll never forget your kindness. I'm thankful God sent me all of you. I know I'm loved."

Everyone had tears in their eyes when Viviane stood to hug each lady, saying a special word to each of them. When she came to Grace, Viviane threw her arms around her in a big hug, "Thank you my friend."

Grace held on tightly, "You're very welcome. We wanted you to know we support you and aren't listening to the mean-spirited people. We love you, and I consider you a dear friend."

Recognizing a special bond, Viviane easily said, "I feel the exact same way."

The two ladies spoke a few minutes more and everyone spent the rest of class talking. No one spoke about the gossip but decided to practice what God spoke in Ecclesiastes 4:12. "Though one may be overpowered, two can defend themselves. A cord of three strands is not quickly broken." It was from the lesson Grace taught last Sunday, and each lady remembered it when the gossip started.

When it was time for the service, Viviane wasn't worried about facing anyone. *I feel support from God and my friends, and know I'll get through the service with my head held high.*

Cole wasn't feeling calm, nervously flipping the worksheets he needed to hand out when the middle school boys finished staggering in for class. As the last boy sat down, he asked himself, *Can I make it through this half hour without falling apart?*

Thankfully it would be a short class, because the students had to set up for service. He had been calm since his early morning prayer time until he looked at the clock and realized Viviane would be arriving any moment.

He was worried about Viviane in her Sunday school class but knew Grace wouldn't let anyone be mean to her. The feisty redhead wouldn't allow it, she protected her friends fiercely. Vee would be fine, and sending up his millionth prayer, before turning his focus on the eleven middle school boys. *If I don't keep a watchful eye on them, they'll run amok and I'll have a real problem on my hands. I've never forgotten a substitute last year missed two of the boys sneaking out to flood the bathroom.* Clearing his throat, he began to tell an animated story of Joshua and the walls of Jericho tumbling down.

Chapter Thirty-Seven

The service was going extremely well, everyone was on their feet singing and clapping along as the kids sang their hearts out. It reminded Cole of why he became a youth pastor. The teens performed the skit during the offering with only one kid forgetting his line, but the girl next to him loudly whispered it to him, much to the amusement of everyone. Cole felt the pride radiating from both him and the crowd.

In just a few moments, the last song would end and it would be his turn to deliver the sermon. Cole prayed for guidance as Sara finished her song. He stood up to thank the kids for a great job as the congregation applauded the youth.

After the noise settled down, Cole cleared his throat with one last plea for God's will and asked everyone to turn to Joshua 6:20. Opening his Bible, he read, "When the trumpets sounded, the army shouted and at the sound of the trumpet, when the men gave a loud shout, the wall collapsed; so, everyone charged straight in, and they took the city."

Cole ignored the strange looks, *I've got a feeling people are expecting me to deal with the Viviane issue from the pulpit. Won't they be surprised how God's led me to preach?*

"God spoke only to Joshua, telling him the Israelites would march around the city, once a day for six days with the only noise coming from the trumpets, not the voices of men. On the seventh day, they would march around the city walls six times, before shouting on the seventh march. Can you imagine what was going through Joshua's mind, not just the strange request from God, but wondering how to convince his army to walk around in silence behind the Ark and musicians?"

Everyone was focused on Cole's message, Viviane sitting in her normal spot off to the side was wedged between Grace and Grand. They were mostly ignored by the church with only a handful of people greeting them. Viviane was grateful Cole's parents were the first to hug her and wish her a good morning.

Cole continued, "I've always found it funny Joshua didn't tell his army anything, only to march around the city without making any noise until he gave them permission to shout. I would imagine the men thought their leader had lost it. Many of them probably wondered when they would get to use the swords they had been carrying around for a long time. As you know, the men followed Joshua's orders and the wall came down with a shout on the seventh day, after the seventh trip around."

Viviane was having trouble focusing on Cole's words as she remembered the cold reception she received. *I was only able not to run because of all the ways God's shown love to me today. Plus, Maddy came running down from the choir loft to hug me, so excited I had shown up.* Talking nonstop until the service began, Viviane hugged Maddy and was glad she came. It helped when Jill Adams' family hugged her and sat down behind her next to Cole's parents forming a hedge of protection.

Holding onto the warm feeling, she was intrigued with Cole's story. *He's right, I always thought it was weird.*

Viviane smiled as Cole made the same point, "I want you to consider something. Joshua didn't tell his army when to shout until just before it was time, even though God told him." Cole closed his Bible and leaned back to look at the congregation. "Many times, God tells us things to do, clearly with precise directions, sometimes He speaks quietly through the Bible, or in Biblical times through a prophet, but most of the time in our daily walk with God, we don't hear from Him as loudly as we'd like and feel His guiding hand less than we want."

Cole paused as he focused his thoughts, "When I was called into ministry, I was a senior in high school, but extremely unaware of where God was leading. When I finally decided to go to school to be a pastor and embrace the life God called me to, I decided He meant for me to do it alone. The problem was I decided what God wanted without asking or waiting for an answer. I used the fancy title of minister to hurt someone I loved, judging her worth by what I felt God called me to do, versus what He called her to do."

Cole's microphone had to be turned up a bit, because his voice dropped low when he laid his guilt before a proven judgmental crowd. "God used an unconventional way of defeating Jericho to teach His people that He and He alone will be victorious. This simple Sunday school lesson taught me God does this to teach us to rely on only Him.

Cole saw out of the corner of his eye, Pastor Winston seated by Pastor Jennings sitting off to the side. Both men were nodding in approval, allowing Cole to continue, his voice steady once again, "A few months ago, I was given the chance to mend a wonderful friendship with someone I hurt with my thoughtlessness, but even after we mended our relationship, I never stood up and told anyone it was my fault we broke up, my actions not hers. I was so caught up in being a perfect minister, I forgot how imperfect I truly am. It's a lesson I fail, time and time again."

Cole tried to see Viviane in the crowd but couldn't and knew it was time to come clean. "I've spent the past few months happy as I've ever been. I've been falling back in love." Cole could see Pastor Winston give him a thumb up sign. "It's a deeper, more mature love with the only woman I've ever asked to marry me. Though, I should mention I proposed when we were fifteen and she made the most awesome catch at my family's annual Christmas football game." He chuckled, "A catch that's still legendary in our family."

Silent no longer, Cole heard whispers, but continued not missing a beat, "I've heard the gossip spread about a wonderful, kind, and thoughtful woman who didn't deserve the slander being spoken about her. It was said to hurt, and as Christians we're called to be above such things, to obey God and lift each other up in our daily struggle on Earth. I want to be the first to apologize, not only to her, but also to anyone else I've used religion as a way to justify any words that criticized, judged or wounded."

Smiling because he meant every word, he continued, "I know it's easy to question why God does things in a strange way, but I've found many times it's because it's the only way to get our attention. I don't judge anyone for their comments the past week, because I'm the last person to say I'm perfect..." Cole paused, looking at his hands before lifting his face to where he knew Viviane was sitting. "I want everyone to know the woman I love is healthy, happy and my ideal woman in every way. The two of us are a perfect example of God's restoring grace."

Cole was unsure how this statement would go over, but when he finished, many people began to clap. Cole smiled graciously to the cheers and thunderous applause. After the noise died down, he raised his hand and said, "Today is the youth celebration day and we've prepared a slideshow of photos from the youth trip. We went to a small community in Alabama to help others in need. Your kids worked hard to show Christ's love and I hope you get a small glimpse of their efforts." Smiling broadly, his chest puffed out, Cole said, "On a side note, my lovely girlfriend took most of these pictures. I'm very proud of the work she put in and I think you'll be able to glimpse a small part of her immense talent."

Cole signaled the audio-visual team to start the slideshow as the youth handed out fliers with the upcoming youth events. The congregation watched the six-minute slideshow, and Cole saw many people were impressed.

I was overwhelmed with the work Viviane sent Friday. She put in a lot of extra work, adding text to detail the kid's work on the trip. I had a hard time choosing between the 300 photos she took. I know she did the editing after the talk with Mrs. Blake, which only proves how amazing Vee is to put in so much time and effort for the kids after the way she was treated.

Viviane divided them up by kid to send copies to the families, which was a good thing because as soon as the slideshow was over, he was smothered by parents asking for copies. When Cole finally made his way to the back of the sanctuary, he didn't see Viviane but knew she was around because a huge crowd descended on her after the slideshow was over.

Cole felt a large hand clamp down on his shoulder, "What a great service. The kids did awesome."

Cole turned to see the senior pastors standing behind him. "Thank you. I'm very proud of them."

They talked a few moments, and both pastors congratulated him on a well-timed sermon. Cole extended his hand to Pastor Jennings before he walked away and then turned to hug Pastor Winston. "Thank you, sir for your advice and guidance. I couldn't have done this without your blessing."

"It was the right words for the right time. You handled it very well without judgment or anger. We can't let gossip stand, because it harms churches and people. Plus, it isn't good to have rumors about a future Pastor's wife floating around." Pastor Winston winked at Cole and walked away as Grand came strolling over. *She looks like a woman on a mission.*

"Cole," Grand said hugging him, "I just found out from Jill you're invited to the Adams' for lunch!"

"Umm... yes they invited me Wednesday."

Grand nodded, "Good, I think you should take Viviane. I've got to go home and pick up food. I told Jill, I'd come early and help set up."

Cole watched Grand, a sly grin spreading across his face, "Now Grand, I thought you'd given up on matchmaking?"

Grand smiled, before hugging Cole, "It isn't match making, it's getting a ride for my granddaughter." Hands on her hips, she asked, "Do you want to drive her or not?"

Cole raised his hands in surrender, "Okay, okay. It's the least I can do." *It will actually make things easier.*

"I'll tell her. See you soon."

Grand waved goodbye as another family walked up. After he finished speaking to the last family, the sanctuary was empty. He decided to walk to his office and hoped he would see Viviane along the way.

Cole carried a box of props and turned the door knob when he heard a noise behind him. He turned to see Viviane standing shyly in the hallway. Cole smiled thinking, *she looks beautiful wearing an outfit that fits her creative personality. Wearing green has to be a good sign, Lord.*

"Grand said you're taking me to the Adams' lunch?"

He heard the shyness in her voice, "Yes, Grand said she needed to help Mrs. Jill set up. Is that okay?" Cole looked deep into her eyes wanting to see her honest answer.

"Yes. Thank you for the ride."

"You're welcome, Vee." They stood in his office staring at each other, unsure what to say.

Cole fumbled for his keys as he stuttered out, "I need to run home and walk Moses. If it doesn't look like rain, I'll bring her. We've had youth cookouts at their place and Moses loves their big yard. Jill's grandkids adore her."

Ignoring Cole's clumsiness, Viviane replied, "I bet they do, Moses seems to be good with kids. She loved your nieces when they came for Christmas."

"If it isn't raining, she'll play outside with them." Cole grabbed his bag and moved to lock his door. Viviane moved out of the way as Cole said, "Otherwise, she'll sit on the porch glaring at me for bringing her out in the rain."

Viviane laughed as they walked to the car, reminding him of September when they were getting ready for the auction. *So much has happened in just a few months.*

Cole opened the car door and neither talked, just sitting in comfortable silence. Closer to the house, Viviane asked, "Do you usually have to walk Moses midday?"

Keeping his eyes on the road, Cole said, "No, but I was up early this morning and she didn't get a walk, I just let her out for a few minutes."

"Oh, that's nice."

Viviane stared out the window, *I don't know why I'm having such a hard time when I was so touched by his words. When he finished his sermon, I wanted to run up and throw my arms around him, but this Sunday was to highlight the youth group and I want that thought clearly in everyone's mind.* Adjusting in her seat, she mused, *I wanted to talk to him alone, but I'm unable to say anything on my heart and feel bad since he clearly laid his heart out in front of the whole church!*

When Cole pulled into his driveway, he parked by the front door and helped Viviane. "Please come in? We have some time before we need to be at the Adams'." Cole fumbled with his tie, nervous about what he planned for after lunch, being moved up. *This will be better, a perfect moment was what I had planned.*

Viviane nodded, still not trusting herself to speak.

When they walked through the front door, she was immediately pounced on by an excited Moses. "Hi, Mo! How are you girl?"

Viviane petted the lab, and Cole loved watching his favorite girls. *I've been going over what to say for weeks, and suddenly I'm extremely nervous. I hope Mo does her part like we've practiced.*

Viviane must have felt his nerves, because she looked up at him, smiling slightly, worry in her eyes. She saw him standing farther back, next to the fireplace with a funny look on his face. She started to ask him what was wrong, when she saw the photos hanging over the mantle.

"Cole?" Ignoring Moses, she walked over to the large blue-gray slate fireplace in the living room. She didn't speak again but moved to within inches of the mantle where two large photographs in matching dark wood frames showed the same view of downtown Cartersville.

The first was taken at sunset, the second at dawn and it amazed her seeing them side by side how it was almost the same photograph. A storefront or two was different, a few more cars at sunset than dawn, but otherwise it was the exact same view of the shops under the bridge.

"Cole, I know the second photo was the one sold at the auction that I took in September. I didn't know you bought it..." Cole only nodded as Viviane continued to point, "But the other one...it's..."

"The one you took on our very first date," Cole finished for her. "With the first camera Grand bought you as an early Christmas present. I saved the photo you gave me. You were so proud of your first professional looking photo."

Viviane stood there stunned. *I can't believe he has had both photos this whole time.* "I was here months ago, why haven't I seen them before?"

Cole looked a little shy as he ducked his head, "When I saw the photo in the auction, I knew I had to have it. It was the twin to the first one. I didn't think you realized you'd taken two similar photos. I had the first one matted like the auction photo, but I couldn't bring myself to hang them."

While Viviane was focused on the photograph, Cole motioned to Moses to follow him. He handed the lab a bouquet of calla lilies, which Moses held carefully in her mouth. Cole whispered to Moses, "Go to Vee, girl."

Moses padded softly to Viviane and brushed the back of her knee with the flowers. Viviane looked down and said while bending down, "What have you got Mo?"

Moses wagging her tail and released the flowers into Viviane's hands.

Viviane stood back up and looked at Cole expectantly as he moved forward speaking, "I didn't know where we stood, or how I felt when I first bought that photo and I couldn't hang them up until I knew."

"Knew what?"

"That I loved you and wanted to marry you."

Cole moved closer taking her hands, "Viviane, I love you and have loved you since you took that photo fifteen years ago. I'm sorry I've been such a jerk for the last few years, but now I realized how truly special, loving, kind, amazing, and perfect for me you truly are."

Cole got down on one knee, "Elizabeth Viviane Stanton-Mays will you marry me and be my wife... as a partner in both my life and ministry for the rest of our lives?"

Cole pulled out a small box from his pants pocket, and Viviane's eyes grew large with wonder when he revealed an elegant emerald and diamond engagement ring.

Tears welled up in Viviane's eyes, as she nodded her head yes and held out her left hand. Cole slipped the ring onto her finger and she felt the tears fall. She threw her arms around him saying yes over and over.

"Oh, Cole it's beautiful. I've never seen anything like it."

He held onto her swinging her around the living room. He happily told her, "I found it at an antique jewelry store several months ago. I wanted to get you something unique that fit your style and personality. I saw this and immediately thought of you. Mo and I have been practicing the flower trick for weeks."

Viviane held onto him and could see her photographs over his shoulder. *It's a wonderful way to start a new beginning to our lives. Grand will be over the moon her plan worked.* "They'll be no living with Grand now, she's been working toward this from the very beginning."

He laughed, holding onto Viviane, "Well, let's go tell her the happy news! Besides, soon you'll be living with me and that's what Grand wanted the whole time... the two of us married and happy!"

Cole felt like shouting to the whole world, Viviane was his, now and forever. The three of them, including Moses walked to his car. Grand wouldn't be the only one celebrating their upcoming wedding, the Adams' clan and the whole church would celebrate this wonderful news!

The End

Dear Reader,

Thank you for taking the time to read my first novel in the Grace Series. I hope you enjoyed Viviane's story and learned more about God's restoring grace. His grace is never ending and has inspired me to write more stories for this series.

Be sure to check out Hillary Blake's story in Accepting Grace coming in September, followed by Bailey Evan's story in Trusting Grace coming in October.

I'm enjoying writing this series so much, I have even more characters I'm writing about. Be sure to check out my website to keep up with future novels.

I love to hear from my readers and would enjoy getting to know you better. Please feel free to reach out to me!

www.acboulier.com
www.facebook.com/acboulier
twitter.com/acboulier
www.instagram.com/acboulier_author
www.pinterest.com/acboulier

Just a note about SPLASH Bartow:
Splash started in 2008 when a group of local youth pastors asked what if? What if we started teaching our kids about mission work, local mission work. What if we empowered them to make a difference now, and not when they get older? What if we showed them how to Show People Love And Share Him- now instead of later?

Splash has grown to over 400 students, plus several hundred adult volunteers who work each summer in July to show how God can use you now, wherever you are to Show People Love and Share Him. It spans church denominations, age and race- people coming together from all over to spread Christ's love.

If you would like to know more about this special ministry, please check out www.bartowbaptist.org/splash for more information.

Until next time, may God's grace surround you,

Anna Christine

Coming in September 2018

Accepting Grace

Book Two in the Grace Series

A Bad Day Followed by a Grumpy, Gorgeous Boss

Hillary Blake is having a very bad last day of school. Called into the principal's office she is accused of cheating and will be put on unpaid leave until she can be proven innocent. Her day gets worse when she arrives back at her rental apartment only to be told she has three days to move out.

Desperate for a job, Hillary hears about a young fireman left with his sister's orphan children after her sudden death. Luke Toledo needs a nanny, but one look at tall, platinum blonde Hillary, and Luke can't decide if a nanny-princess combo will work for his new family.

Both too desperate to walk away, will the obvious attraction keep them from working through their differences and past hurts to create a ready-made family?

Chapter One

Ok, everyone put up the crayons and grab your book bags. The last day of school is officially over in two minutes."

The sounds of children laughing and scraping their chairs back to follow her instructions filled the classroom as Hillary's third grade class finished out the last end of the school day ritual for the year. As she watched them lining up at the door, she felt immense pride at the twenty-three third graders making it through another year.

Miss Blake, Timmy won't get in line." A feisty red-haired girl called to her from the front of the classroom.

Rising from her desk, Hillary walked over to Timmy and helped him finish putting up his crayons. "It's ok, Cicely."

Any comment from Cicely was stopped when the intercom blared. "Car riders to the front." The day was almost over.

Nodding her head to the eight children in the front of the line sent them fleeing from her classroom for the start of summer break. She was going to miss this class, especially since this was the first time she tried some new techniques she acquired last summer for children with various learning disabilities. With the rising number of students struggling to master an ever-changing curriculum and standards, she researched a conference in Canada and went last June to learn some innovative ideas to apply to her classroom. She had been pleased by how well the ideas worked and felt her students had responded better than anyone anticipated.

Bus riders to the loading area." The remaining kids waited with bated breath for Hillary's nod, and she waved as she sent them out one last time. "Have a great summer," she called to the back of the heads.

As she watched them leave, she said to Timmy, "I can put this up, Tim. You don't want to miss your bus."

The little boy nodded but didn't move to grab his backpack. He stood at his desk holding a red crayon tightly in his clenched fist. "Miss Blake, I umm..." Moving toward her, he grabbed her in a tight hug. "Thank you, Miss Blake. I had fun this year, and I learned a lot." Moving a fist across his wet eyes, he blurted out, "I know it's because of you."

Before she had a chance to reply, the little man was out the door. Hillary felt tears fill her eyes, *I knew the extra work, the money on worksheets and games and other learning tools I employed this year would be worth it.* She had paid for the conference herself, since she had been so passionate about helping her kids, because the school couldn't afford to pay her to go out of the country.

Bye Tim," she whispered, "and thank you!"

She knew he couldn't hear, but she was most proud of that young man. He was diagnosed with ADHD, along with other behavior and learning problems. Both of them had worked hard, she in helping him find new ways to learn and he in putting extra effort, even working during recess when he was struggling with a difficult subject.

Looking down at his desk, she saw a card he left for her with a picture of him on the stability ball with what she assumed was her standing next to him with an A+ on his spelling test. Smiling, she picked up the paper and placed it on her desk, knowing she would treasure it always. She rolled his special stability ball to the closet, because she had promised him that once she knew what classroom he would be in next year, she would give it to his 4th grade teacher. She had started praying for him to get a great teacher to help him to continue to grow in his new love of learning.

Praying for her kids' safety over the summer, Hillary moved to shut down her computer and finish putting her papers away. She was to have three days of post planning to finish packing up for next year but wanted to go home and rest tonight. The last week of school was exhausting with the high energy from the kids. Keeping them calm to review a few last pieces of knowledge, and the long hours preparing for a fun end of the year had worn her completely out.

Hillary?"

Yes?" Surprised to hear the office calling her.

Principal Peters would like for you to come to his office right now, please."

Rising from her desk, Hillary grabbed her purse on the way out the door. "Be right there."

She would leave from the front office and deal with everything tomorrow. It was strange the principal wanted to see her now. Most of the staff were ready to leave as soon as the kids were gone. She knew it had to be important, and hoped it wasn't one of her kids. At the beginning of the year, Timmy had gotten in a fight with another child and it was mess, that's was when she decided to try the new learning techniques with him, because he was a little boy crying out for help.

As she walked down the hallway students called out to her, some she had taught, but others she knew by sight. She knew she was well liked by the students, and often they were thrilled when they were in her class. She was a strict teacher, but she let her kids have fun, too.

The sunlight glinting on polished floors and decorated hallways caused her heart to swell, she loved this time of year seeing the kid's achievements. *The fun part is in a few months when I get to start over and see how God works miracles with a new group of little ones.*

Opening the back door to the office, she walked past an empty copy room and saw most of the staff had already snuck out. *Just like I'm hoping to do in a few minutes.* Seeing Principal Peters' door open, she knocked softly and stepped in after he waved for her to come in. She saw the older gentleman sitting at his desk and was surprised to see the frown on his face. He was usually a genial man, only becoming stern when he had to discipline a child, but as soon as the serious part was over he would smile and become the friendly Santa Claus he was known to be by staff and students. He even played the character every Christmas, he fit the part so well for photos as a fundraiser for the school.

Mr. Peters?"

Hillary, good, you're here. Please have a seat." Rising a bit, he sat back down after she was seated in the leather chair in front of his big desk. It felt intimidating sitting across from him, like a small child in trouble.

Clearing his throat, he looked at her with sad eyes. "I'm afraid I have some bad news and wanted to tell you after everyone was gone."

Worried she asked, "What's wrong? Is it one of the kids?"

Not exactly." Seeing her eyes widen, he continued quickly, "No, the kids are fine. I've been talking with the superintendent and a complaint against you has been made. That along with the evidence of your kids doing so well on the CRCT test in April..." He paused, sighing as he said, "All of your students scored amazingly well this year."

I don't understand." Shaking her head in confusion, she asked, "How can my kids doing well be a problem?"

Squirming in his seat, the large man looked uncomfortable as he answered, "A parent has made an accusation you helped your students cheat during the CRCT test and when the high test scores came out last week, well the superintendent has to actively deal with this matter. It wouldn't be good for our school system to look like we were not taking this very seriously. We don't want a scandal."

I've never...." Hillary was so stunned, she couldn't finish defending herself. Her mind raced, *what's going on God? I didn't cheat... I thought going to Canada to get helpful tips to teach my kids was from You....an answer to prayer to be the best teacher I could be! What's going to happen to me? I'm a teacher, I've always wanted to teach from the time I was a kid making my cousins play school all summer.*

Jackson Peters could see Hillary was upset and knew the rest of his news wasn't go to help. "I'm afraid there's more. Part of the way this is being dealt with is to suspend you from school without pay until the students can be retested in August to see if they can get similar results to the ones in April."

Hillary couldn't believe her ears. *Suspended? Like a naughty child? I can't wait until August for this to be resolved.*

I didn't do anything wrong, Sir." Standing up her purse fell to the floor as she firmly said, "I did not cheat, or allow my students to cheat. I've taught them better than that and I stand behind their work this year. You've seen the test scores EVERY week, all of the grades for my kids improved– the CRCT scores are just proving what's been happening all year."

Hillary, I don't believe you cheated. I think the conference and techniques you employed this year have been remarkable, but I can't go against policy and an accusation from a parent."

Do I get to know who's falsely accusing me?"

Shaking his head no, he was unable to look her in the eye. "Not until after the kids have been retested and a panel can be convened to go over the accusations and test results."

Sinking into her chair, Hillary's voice trembled as she spoke, "We both know kids forget a lot over the summer and the first few weeks of school are to remind them of what the sun and fun has caused them to forget."

Catching her eye, Jackson said, "I assure you that will be taken into account. I believe the second test will prove your results, Miss Blake. You're an excellent teacher, but my hands are tied. As of today, you are not to come back to the school until the panel requests you in early September. I'll have one of the para pros finish packing up your classroom for the summer."

Head held high to hide tears in her cornflower blue eyes, she said, "I understand. I will get my things and see you in September."

Hillary, I'm sorry and want you to know I'm going to fight for you. I believe you're one of the best teachers I have and I won't lose you. This isn't over, it's just moving into half time for a while."

Unable to reply, Hillary only nodded as she picked up her purse from the floor and moved to the door.

I'll need your keys and security badge before you leave." He said quietly.

Hand on the door, she didn't turn but said, "I'll drop them off after I clean out my desk."

Walking back to her classroom, she didn't see anything, but mindlessly walked to her door, tears started to fall down her pale checks. *Oh, Lord, what now? How can this be a part of Your plan?*

Turning on the lights, the first thing she saw was little Timmy's picture with his hand written thank you. Seeing his tidy penmanship, she couldn't control her tears any longer, she knew how hard the little boy worked to get the letters just right, even the letter s in miss were turned the right way and she knew how he struggled with getting them right.

Laying her head on her desk, tears fell unchecked and she didn't try to stop them or quiet herself. She felt she was alone, and not just physically in the room. It seemed God had abandoned her. After she cried every drop of water out of her system, she sat up and looked around her empty classroom. Struggling not to lose it again, she pushed a few wisps of her platinum blonde hair out of her eyes, as she began to go over what she needed to take with her. *This isn't the packing up I had in mind earlier.*

She gathered the most important things: notes from students and parents she had collected over the years, little mementos she kept in her desk, a spare sweater, along with her favorite mug a student had made for her a few years ago, plus the new teacher gifts from students for today's last day of school. She hiccupped, *my last day.*

Throwing everything in an empty box, she couldn't believe how much her life had changed in forty minutes at least according to the silver watch on her slim wrist, a college graduation gift from her parents.

My parents! What am I going to tell my parents? They'll be so upset. Pausing by her door, she realized her mother would storm the school, irate and angry as she yelled at everyone about how horribly they were treating her precious daughter. *It would be embarrassing, unprofessional and completely out of my control.* She had never been able to stand up to her mother, and she was in her late twenties. *Lord, please don't let my mother find out.*

On autopilot she walked back to the office and laid her keys and security badge on Peter's desk. Glancing at the photo ID, she saw the smiling, younger version of herself and couldn't believe only six years later she would be turning in her badge.

Hillary?"

Yes?"

I'll be praying for you and for all of this to work out."

Thank you." Unable to say more she walked out the double door entrance and refused to look back as she found her little silver Prius alone in the teacher parking lot. She put the cardboard box in the back seat and slowly got into the car to drive to her apartment.

She worked in Cobb County which meant she had a long commute to Cartersville, but since she usually left before traffic was heavily congested it wasn't bad and she liked listening to books on cd to keep alert. Shock made the usual thirty-minute drive seem short, and before long she was at her exit, pulling off the interstate and making her way to her basement apartment. Her plan was to go to her room, pull the covers over her head and pray this was just a nightmare.

Surely, this day can't get any worse!

About the Author

Anna Christine Boulier has been a writer/storyteller since she begged her mother to learn to read before she entered first grade- to the bane of her first-grade teacher. Since then she has written short stories and had characters that lived in her head for years. In May of 2013, God gave her a story and she wrote it in six weeks. Once the first book lived on paper she couldn't stop. She currently has three books written with more on the way.

She grew up in Cartersville and except for a brief stint in Atlanta for college, she's been there ever since. If you meet her, she can tell you more, because it's a story! Writing is not full time, she pays the bills with a full-time job that helps her stay creative.

Writing is my testimony- Grace my story!
It isn't just a tagline, but a way of life.